BLOOD
LINES

THE AMERICAN VAMPIRE SERIES

BLOOD

LINES

VAMPIRE
STORIES
FROM
NEW ENGLAND

LAWRENCE SCHIMEL AND MARTIN H. GREENBERG

CUMBERLAND HOUSE
NASHVILLE, TENNESSEE

Published by Cumberland House Publishing, Inc., 431 Harding Industrial Park Drive, Nashville, TN 37211-3160.

Distributed to the trade by Andrews & McMeel, 4520 Main Street, Kansas City, Missouri, 64111.

Cover and interior design by Joel Wright.

Library of Congress Cataloging-in-Publication Data

Blood lines : vampire stories from New England / edited by
   Lawrence Schimel and Martin H. Greenberg.
      p. cm. — (American Vampire Series)
   ISBN 1-888952-50-4 (pbk. : alk. paper)
   1. Vampires—Fiction. 2. Horror tales, American—New England.
3. New England—Fiction. I. Schimel, Lawrence. II. Greenberg,
Martin Harry. III. Series.
PS645.V35B57 1997
813'.08738375—dc21   97-13299
                                                         CIP

Printed in the United States of America
1 2 3 4 5 6 7—02 03 01 00 99 98 97

For my mother,
since the apple doesn't fall far from the tree
when it comes to an interest in vampires.

—L. S.

Contents

Introduction

Stereotypical of small New England towns is a mistrust of outsiders and strangers. Even though we are almost all of us newcomers to this land, those whose ancestors were among the first Europeans to set foot on this soil and brave the harsh winters in those early settlements have been fiercely possessive of their claim to this country. Families who arrived a mere two hundred years ago are viewed as newcomers by comparison.

This New England memory for lineage is akin to the longevity of the vampire, stretching back through centuries, as its life (or umlife) is extended by draining the lives and blood of others.

From the New Englander's perspective, the "literary" vampire popularized by Bram Stoker, which gave rise to all the things we think we know about vampires—that they turn into bats, do not cast reflections, are deterred by holy symbols or garlic—is a newcomer. Reports of vampirelike creatures or activities litter New England newspapers from the 1800s, long before Dracula was first published in 1897. Because the idea of germs was not understood, it was believed that, when a person died of consumption or a similar disease, and later other family members began to sicken, the dead must be returning to drain the life from their living relatives in revenge. Bodies were often exhumed and the hearts burned.

This idea was supported by the belief that consumption was a spiritual rather than physical disease passed on through human contact. The Puritans, who were the first to settle in this land they named a "new" England, believed that all sorts of evil creatures tried to lure souls away from God; they lumped many beliefs—in witches and devils as well as vampires—as minions of Evil, to be battled with by whatever means necessary. This need to "battle" evil became the hysteria that resulted in the trauma and turmoil of the notorious Salem witch trials. In this mindframe, any stranger was automatically suspect as a possible source of evil—witch, devil, or vampire.

One manifestation of this intense xenophobia is that New Englanders did not look far from home for victims. A corollary to the belief that vampires caused disease within a family was the idea of vampirism as a curse that afflicted generation after generation of a particular family.

The stories in *Blood Lines* explore all of these themes, as well as more contemporary notions about vampires derived from the rich literary tradition begun with Lord Byron and with Bram Stoker's Dracula—a heritage that, while not as old as that of many New Englanders, is nonetheless a powerful ancestry traced through a bloodline of text—including this volume.

—Lawrence Schimel

Acknowledgments

This book would not exist without the assistance of Stefan Dziemianowicz, which is greatly appreciated by both editors.

John Helfers also provided invaluable help in compiling and processing this project.

Thanks are also due to many others, for suggestions and other help in tracking down some of the stories included, but especially to: Greg Cox, Ellen Datlow, Keith Kahla, Michael Lowenthal, and Gordon van Gelder.

Norine Dresser's book *American Vampires* (Vintage) was a useful resource for historical data.

Only the IRS could ferret out a community of bloodsucking vampires.
It takes one to know one!

Investigating Jericho

BY CHELSEA QUINN YARBRO

aper rolled from the printer in waves, and Morton Symes gathered it up from the floor, scowling at the columns of figures printed there. It was exactly what he had feared. He dragged the material back to his office and began to separate the pages and arrange them.

William Brewster was waiting impatiently when Morton finally came into his office. He wasted no time with polite trivia. "Well?"

"I think it's a taxpayers' revolt, sir," said Morton, holding out his newly assembled file. "According to our records, no one in Jericho has filed income tax returns for the past two years. No one."

"Jericho," said Brewster, his eyes growing narrow behind his horn-rimmed glasses. "Where is this place?"

"North of Colebrook, in New Hampshire. Near the Canadian border." He held out a photocopy of a Rand McNally map. "I've marked it for you in red."

"Is that a joke?" Brewster asked suspiciously.

"No," Morton said, horrified. "No, sir. Not at all."

Brewster nodded, satisfied; then he said, "It might have been a good one, though."

"Thank you, sir," Morton said promptly. He stood more or less at attention while Brewster opened the file and scanned through it, pausing from time to time to click his tongue.

"Not a very big place by the look of it," said Brewster as he put the file down some twenty minutes later.

"'Population: 2,579,'" Morton said. "As of two years ago."

"When they stopped paying taxes," Brewster said with that cold disapproval that made his whim law in the office.

"Well, you see," Morton pointed out as diplomatically as possible, "last year there were still a few paying taxes, a few. For the last taxable year, not one citizen sent in W-2's or anything else. Not even those entitled to refunds filed. It has to be a taxpayers' revolt." He waited while Brewster considered the information.

"I wonder why it took so long to find it?" Brewster mused, his expression suggesting that anyone lax enough to have let this pass might expect a very unpleasant interview.

"Well, it took awhile for the random sampling to catch up with a place that small. With nine states filing in our office, the computer has an enormous number of returns to deal with. And tax reform made it all so complicated. . . ." He smiled miserably. "I guess we weren't looking as closely as we should have. There were other things on our minds." It took the greatest self-control for him not to twiddle the ends of his tie.

"It's very small; as you say, it wouldn't turn up quickly in a random comparison." Brewster was letting him and the rest of the office off the hook, and his expression said he knew it. "So. What are your plans?"

This time, Morton did pull his tie, but just once. "I thought . . . I thought I ought to go look around, investigate the situation, see what's happening up there." When he received no response from Brewster, he opened the file and indicated one set of figures. "You see? There's a small lumber mill that provides employment for over two hundred men and about a dozen women; none of them have filed, and neither has the lumber mill. It might mean that the mill has shut down, in which case there could be a minor recession in the town. I have to check the courts to find out if there's been a bankruptcy hearing on the mill. And the other large income is from the Jericho Inn, which specializes in sportsmen. There is no indication that it's still in operation, so I thought . . . well, it might make sense to go there and see for myself. . . ."

Brewster glowered as Morton's words faded. "How long were you planning to be away?"

"I don't know; a week, maybe two, if the situation warrants the time." He shifted his weight from one leg to the other. Brewster always made him feel about eight years old.

"What would make the situation warrant it?" Brewster asked sharply.

"If the town turns out to be prosperous and is actively refusing to cooperate with us, then I might not need as much as a week; a few days ought to be enough to get a full report. But if the town is having trouble with unemployment, then I might have to stick around, to see how deep the rot goes." He could not read the cold look in Brewster's magnified eyes. "We're supposed to be compassionate, aren't we, sir? Not make snap judgments or arbitrary rulings? With the reform and all the changes, we were told to be understanding, weren't we? If the town's out of money, it could account for what they've done."

"It might," Brewster allowed. He leaned back and regarded Morton down the length of his long Roman nose, a maneuver calculated to be intimidating. "Why should I send you? Why not Callisher or Brody?"

"Well, I found it, sir," said Morton, as if he were about to lose a favorite toy.

Brewster nodded once, but returned to the same dominating pose. "That you did. That you did." He drummed long, thick fingers on the immaculate surface of his desk. "That's a point." His next question was so unexpected that Morton was shocked almost to silence. "Where do you come from?"

"I live in Pittsford, just south of—," Morton began.

"I know where you live," said Brewster in his best condescending manner. "Where do you come from?"

"Oh." Morton was afraid he was blushing. "I come from Portland. In Michigan. Between Grand Rapids and Lansing." He was afraid that if he said anything more, he would stutter.

"Family still there?" Brewster inquired.

"Dad's in Chicago; Mom's dead; my older sister lives in

Montana, running some kind of tourist ranch—I forget what you call them—"

"Dude ranches," Brewster supplied.

Morton bobbed his head up and down several times. "Yeah. That's it. She works there. My younger sister is married to a colonel in the army. They're stationed in Texas. They were in Europe." He did his best to look confident. "No family in New England anywhere that I know of."

Brewster straightened up. "That's something." He looked down at the file once more, thumbing his way through the print-outs. "I'll authorize you to travel for a maximum of ten days. I expect a phone report every two days, backed up by a written report when you complete the investigation." He handed the file back to Morton. "You better come up with something. We don't want the evening news saying the IRS is persecuting innocent citizens. Best go over that village name by name."

"Of course," Morton assured him, doing his best to contain the panic he felt. "I'll be very careful, Mr. Brewster," he vowed, his ordinary face taking on as much purpose as it could. "I'll report each day if you like. Tell me when you want me to call."

"Midafternoon should do," Brewster said, suddenly sounding very bored.

"Midafternoon, every day," said Morton.

"Every other day," corrected Brewster. "If I'm not available, my secretary will record your report, and I'll review it later. I expect to have numbers where I can reach you while you're gone."

"Certainly. Of course," said Morton, daring to give the hint of a smile.

Brewster made sure that did not last. "I expect you to have an evaluation for me within the first twenty-four hours as to the general economic condition of the community and some observations on the political disposition of the citizens." He indicated the file. "You don't want to end up on Dan Rather's bad side, do you?" He made it very plain that if anything went wrong, Morton would take all the heat himself.

"No," said Morton, blanching.

"Keep that in mind, and you should do well," said Brewster as he leaned forward. "Be astute, Symes."

BLOOD LINES

Morton had never been admonished to be astute before, and did not quite know what would be an appropriate response. "I'll do what I can, sir." He wanted to make his escape while Brewster still seemed disposed to give it to him.

"Carry on, Symes," said Brewster, and at once ignored Morton, not so much as if he had left the room, but as if he had disappeared altogether.

◊◊◊

Northern New Hampshire was quite beautiful, the worn mountains dozing in the early-autumn afternoon, their trees still green, though no longer the deep, heady color of summer. The drive was so pleasant that Morton Symes castigated himself for lack of purpose as he drove northward, into increasingly remote regions, his chocolate-colored BMW humming efficiently, the tape deck playing some of Symes's favorite soft-rock hits. The one delay, caused by a road-repair crew blocking traffic for the better part of forty minutes, brought Morton to North Poindexter, near Colebrook, at sunset. He flipped a mental coin and elected to find a motel for the night rather than press on to Jericho.

"Just the one night?" asked the clerk in the insufferably quaint inn Morton found off the main street."

"Just the one."

"On your way to the lakes?" asked the clerk, making small talk while Morton filled out the necessary forms.

"No, Jericho." Morton looked at him over the rims of his glasses, a move he thought might discourage conversation.

"Jericho?" said the clerk in some surprise. "Why there?"

"Business," said Morton, even more tersely.

"In Jericho?" The clerk laughed once in disbelief.

"Why not in Jericho?" asked Morton, in spite of himself.

The clerk hesitated a bit longer than he should have. "Oh, nothing. Just don't get many . . . flatlanders going there; that's all. People from North Poindexter don't go there." He handed a key to Morton. "Second door on the left, at the end of the walkway."

"Thanks," Morton said automatically as he took the key. He

was about to pick up his suitcase, when he could not resist asking, "Why don't people from here go to Jericho?"

This time the clerk considered his answer very carefully. "Not that kind of place," he said, and turned away, unwilling to say anything more.

Morton pondered over what the clerk had said, and decided that he might have been right in his assumption that the town was in some form of depression. If it had little tourist trade and the lumber mill was not doing well, it could be that the whole village was hanging on by the proverbial shoestring. He made his first, meticulous notes, with records of mileage and amounts spent on fuel and food, then went to the most promising restaurant in town, certain that he was off to a good start.

Over baked chicken in the North Poindexter restaurant, he decided that he would do his best to be helpful to the people of Jericho. If, like their biblical namesake, their walls were "tumblin' down," he would offer to help the citizens shore them back up. He remembered the seminar he had attended three months ago, a seminar that stressed learning to relate to the problems of the taxpayer and to be compassionate and sympathetic in regard to their needs and their problems. He rehearsed in his head the right way to say things, so that he would not sound too much like a cop or an inquisitor.

◊◊◊

Morning found him out of North Poindexter and on the road to Jericho by nine. He had taken great care to dress less formally than usual, in a tweed jacket and gray slacks instead of his usual three-piece suit. One of the things he had learned in the seminar was that most people found casual attire less intimidating, and Morton did not want to get off to a bad start with the citizens of Jericho. He listened to light classics—they seemed more appropriate to this warm, windy day—and admired the scenery. In another month, with the trees in their autumnal glory, the drive would be spectacular; now it was pleasant, even refreshing. Morton made a mental note to take a few pictures before he left, so that he could recapture his sense of enjoyment, which led him to think about his destination. A remote village like Jericho might easily become his secret vacation haunt, where he could spend a few days away from the pressure of his work in an unspoiled place. He permitted himself a flight of fancy: his work with the townspeople had earned him their respect and possibly the affection of some, and he was regarded as their welcome outsider on his annual returns. Returns. He chuckled at his own mental pun. Then he concentrated on his driving and the road, making special note of the few buildings he saw at a distance, and then the ones that were nearer.

Two tall Victorian atrocities at the bend of the road were Morton's first sight of Jericho. The houses were run-down, with peeling paint and broken windows, but even in their heydays, neither would have been a sterling example of the carpenter Gothic style, in large part because both were so overdone, with turrets and cupolas and widow's walks and piazzas and fan windows in such frenzied abundance that the basic lines of the houses themselves seemed to be lost behind it all. Morton slowed as he went past the houses, and fancied that they were leaning together, whispering—two ancient crones bedecked in elaborate gowns no longer in fashion. He chided himself for his overactive imagination as he slowed the car just as the rest of the town came into view.

The main street was predominantly nineteenth century, but with a few older buildings at the far end of the town. Two churches, both austere white buildings, one with a spire and one with a turret, were on opposite sides of and opposite ends of the street; the older of the two—with the turret at the far end on the left—had been unpainted so long that the wood beneath had weathered to a scaled gray. Next to that church was a Federal-style building with an ancient and faded sign that proclaimed it the Jericho Inn. Between Morton and the Inn were a town hall; a single-story building with an imposing Victorian facade (Morton learned later that it was the bank); a 1930s-vintage post office; a café of sorts, in a building that had once been a private home and was now given over to offices; a small, neglected park; a barnlike building advertising feed, fuel, and ice; a hardware store with a display of plumbing tools and supplies in the window; two small wooden houses, both dating from about 1850, one with a sign tacked by the door saying, "Knitting and Sewing: reasonable rates," and a more recent house with an Art Nouveau stained-glass window over the front door; then a fifties ranch-style house, hideously out-of-place. Opposite that house was the steepled church; and next to it, an open block overgrown with weeds, identified as the "Jericho Park" by a sign near a rusty children's playground that ended at a fenced schoolyard; next to that, opposite the two houses, was a medium-sized grocery store, its windows dusty and its doors closed; beyond the store was another house that had been converted to office space that advertised the services of John H. Lawler, accountant; then a more recent building: in the concrete-slab style, with "Jericho Lumber Company" over the entrance; across from the post office was the Wallace's Department Store, its window displays at least two years out-of-date, the mannequins looking like escapees from a 1940s *film noir;* after that two small shops, one selling candy, the other a bookstore; then a box of a building, opposite the town hall, which housed the two-man police force and the three-cell jail; the place across from the Jericho Inn was much larger, the whole of a block and a half given over to the gardens—now in riotous ruin—of a grotesque mansion, which had started out Federal and had been added to in two distinct layers of Victoriana. Along the street, there were five different vehicles parked: a twenty-year-old Chevy pickup by the hardware store, a muddy Edsel in front of the post office, a four-year-old Cadillac across from the bank, a step van by the department store, and a cherry 1956 Thunderbird sports car by the park.

Morton stared at the town, noting that most of the secondary streets were filled with single- and two-family residences, and that no one seemed to be up and about, though the morning was closer to lunch than breakfast. He started down the main street, looking for signs of life.

In the distance a school bell rang, but there was no change apparent on the street.

After a brief period of consideration, Morton pulled in across the street from the town mansion and settled down to watch Jericho, wondering why the school bell seemed to attract no response other than the occasional answer of hoots from the volunteer fire department, a block and a half away.

An hour passed; two. Morton was hard put to keep his eyes open, or to pay attention to the main street, and when he did, he could detect no change. No wonder the town was depressed; no one appeared to work in it. In fact, no one seemed to live in it. Over his greatest determination, Morton began to doze.

He was awakened at sunset by a tap on his window and a face all but pressed against the glass. He straightened up and adjusted his glasses, trying not to appear startled.

"Something the matter?" asked the uniformed cop as Morton rolled down the window.

"No," said Morton at once, adding, "sir," as an afterthought. "The afternoon. . . . I got drowsy."

"It happens," said the cop, standing up. "You're new in town."

"Yes," said Morton, reaching into his pocket for his wallet. He opened it to show his IRS identification and his driver's license. "Morton Symes."

The policeman inspected these two documents narrowly, then gave a grudging nod. "It appears you are."

"And you?"

"Wilson, Dexter Wilson," he said, not offering his hand. "You passing through or staying?"

This was not a very promising beginning, but Morton was not deterred. "I have some business to do here."

"Uh-huh." Wilson rocked back on his heels. "Well, lots of luck with it." He made a gesture that was not quite a salute, and then ambled away.

Watching him go, Morton noticed that there were a few other people on the street, strolling in the last fading light of day. They moved silently, in pairs or singly, making no effort to stop for conversation. When they met, there was scarcely so much as a nod exchanged, and never did anyone hail one of the others moving along the sidewalk. This puzzled Morton, though he supposed that people living together in the same small town might not have much to say to each other after a time. There was also the taciturn nature of New Englanders, he reminded himself, their disinclination to small talk. He rolled up his window and locked the passenger door before he got out of the car.

There was no one at the reception desk in the Jericho Inn,

which had the same dusty look of neglect as the rest of the town. Morton hesitated, then gave his attention to the large, old-fashioned register, noticing that the most recent guest had stopped there fourteen months ago. He frowned, then took a pen and added his own name, address, and occupation to the required lines. Assuming the Inn had no guests at the moment, he wondered if it would be proper simply to inspect the rooms and choose the one he liked best. He was weighing the possibilities, when he heard a voice rusty with disuse behind him.

"Get anything for you?"

Morton turned and saw a man in late middle years, rather scrawny and rumpled, standing in the door to the dining room.

"Why, yes," he said when he had recovered from the shock of being discovered. Little as he wished to admit it, the silent arrival of the man had terrified him for an instant. "I'd like a room. With a bath."

The man did not move; he regarded Morton with a measuring look. "Fixing to stay long?"

"Probably a week," said Morton.

"Not much to do around here," said the man.

"I'm here on business, not pleasure," Morton informed him. I will need a week to complete it."

"Business?" repeated the man. "In Jericho?" He laughed unpleasantly as he shambled closer. "Don't have much fancy here," he said.

"You mean in the Inn?" Morton asked with a significant raise to one eyebrow.

"That; Jericho, too." The man was now behind the reception desk. "Might take less time than you think, your business."

"I doubt it," said Morton, determined to assert his authority and establish a more reasonable level of communication between them.

"Suit yourself. You want a room, do you?" He read the signature Morton had just put in the register. "IRS. Well, well, well."

"We have some questions about Jericho." Morton once again offered his identification. "I trust you take Mastercard."

"Cash," said the man. "Don't hold with plastic here."

Morton shook his head; uncertain if he had brought enough cash to pay for the whole week. His head ached at the thought of reviewing cash transactions with their lack of supporting paper. He wondered if the rest of the town were as unorthodox. "How much for a week?"

"Two hundred forty dollars for seven days," said the man. "No meals included. Linen changed twice a week. Coffee available in the morning upon request, two dollars extra."

Sighing, Morton drew three hundred dollars from his wallet and hoped that the remaining hundred would be sufficient. He hoped that the bank would be willing to honor one of his credit cards if none of the businesses were willing. "I'll want coffee every morning, so that means $254; $46 change."

"Fast with those numbers, aren't you?" The man opened a drawer under the counter and handed four worn bills to Morton. "'You want a receipt?"

Morton blinked. "Of course," he said, knowing that not getting one was inconceivable.

"Now or when you leave?"

"Now," said Morton.

The man shook his head, but brought out a receipt pad and scribbled the date and amount on it. "Need anything more than that?"

Morton grew irritated. "Please state what the money is for, including the length of the stay and morning coffee."

Grudgingly, the man did as Morton requested. He tore off the receipt and handed it to Morton. "You can have the front center room," he said, pointing toward the ceiling. "First floor. Bay window. It's the Ivy Room. All our rooms are named for plants." He handed over a key. "The hot water don't work real good."

This information, under the circumstances, did not surprise Morton. "I'll keep that in mind," he said, and picked up his suitcase. "Is there a phone in the room?"

"Pay phone's by the rest rooms. That's all we got." The man jerked his thumb toward a narrow hallway. "Down that way."

"Thanks," said Morton, aware that he was late in phoning in. Brewster would be displeased, but that could not be helped. Morton started up the stairs, watching the desk clerk covertly, noticing how pale the man was. Perhaps he was ill, which would explain his rudeness. Then the clerk returned the stare, and Morton, abashed, averted his eyes and continued to his room.

The Ivy Room had ancient wallpaper covered in ivy twines. Luckily, it was faded, or it would have been hideous; as it was, there was an air of decayed gentility about the room, and Morton, while not delighted, was not as upset as he had feared he might be. The bathroom had an old-fashioned stand sink and a legged bathtub as long and narrow and deep as a coffin. The medicine cabinet of the sink lacked a mirror, though from the look of it, there had been one some time ago. Morton set out his shaving gear and took out the mirror he always carried when he traveled. When he was satisfied with the arrangement of his things, and that the enormous towels were clean and fresh, he went back into the bedroom and set about hanging his clothes in the antique armoire that dominated one side of the room. It was too late to call Brewster now, he knew. As he sat down to make his report for the day, he did his best to suppress a twinge of guilt. The next after-noon he would explain it all to Brewster— from the pay phone.

By the time he finished his report, it was quite dark. The two forty-watt bulbs in the ceiling fixture barely got rid of the gloom, and the desk lamp was not much brighter. With concealed exas-peration, Morton changed his shirt and tie in preparation for finding supper. "It is supper in this part of the world, isn't it?" he said to the walls. Perhaps tomorrow he would also invest in some stronger light bulbs. Then he hesitated. The wiring in many of these old buildings could not take bright lights. He could get one of those battery-powered reading lights at the hardware store; that would do it.

To Morton's surprise, there were a number of people on the street when he walked out of the Inn. He noticed the same odd silence about them. He could tell they were curious about him, but no one approached him, and when he got too near any of the pedestrians, they moved away from him, avoiding him. He thought that perhaps the clerk from the Inn had mentioned his work. How sad that so many people mistrusted the IRS, Morton thought as he found a coffee shop on one of the side streets not far from the post office.

A single waitress was behind the counter, a middle-aged woman with her hair in an untidy bun. She squinted as if she needed glasses as Morton came up to the counter. "We don't have much tonight," she said, her voice unusually low and full of disturbing implications. It was a voice made of spices and madness, and it turned her from a frump to a femme fatale in disguise.

'That's fine," said Morton with his best sincere smile. "I guess the rest have eaten."

She gave him a quick look. "You might say that."

Morton was more puzzled than ever. "Well, I've heard that some of these remote towns roll the sidewalks up early. Though you have lots of people out still."

"Uh-huh," said the waitress as she got out some flatware and set it in front of him as if she were unfamiliar with the task. "It's lamb stew—that's with vegetables in the stew and biscuits with gravy on the side."

"Fine,'" said Morton, who hated lamb. "That's fine." He looked around for a menu to see what he might have the next day, but could find none.

The waitress saw this and said, "There's a chalkboard. Most of the time, I tell anyone who wants to know."

"I see," said Morton, baffled.

"It'll take a couple minutes." She went through the swinging doors to the kitchen, and Morton listened for conversation or the banging of pots, but there was only silence.

You know, he told himself in his best inner-jocular style, if I were more credulous than I am, this place would be downright eerie. He looked around for a clock, and saw that the only one, on the wall over the cash register, was stopped at the improbable hour of 2:13. He was becoming more and more convinced that the economy of the town had collapsed, and that those who remained were hanging on by the slimmest of threads. Perhaps that's why I saw no one, he went on to himself. It may be that much of the town's population has moved away. It could be that many of the houses are deserted, that the offices have no one in them. He resolved to find out more in the morning.

The waitress returned with a white ironstone dish with his dinner spread over it "Coffee?" she asked in that disturbing voice of hers as she put the plate down in front of him.

"Yes, please," said Morton, not looking directly at her. "Is there any salt?"

Once again the waitress shot him a quick dagger of a look, and then concealed it with a smile. "Sorry. We ran out."

"That's all right," said Morton, adding one more item to his mental shopping list. He took a too-hot forkful of the stew and burned the roof of his mouth with it. He tried not to look too dismayed, but he panted over the stuff until he was sure he could swallow it without disaster. It was the strangest thing, he thought, that this lamb stew should taste so . . . so characterless, more like a TV dinner that had been in the microwave than a New England supper.

◊◊◊

Morning began with some minion of the Inn leaving a tray with a pot of coffee, a carton of cream, and a few packets of sugar on a tray with a cup and two pieces of desiccated toast. Morton was already dressed and tying his shoes when the knock came on his door and he found this spartan fare waiting for him. Over the coffee—which was strong without being tasty—he looked through his report of the night before. The first thing on his morning agenda was a visit to the lumber mill, to find out if it was in operation at all. After that, he supposed he would have to speak with the banker, not only to learn more about the town, but to shore up his dwindling supply of cash.

The day was glary, with thin, high clouds turning the sun to a bright patch in a white sky. Morton shaded his eyes as he looked down the street and debated whether he should drive or walk. In a town like this, he thought that walking might be the wiser choice, so that he would not appear to be as much a stranger as the townspeople seemed to think him. So he ambled along the main street toward the older church, then made a right turn along the rutted road toward the jumble of buildings that housed the mill. As he strolled toward the small parking lot, he saw there were only two cars there—an elderly Jeep and a seven-year-old Pontiac in need of new paint—and that the incinerator cone was dark. For some unknown reason, Morton began to whistle as he approached the mill.

The first place he looked was the millpond, where a couple

dozen waterlogged trunks rode low. There was no one around. He went toward the nearest building, his whistling making the silence more immense. He stared at the gaping doors, standing open as if to receive the logs, but with all the machinery quiet. Morton decided not to venture inside. Still whistling, he made his way back to the parking lot, taking his notebook out of his pocket and scribbling down his impressions before they left him.

Wending his way back to the Inn, he detoured along side streets, seeing gardens run over with weeds and berry vines. Most of the houses needed paint, and a few of them had broken windows that showed no sign of patching. Just as I thought, Morton observed to himself as he continued to whistle. This town is empty. That's what happened. The mill has closed, and most of the people have moved away.

But, said another part of his mind, they have not got new jobs or addresses, and they have not filed taxes.

When Morton reached the bank, a sign in the door said: "Closed for Lunch. Open again at 1:30." Now that, Morton decided, was a real case of banker's hours. He checked his watch, and noted that he had forty-five minutes before the bank would open again. After a brief hesitation, he decided to go back to the café where he had had supper and get himself a bite of lunch; his breakfast had not been enough to sustain him for long.

To his irritated surprise, the café was closed. A hand-lettered sign in the window indicated they would be open at six. How on earth could they get by doing so little business in a town like Jericho? Shrugging, Morton started up the street to the grocery store he had seen. He would buy some sandwich makings and a little something to augment tomorrow's breakfast.

There were two clerks in the grocery store, both teenagers, both listless, as if they had wakened less than ten minutes ago. Morton wondered it they were on some kind of drug—they moved so lethargically and could offer so little.

"The freezers are—," Morton began to the taller boy.

"Empty. Yes, sir. Power failure." He folded his arms. "There's canned stuff, and like that."

"Yes," said Morton dubiously. "And no fresh produce, I see."

"We got a couple dozen eggs," the boy offered.

"All right," said Morton, thinking he would ask the waitress to boil them for him that night. "I'll take a dozen."

"O.K." The boy moved off sluggishly, his eyes slightly unfocused.

Morton shook his head. He had always associated drug abuse with urban kids and city pressure, but of course, that was naive. In a depressed village like this one, no wonder the kids looked for solace in drugs. He supposed the cops were aware of it, but he decided he would have to remark on it in any case.

The boy returned with a carton of eggs. "They're O.K. I checked them."

"Thank you," said Morton, handing over forty dollars.

The boy stared at the money, then gave a self-conscious shrug and made change. "Oh yeah," he said with a slight laugh, which was echoed nastily by the other boy in the market.

"Is the manager in the store?" Morton asked as he took his bagged purchases.

"Yeah," said the second boy. "But he's resting."

That, Morton surmised, could mean anything. "I'd like to speak to him. If not today, then tomorrow. Will you tell him?"

"Sure," said the first boy, leaning back against the cash register as if he were exhausted.

Morton thanked them and went back to the Inn to put his meager provisions away.

It was 1:45 before the sign in the bank door was removed and someone unlocked the door. Morton, waiting impatiently across the street, hurried over and flung the door open.

The cavernous room was empty. No tellers stood at their windows; no officers sat at the desks beyond the low railing of dusty turned wood. Morton looked around in amazement. Then he called out, "Is anyone here?"

A door at the back of the room opened, creaking on its hinges. "Please come in," said the sonorous voice of a gaunt figure standing in the opening.

◊◊◊

"You're the president of the bank?" Morton faltered, looking around him and becoming more convinced than ever that he was seeing the final death throes of Jericho.

"Yes," said the man. "Please come in"

"Thank you," Morton said, starting to sense some relief, for surely he would now have the answer to his puzzle. He hefted his case and drew out his identification and his business card. "I'm Morton Symes. I'm with the IRS as you can see." He held his identification up so that the tall, lean man could read the documents and see the picture.

The bank president barely glanced at it. "Yes, of course. Please sit down." He directed Morton to a high wing-backed chair covered in dark green velvet that matched the (closed) draperies at the tall window. The president took his seat in a leather-upholstered chair behind a desk that was at least two hundred years old. "Now, what is it you want here, Mr.Symes?"

"Well," Morton said, gathering his thoughts together and launching into his explanation. "We were reviewing the tax returns for this area, as we do from time to time, and it came to our attention that in the past two years, almost no one in this village has filed tax returns with the IRS. Our records show no indication of the cause, and given the economic situation in the country, there have been times that isolated communities such as this one have been subjected to more fluctuations in their fortunes than in other, more largely economically based urban areas; yet, because of the lack of information available, we were in an awkward position—don't you see? Naturally, we are curious as to the reason for your whole village not paying taxes, or even filing forms saying that they made insufficient income, and I have been sent to investigate."

"I see," said the bank president.

Morton waited for the man to go on, to extrapolate or obfuscate, but was met with silence. Awkwardly, he continued. "Since I've come here—only yesterday, I admit—I've noticed that most of the town seems deserted. There don't appear to be pupils in the school—"

"The semester hasn't started yet," said the bank president smoothly.

"—and the mill has been shut down."

"Most regrettable," said the bank president.

"Is that a permanent situation, do you think?" Morton said, reaching for his notebook.

"I believe so," said the bank president, with a very smooth widening of his mouth that did not succeed as a smile.

"How unfortunate," said Morton automatically. He had listened to tales of economic disasters so often that he had become something like an undertaker offering sympathy.

"It creates problems," said the bank president.

"Too much competition from the big companies, I guess, like Georgia-Pacific." It was a safe guess, he told himself, and not bad for an off-the-cuff remark; it made him sound more knowledgeable than he actually was.

"That is a factor," said the bank president. "You understand that since this bank was founded by my family . . . oh, generations ago, and our principal is tied up in tax-free bonds, for the most part—as you undoubtedly know—we are in a position to be able to carry much of those who remain here for a considerable time more. We have an obligation to this village, and to the people in it." He gave a delicate cough. "You said almost no one has filed tax returns for the past two years. Am I the exception?"

"Uh . . . yes." Morton had not found that particular return in his first check of the town because the return was so vast and complicated that he had overlooked the Jericho address. Now he was glad he had taken the time to review. "You have more money in North Poindexter right now than you do in this town. And all over New England, for that matter. Your Boston holdings alone could finance a dozen Jerichos." He did not want to fawn or to appear unduly impressed, though he was startled by what he had discovered. "You're very well connected."

"Yes. That's what old money does for you," said the bank president. "Still, I can see you'd better have an explanation, and I'm afraid I can't offer you one right now—I have other affairs to attend to."

Morton almost said, "In an empty bank?" but held his tongue.

"If you're not busy, let me have some of your time later today. You come to my house this evening for cocktails, say, about, oh,

7:30. Just sherry or bourbon or rum," he went on. "We're not fancy in this place." He leaned back in his chair. "My wife will be delighted for your company." There was a slight change in his expression, as if he were being amused at Morton's expense.

"Is something the matter?" Morton asked, trying to be polite, but without success.

The bank president did not answer at once. "Mrs. Wainwright is a trifle older than I am," said the bank president. "She comes from a very old and distinguished European family. You may find her reserved, what they used to call 'high in the instep.' But don't let this bother you. She's a product of her time and culture, as are we all."

"Yes, of course," said Morton. He paused. "I can obtain the necessary documents, if you insist, but if you're willing to let me examine your records while I'm here—"

The bank president—Hewlett Wainwright was his name—held up his hand. "I'm sorry, but for the sake of the depositors and their privacy and constitutional rights, I must insist that you obtain your warrants and subpoenas." This time he made no attempt at a smile. "You understand I would be lax in my duty and my responsibility if I permitted you to ransack the accounts without the required documents."

"I understand," said Morton, ducking his head. "Certainly that's the prudent thing to do. I was only thinking that with the town in such a . . . depressed state, the sooner the tax situation is cleared up, the sooner you might go about setting things right again."

"Setting things right?" asked the bank president as if Morton had suddenly started speaking in Albanian.

"You know," Morton persisted, though his ears were scarlet, "arranging for federal aid. No doubt some of your townspeople could use a little assistance, a little retrenching, some retraining, perhaps—"

"My dear Mr. Symes," said the bank president, doing his best to contain his temper. "We are not sniveling, whining creatures, to throw ourselves on the dubious mercy of the federal government. As long as I can afford it—and I have every reason to believe I will be able to afford it for some considerable time to come—I will see that Jericho is tended to. There is no reason for the government—federal, state, or any other—to intrude." He held out his hand. "Until this evening, Mr. Symes."

Not even Brewster had routed Morton so efficiently. Stammering an apology, Morton got to his feet and made his way to the door, all the while wondering what could be making such demands on the bank president in this echoing, empty building. He closed the door to the bank president's office and all but tiptoed across the main chamber, finding its vacant teller cages almost sinister. "Don't be absurd," he whispered to himself as he reached the door.

The afternoon air was sweet, and the deserted street intrigued him. It was comforting to stroll toward the Inn, free to stop and stare when he wanted to, or to make notes without being embarrassed. He whistled a tune he had heard last week—he thought it came from *Phantom of the Opera*—and considered going to the little police station, then kept on toward the Inn. If he was going to have cocktails with Hewlett Wainwright and his wife, he wanted to be properly dressed. He also had to make his report to Brewster.

Luckily, he had change enough to place the collect call, but he had to accept the criticism of his boss in return for his taking the call. Morton opened his notebook. "Mr. Brewster," he began in his most official voice, "I'm sorry I wasn't able to reach you yesterday. Things turned out to be a little more complicated than either of us had anticipated."

"Anticipated?" Brewster repeated, some of his bluster still in his voice. "What do you mean?"

"There are . . . difficulties here." He sensed that the desk clerk was listening, but he vowed to continue no matter what. "The mill is closed, and many of the houses appear to be deserted."

"What does that have to do with the delay in your call?" Brewster demanded.

"I needed time to gather some information," said Morton, his patience all but deserting him. "I didn't want to waste your time with telling you simple descriptions. I thought you'd rather have a complete report, not a catalog of ills."

Brewster coughed once, and while not mollified, he was not as overbearing. "That was my decision to make, Symes, not yours. But if you'd had to call collect then, too, I can see why you might wait. How come you didn't use the phone credit card we issued you?"

Morton sighed. "They appear to refuse credit cards here in Jericho. That's another reason that made me assume that the town is . . . failing. They won't take checks or credit cards — nothing but cash. I'll have to get more by the end of the week, or I won't be able to get enough gas to drive out of here." He did not give Brewster time to comment, but hurried on: "I have to be prepared to work with these people on their terms, Mr. Brewster. I don't want them to think that we have no sympathy for their plight, or that we're punitive in our methods. These people need our help, sir. They need social services and housing grants and emergency funds to keep the whole place from turning into a graveyard."

"As bad as all that?" Brewster asked, not quite bored.

"I think it could be," Morton said carefully. "With the mill closed and most of the businesses looking pretty bad. . . . I went to the grocery store, and there was no one shopping but me. I don't think they've done much to restock the shelves." He cleared his throat delicately. "You told us all last month that we need to pay attention to the economic curves in a place before dealing with the tax impact."

"So I did," said Brewster heavily, as if he now considered that a bad idea.

"And I want to be certain that we don't make a bad situation worse. There's no point in running this place into the ground if we don't have to. It's better to have them working for a little pay than on the welfare rolls, isn't it?" Morton hoped that he could find a way to gain Brewster's support. "If we can work out some kind of program for the whole town, it might mean the difference between staying afloat and going under."

"Yes, yes," said Brewster impatiently. "Well, it's something to think about, isn't it? The last thing we want is another one of those pity-the-poor-taxpayer stories on '60 Minutes.' And this is exactly the kind of situation they'd love." He paused, and Morton did not dare to interrupt. "Give it a couple of days,

Symes, and call me again. Collect. I'll see that some cash is transferred to the bank for you, but you'll have to work out the vouchers when you get back, and we'll do what we can to arrange—" He stopped abruptly. "Call me day after tomorrow, at this time. And in the meantime, don't talk to anyone else about this—do you understand?"

"Yes," said Morton, anticipating that Brewster would find a way to take any credit coming from this venture for himself, and attach any blame to be had to Morton Symes. "Sure, Mr. Brewster."

"That's good," said Brewster, turning cordial. "You'll have that cash transfer tomorrow. I'll see that it's wired to the bank—"

"Pardon me, sir," Morton interrupted. "Would you make the transfer to the bank in North Poindexter? I'll drive over and pick it up; it won't take long. I don't know what kind of cash reserves are at this bank, or if there are any. And there's almost no staff."

Once more Brewster considered. "All right; North Poindexter it is. I will tell them to expect you by noon: how's that?"

"Fine. That's great." Morton looked down at his notes. "I haven't seen many kids aside from the two clerks at the store. The school appears to be closed. I'm going to check that out tomorrow, but I'm afraid that it means several families have left town. I'll try to get some figures on that tonight"

"Do as you think best, of course," said Brewster at his smoothest.

"Yes, sir," said Morton, all but saluting. "I'd better get ready for this cocktail thing, and then try to arrange for dinner at the café. I'll call you in two days, when I know more."

"Make sure it's all in your daily reports." Brewster coughed. "Good luck, Symes."

"Thank you, sir," said Morton, and hung up as soon as he heard Brewster put down his receiver. He stood by the phone for a few minutes, curious about the innkeeper: how much had he heard, and what had he made of it? There was no way to ask him, but Morton felt he ought to try at some point to learn more about the man. As he made his way to his room, he decided he had better have a bite or two to eat before going to the Wainwright house, for drink on an empty stomach always made him giddy.

By quarter after seven, Morton was ready, his three-piece navy-blue pinstripe suit and pale blue shirt nicely set off by his discreet medallion-patterned silk tie. It would pass muster for all but the dressiest dinners in Boston and Washington, and certainly ought to do for cocktails in Jericho. He felt awkward that he had nothing to bring his hostess, but decided that on such short notice, he could be excused for not bringing flowers or candy or a bottle of French wine.

He saw there were about a dozen people on the street, including the two policemen who served the village. As he opened the gate to the once-lavish and now-neglected gardens of the Wainwright house, he noticed that several of the people on the street were watching him covertly, almost—he smiled at the image—hungrily.

Hewlett Wainwright himself opened the door. "Please come in," he said formally, standing aside for Morton. "Welcome to our home."

"Thank you," said Morton as he stepped into the dimness of the entry hall. He noticed the authentic Tiffany light fixtures and decided that the house had probably not been rewired since they were installed. No wonder the Wainwrights used low-power bulbs with them; anything stronger would be courting fire and disaster. Still, he thought, as he made his way toward the parlor Mr. Wainwright indicated, it might be worth it; the place was positively gloomy, with all that heavy, dark wood and the low light.

"My wife will join us directly; she takes a nap in the afternoon, you know, so she will be fresh for the evening." He indicated the parlor, which was an Art Nouveau treasure. "Go on in, Mr. Symes. Make yourself comfortable."

Morton said a few words by way of thanks, and stepped into the parlor, marveling at what he saw there. By anyone's standards, every piece in the room was a valuable antique, and all kept in beautiful condition, but for a fine patina of dust, one that could not be more than one or two days old. Aside from the Tiffany lamps, there were small statues of superb design, three of them most certainly tarnished silver. As Morton stopped to look at the largest of these—two lovers with attenuated bodies entwined like vines in an arbor—he heard a step behind him.

"Ah, there you are, my dear," said Hewlett Wainwright.

The woman in the door was elegantly attired in heavy black damask silk topped with a bodice of heavy Venetian black lace. Her hair was abundant and of a glossy white, waved back from her face and caught in some sort of twist that emphasized her slender neck and high brow. Certainly she was not young, but she was magnificent enough to catch Morton's breath in his throat. She smiled faintly, her full red lips turning up; she extended her hand to be kissed, not shaken. "Welcome to our home," she said as Morton took her hand.

Though he felt incredibly awkward, Morton bent over and kissed her fingers, trying to appear more practiced at this courtesy than he was. "I'm pleased to meet you, Mrs. Wainwright"

"I am Ilona," she said. "That is one of the Hungarian variants of Helen." It was an explanation she had made many times before, but she had a way of speaking that created a kind of intimacy with her guests such that each of them felt they were being offered a special secret: Morton was no exception.

"Mr. Symes is concerned for our village," Mr. Wainwright told his wife. "He is from the Internal Revenue Service. You recall my remarks earlier?"

"Oh yes," said Ilona, her dark eyes not leaving Morton's face. "Those are the tax people, aren't they?"

"Yes. They are worried because we are the only people in Jericho who still pay taxes." He went to a gorgeous cabinet opposite the fireplace. "What would you like to drink, Mr. Symes? I ought to warn you: we have no ice."

"Oh," said Morton with an effort, "whatever you recommend. I'm afraid I'm not an expert on such things." He knew he should not be staring at his hostess, but there was something about her, and it was not her elegance or her beauty—not at all faded by age—that held him fascinated.

"Ah," said Mr. Wainwright. "Well, in that case, I can recommend a Canadian whiskey; it isn't much available in this country, but, living so close to the border, from time to time I pick a bottle or two up when I'm north on business." He had taken out a large, squat glass with a hint of etching on it. "I'll pour you a little, and if you like it, I'll be happy to fill you up again" He poured

24   B L O O D   L I N E S

out the whiskey and brought the drink to his guest. "I see you're captivated by Ilona. She is so lovely, isn't she?"

"Yes," said Morton, blushing with the admission.

"I don't blame you for staring. I remember the first time I set eyes on her; I thought I'd die if I looked away. You were very sweet to me then, my darling," Mr. Wainwright said, addressing this last to his wife.

She lifted her shoulder; on her, even so mundane an action as a shrug was graceful. "And you were sweet to me. You had such savor then."

Morton blinked at her words, startled at her choice of words. Then he recalled that English was not her first language, and he supposed he ought to expect an occasional strange turn of phrase from her. He tasted the whiskey and tried hard not to cough. "Very . . . unusual."

Hewlett Wainwright took that as a compliment. "Thank you; let me give you some more. And in a short while, I'll have Maggie bring in something to sop up the alcohol." He winked at Morton. "Nothing special, just a little cheese and some crackers, but it'll tone down the whiskey. Not that you have to worry about it tonight. The Inn's close enough, and you're not driving anywhere." He chuckled. "Enjoy our hospitality."

"What about you?" asked Morton, noticing that only he had a glass in his hand.

"Oh, Ilona never developed a taste for whiskey, and I've had to give it up." He patted his stomach. "You know how it is: after a certain age, you must watch what you eat and drink, or your system takes revenge. You wouldn't know that yet, but one day it will happen to you, too."

"I feel awkward—" Morton began, only to have Wainwright make a dismissing gesture.

"Don't bother, Mr. Symes. It's a pleasure to be able to offer you our hospitality, and it would be very disappointing if you were not pleased with what we offer." He indicated one of the rosewood chairs near the fireplace. "Sit down. Be comfortable. Ilona, persuade him for me."

Mrs Wainwright looked directly into Morton's eyes. "Please. Sit down. Have your drink. Be comfortable."

A trifle nonplussed, Morton did as he was told, thinking that if the situation became too awkward, he could always make his excuses and leave. "Thank you."

"Now then," said Hewlett Wainwright, coming to stand in front of the hearth. "I told you I'd explain what has happened in this village to account for our change of fortune here. I imagine your superiors are going to wonder about it, no matter what you do here. In a way, that's too bad; I hate to think of Jericho drawing attention to itself in its present state. However, I suppose we must accept our predicament as unavoidable. Eventually someone would notice our . . . absence."

Morton was trying not to look at Ilona Wainwright, but was not succeeding. "Your absence," he repeated as if the words made no sense at all.

"Certainly we have to contend with . . . many problems here.Once the mill closed, there was so little to hold on to, you must see. The mill, directly or indirectly, accounted for more than half the employment in Jericho, which meant that a sort of domino effect resulted from the closing. There have been some businesses that have been able to hold out, but generally we have not a wide enough economic base to keep the town going. Which is why I've been extending credit to so many of the villagers through my personal fortune, which is quite extensive."

"Hewlett is of the old school," said Ilona with a fond glance at her husband. "I sometimes think that was why he wanted to marry me."

"Oh dearest!" Hewlett Wainwright guffawed. "I didn't care what you were or who you were or anything else about you; I cared only that you wanted me as much as I wanted you." He paused and turned toward Morton. "It was a second marriage for me; my first wife died ten years ago. She—my first wife—was the daughter of my father's closest business associate. You might say that our marriage was set from birth, and you would not be far wrong."

"You're worse than the old aristocracy," said Ilona fondly.

"Be that as it may. The second time I married, Mr. Symes, I married to please myself, and when I brought my wife back here to Jericho, I was the happiest man in the world." He indicated the parlor. "It's no Carpathian castle, but it's not a hovel, either."

"Carpathian castles are cold," said Ilona. "More than half of them are in ruins." She looked at Morton with a strange expression in her mesmerizing eyes. "You think this place has become lifeless—you know nothing of it. There are places in the mountains of my homeland that appear to be on the far side of the grave, so lost are they."

"Don't exaggerate, my dear," Hewlett Wainwright asked with a playful grin. "Every part of Europe has some village or ruin that makes Jericho seem lively."

"I suppose so," said Morton dubiously. He had another taste of the whiskey, and hoped he could keep his head clear. "It must have seemed strange, coming here after living in Europe. There is so much history in Europe."

Ilona smiled, this time widely. "We make our own history, don't we?" She turned her head as a small, shapeless woman bustled into the room with a little tray. "Here's the cheese. I hope you enjoy it, Mr. Symes."

Morton looked at the hard yellow cheese and did his best to appear interested. "It's fine." He was glad he had had a little to eat before coming to this meeting, and at the same time felt so hungry and uncomfortable in this strange company that he hardly cared that the cheese looked almost inedible.

"I'll cut you a slice, if you like," offered Hewlett Wainwright, motioning the maid away. He picked up the cheese slicer and set to work sawing. "You'll find this has a lot of character. Not many places you can get this kind of cheese today."

"I see," said Morton, accepting the long shard of cheese laid across a dry cracker. "Thanks." It was quite a job getting through the cheese and cracker; in the process he consumed most of the whiskey only to make the other swallowable. His head rang, but he did his best to smile as he set his glass aside. "You're very gracious. Tell me more, will you, about how the town ran into financial difficulties? Wasn't that two years ago?"

Hewlett refilled his glass as he embarked on a complicated tale that would have been hard to follow if Morton had had all his wits about him. As it was, he discovered that he was not able to make sense out of most of it, though he had a general description of a mill unable to keep up with modern big business, and a town that lived on its bounty; it was theme and variation on what he had already learned, but told with more convolutions. Still with or without the embellishments, the story was basically a simple one: when the mill was closed, jobs and money disappeared, and most of Jericho was lost.

"My husband has made it more cut-and-dried than it is," said Ilona when Hewlett at last paused. "He hasn't mentioned his own role in preserving the place. His personal concern for the village has provided a livelihood for many of those who have remained here."

"But . . . but they haven't filed their taxes," said Morton, doing his best not to slur this statement.

"They had no reason," said Hewlett. "Most of them had very little income. There was nothing to report."

"But you know better than that," protested Morton, striving to keep his thoughts clear enough to continue. "We have to know when there is nothing to report, just as when there is. It's the information that's crucial—don't you see? The government cannot provide needed assistance if there is no record of the need—don't you see?" His head hummed like a shell against his ear, the sound that was supposed to be like the sea and was not. "We have to be able to show that the circumstances have changed, that you are not . . . taking advantage, or. . . ." He swallowed hard and tried again. "If you have new problems, there are other consequences than. . . . Don't you see: if you haven't made money, then there are fewer penalties for not filing. But you have to file—don't you see?" He knew he was repeating himself, but was unable to stop himself. That one phrase—don't you see—was stuck in his thoughts, persistent as allergy sniffles, and he could not rid himself of it.

"No," said Hewlett. "Oh, I've read the publications, but I cannot see why it is essential for you to have paperwork for no reason, because we have no money to report. Why, even the police chief and his assistant are paid from my personal accounts, not from the village budget, because those coffers are empty. If you like, they're the village's private security force now, and as such are my employees." He looked at Morton. "Would you like a little more whiskey?"

"Not right now," said Morton, who was astonished when Hewlett put a bit more in his glass.

"Just in case you change your mind," said Hewlett. "More cheese?"

The room grew darker as the three of them conversed. Morton soon began to lose track of what he was trying to say, and after a while, that no longer bothered him. He noticed that his host and hostess hovered close to him, which he decided was flattering, since it was not typical of New Englanders. He could feel them bend over him, and he tried to think of an adequate apology for his bad manners, for he was more than pleasantly tipsy. He knew he ought to make an excuse for his behavior, but he could not string the words together sensibly. He was simply aware of stretching out on the sofa—unthinkable behavior!—and of Ilona Wainwright fussing with his tie to loosen it, her eyes boring into him as she did.

"Not too much, my dearest," Morton heard Hewlett say. "Not all at once, remember."

Whatever Ilona had answered was lost to Morton, who felt overcome by fatigue, unable to move or think. He tried to explain how sorry he was, but, to his intense chagrin, he passed out.

◊◊◊

He woke in the Ivy Room of the Jericho Inn, his clothes neatly put away and his pajamas on, the blankets tucked under his chin. It was midmorning, to judge by the position of the square of light from the window. Morton rubbed his eyes, groaning as he moved. He started to sit up, but stopped as dizziness made the room swing; he lowered his head and sighed. He damned himself roundly for getting drunk, and he shuddered at what the Wainwrights must have thought. He moved again, more slowly and gingerly, and this time made it to his elbows before vertigo took hold of him. "Damn it," he muttered. "Damn, damn, damn."

The few times he had drunk too much, he had been left with a thumping headache and a queasy stomach, but never before had he felt weak. As he made himself sit up, his arms trembled with the effort, and a cold sweat broke out on his chest and neck.

"This is absurd," he said to the wallpaper, embarrassed at how little strength he had, and how much work it took merely to drag himself to his feet. With a concentrated effort, he got out of bed and, steadying himself against the wall, he went toward the little bathroom, breathing as if he had just run two miles.

His waxy pallor surprised him, and the dark shadows under his eyes, as if he had been beaten. Morton stared in the mirror, appalled at his own wan features. His hands shook as he did his best to shave, though when he was through, he had several minor nicks, including one on his neck that bled more persistently than the others. As he toweled his face dry, he inspected the cuts and dotted them with iodine. How was he going to explain this to Brewster? he wondered. How was he going to account for his failure to gain the needed information? What excuse could he offer for his conduct? He puzzled over this, his wits moving more slowly than his body, as he dressed. Belatedly, he remembered he had to drive to the bank in North Poindexter to get his cash. The thought of such a journey left him troubled, but he knew he had to go there before he ran out of money, and he had to be there this morning, or Brewster would be curious and critical.

There was no one in the lobby of the Inn when Morton made his way down the stairs, and the street, once again, appeared all but empty. A face appeared at the window of one of the offices near the general store, but aside from that, there was no one to be seen. Morton got into his chocolate BMW and started it cautiously, wincing as the engine erupted into life. Ordinarily he would have taken pleasure in the sound, but not this morning He drove off at a sedate pace, and once on the two-lane state highway, he did not risk going faster than forty.

By the time he reached North Poindexter, the worst of his dizziness had gone. His hands still felt weak, his thoughts seemed disordered, and his eyes squinted against the sun, but he no longer felt as if he could not keep steady. The busy, narrow streets pleased him, and he almost enjoyed having to hunt for a parking space.

The senior teller had Morton's voucher for cash, and after checking his credentials and getting his signature on the necessary documents, gave him eight hundred dollars. "Odd, you needing cash," she remarked as she slipped the papers into the appropriate files.

"Yes it is," said Morton, adding, "Can you recommend a good place for lunch?" Now that he had said the words, he decided he was ravenous. It was not just the drink, he realized, that had made him so much not himself, but the lack of food. Whiskey and no supper, and no breakfast. No wonder he had felt poorly. "I want something more than a sandwich," he went on.

"Well," the senior teller said, "I don't know what to tell you. There's Edna's down the block; they're quite good, but they're pretty much soup-and-sandwich. Then there's the Federal Restaurant. That's expensive, but the food is good, and they have a large lunch." She looked at him more closely. "We don't have much in the way of fancy eating in North Poindexter."

"You have more here than in Jericho," said Morton in a tone that he hoped was funny. "That place was—"

"Jericho?" echoed the senior teller. "You mean you've been over in Jericho?"

"Yes," said Morton, baffled at the peculiar expression in the senior teller's eyes. Speaking the word carefully, he asked, "Why?"

"Oh," said the senior teller with a belated and unconvincing show of disinterest, "it's nothing—the place is so remote, and with the mill closed and all. . . ."

When she did not go on, Morton grew more intrigued. "Has there been trouble in Jericho? Other than the mill closing and people being out of work, I mean?"

The senior teller shrugged. "You know how people say things about places like that. It's gossip and rumors; all these little places in New England have some of it. They're glad to think the worst of villages like Jericho, so their own place seems better." She lowered her voice. "It's not as if I believe what they say about the place, but it is spooky; you'll give me that."

"I wouldn't use that word, perhaps," said Morton with caution, "but I can understand why someone might."

"Yes; well, you see why there are stories about the place. Most of them sound like some kind of horror movie, you know; one of those George Romero things. You hear about weird creatures, or worse than that, roaming the streets, preying on decent folk. It's silly. It's just talk. It's because the place is so . . . empty." She made a dismissing movement with her hands. "I probably shouldn't be saying this. It's not at all responsible."

"I appreciate it," said Morton. "It's always disconcerting to be in deserted places. While I've been there, I don't think I've seen more than a dozen people. During the day, there's almost no one around, and in the evening, the people on the streets don't say much. I think having the mill gone makes it all so precarious that they don't like to talk about it."

"Probably," said the senior teller, and moved away from him. "I'm sorry, but I got work to do."

After Morton ordered a generous lunch at the Federal Restaurant, he caught up on his report, trying to gloss over his misbehavior the night before. "I don't know," he muttered as he read what he had put down, "how else to account for it."

"Did you say something?" asked the waiter as he brought calves' liver and onions with a spinach salad on the side. "More coffee?"

"Yes, please," said Morton, adding, "And a glass of tomato juice, if you would."

"Naturally," said the waiter, departing at once.

When he had finished his lunch and indulged in an excellent carrot cake with extra raisins, Morton decided he was getting better. Food was what he had needed. He no longer felt as light-headed as before, and some of his strength was returning. "That'll teach me to skip dinner," he said softly as he paid the bill.

Before he drove back to Jericho, he stopped to get some protein snacks: jerky, a few slices of ham and turkey, and a box of crackers. He had his hard-boiled eggs, and this ought to make things easier for him.

◊◊◊

The police chief, a bulky man everyone called Willy, regarded Morton's identification askance. "I wondered when you'd be getting around to me," he said, his accent ringing with the flat vowels of New England and the east coast of Britain. "I don't know what I can do for you, and that's a fact."

"It may be," said Morton, feeling restored and just guilty enough to persevere with his investigation. "I have to ask. I hope you appreciate that."

"Of course," said Willy with resignation. "What do you need to know?"

"First, I need to know how many people have moved out of Jericho in the past eighteen months." Morton drew out his notebook and made a show of getting ready to write down the information.

"Oh, four, maybe five," said Willy after giving his answer some thought. "No more than that."

Morton stared at him. "That's absurd."

"Preacher Stonecroft, he left; him and his wife, that is. They went, oh, more'n a year ago. Sad to lose them, but the way things are around here. . ." He indicated the window, as if the view of Main Street provided the explanation. "They weren't our sort, not them. So they left."

"I see," said Morton, trying to guess why this man was lying.

"Over a year ago. So did the minister; he took those two orphaned boys and went west. That was before the Stonecrofts left, by maybe a couple months." Willy looked at his three empty cells visible through the open door.

"Also not your sort?" Morton ventured.

"That's right. And the two boys probably needed to get out, with their folks newly dead and all." Willy sighed. "Henry and Dinah Hill."

"They were the boys' parents?" Morton asked, finding the police chief's remarks a bit hard to follow.

"Yeah. They died, and Reverend Kingsly took them away. He said it was for the best. He might have been right," said Willy.

"Where did they go?" Morton wanted to know.

"West," Willy told him, with a wave of his hand in that direction.

"But where west? Don't you know?" He would have to tell Brewster about Reverend Kingsly; somehow it ought to be possible to trace the man and the two orphans.

"He didn't tell us. I don't think he knew." Willy sighed. "Not that we hold it against him, you understand. In a case like his, he had to leave."

Morton scowled. "How do you mean, in a case like his?"

"The way things were going. Churchmen have to have a congregation, don't they?" Willy sighed again, this time letting his air out slowly.

"And because the mill closed, people stopped going to church?" Morton asked, and decided at once that what the chief of police was trying so politely to say was that there was no money to support the churches in town; with the Wainwrights paying the villagers out of their own pockets, there would not be much left for the two ministers.

"Well, it wasn't quite like that, but. . . ." He looked toward the window again. "This isn't a very big place; it's never been a very big place. Things get hard in a town like this. We know what it's like to be cut off."

"You mean your isolation is working against you?" Morton asked, hoping he had interpreted Willy's remark accurately.

"Well, some of us think it works for us, but it's all in how you look at it." He nodded twice. "I can't give you much more, Mr. Symes. You've seen Jericho for yourself; you know what it's like here. No matter what the government does, things aren't going to change here a whole hell of a lot, if you take my meaning."

"Yes," said Morton, not at all certain he followed Willy's implications. "Do you think you'd have time to draw up a list of the names and addresses of those people still living in town?"

"Still living?" repeated Willy. "Sure, I can do that."

Morton gave him his best stern but sincere smile. "Thank you very much for your help, Willy. I know this can't be easy for you."

"We get by," said Willy as Morton let himself out of the police station.

◊◊◊

At the diner, Morton made a point of having a second order of pot roast and a dish of ice cream for dessert. He noticed once again that no one else was in the place, and this time he said, "Is it always this slow?"

"Most folks around here like to eat in," said the waitress without looking at him. "You know how it is."

"Yes," said Morton, thinking that at last he did.

"We keep to ourselves around here, especially since the mill closed." She regarded him with taunting eyes, the rest of her apparently consumed with boredom.

"It has had serious repercussions for the town, hasn't it?" Morton looked at the waitress once, then gazed toward the window so that she would not feel he was questioning her too closely.

"It's one of the things," said the waitress. "There are others."

"Yes," Morton said at once. "Of course there are." He paid for his supper and left a 22 percent tip, more than was allowed, but he wanted to let the waitress know he appreciated all she had told him.

As Morton went out the door, the waitress called after him, "You've not found out everything yet."

Morton paused, his hand on the latch. "What did you say?"

"You heard me," she responded. "Think about it."

"Of course," said Morton, wondering what she intended to imply. He thought about it as he stepped out onto the street, feeling a peculiar exhilaration from the darkness he had never experienced before. He strode back toward the Inn, but found himself reluctant to return to his room. Inadvertently, he was drawn to the Wainwright house, his thoughts disordered as he looked up at the faded grandeur of the mansion.

"Mr. Symes," called Ilona from a second-story window. "How nice to see you again."

"Thank you," said Morton, overcome with a sudden and inexplicable rush of desire that left him all but breathless. His pulse thrummed; his flesh quivered; he seemed to be burning with fever and locked in ice all at the same time. It was most improper for him to stand staring up—and with such naked longing in his face—at the aristocratic features of Ilona Wainwright.

"It was a pleasure to have you with us last evening," she said, her red lips widening in a smile.

"You're very . . . kind," Morton faltered. What was it about this woman that aroused him so intensely? What fascination did she work on him, that he felt drawn to her in a way he had thought existed only in fantasy? And how could he ever account for his reprehensible behavior to Hewlett Wainwright?

"Not at all," Ilona said, her voice low and seductive. "I only wish to . . . to entertain you again," She stepped out onto the little balcony that fronted her window. "Will you come in?"

"I . . . I don't know. . . ." Morton was almost certain he was blushing, and that made his embarrassment more acute. "Is your husband at home?" He could hardly believe that he could be so callous, so impolite to speak to her that way. He moved back a few steps. "I'm sorry."

"Why?" Ilona asked, and that single word was as thrilling as a symphony.

"It's . . . it's all very awkward," Morton began. "You see, Mrs. Wainwright, I don't . . . that is, I ought not. . . . It would not be right to take advantage of you." Be sensible, he told himself. This woman is older than you, and she is married. You have no right to want her; you have no right to speak to her. It is wrong for you to do this.

"Is something troubling you, Mr. Symes?" she asked, and there was the faintest suggestion of haughty laughter in her question.

Morton squared his shoulders. "I have an obligation as an investigator for the IRS not to abuse my position, which is what I would probably be doing if. . . . It would be unforgivable of me to use my . . . power to . . . to compromise you." As he spoke, he moved closer to the house.

Ilona appeared not to have heard him. "It has been so long since there was someone new in the village; I have been beside myself, wanting to meet someone new. Will you come in?" She leaned down, one long, pale hand extended. "I would be so grateful to you, if you would come in, Mr. Symes."

"But . . ." All the protests he had intended to make faded from his lips "Certainly, if you would like that."

"Very good, Mr. Symes," said Ilona, her smile growing more vivid. "You will find the side door, there by the conservatory, open." With that, she left the balcony.

Morton all but fell through the door in his eagerness to see Ilona. Though part of his mind still tried to reason with him, to make him resist the favor that Ilona appeared to offer, it was quickly stilled as Ilona herself came into the sitting room, her face alight with anticipation. Morton made one last attempt to break away from her. "It's wrong of me to be here. I owe you and your husband . . ."

"If you believe you owe us something, all the more reason for you to stay," she said, coming to his side and resting her head on his shoulder. "How vigorous you are. How the life courses through your veins."

That odd compliment puzzled Morton, but not for long. Ilona turned her face to his, and her carmined lips fastened on his as she seized him in a surprisingly powerful embrace. Morton stopped thinking and gave himself to delirious, erotic folly.

◊◊◊

It was almost time to phone in his report when Morton woke in his bed once again. His dizziness had returned threefold, and his weakness was far greater than it had been previously. Morton put an unsteady hand to his forehead and tried to organize his thoughts before he made his call to Brewster.

"You sound as if you're coming down with something," his superior observed critically after Morton commenced his report.

"I think I might be," Morton allowed. "I feel . . . drained." He sighed. "I wish I understood it."

"Have the doctor check you over before you come back to the office; I don't want you starting something with the other investigators."

"Of course not," said Morton, then got on with his report. "According to the chief of police, not very many people have left town, though I personally have seen few of the remaining townspeople. If they still live here, they must work somewhere else during the day."

"You say the town is empty?" Brewster demanded. "Make yourself plain, Symes."

"Yes sir," said Morton, squinting to read his notes. "It might as well be a ghost town during the day."

"I see," said Brewster in his best significant voice. "And where do you think the people work?"

"I want to find that out," said Morton, stifling a yawn. "I don't think it's North Poindexter, if that's the issue. I'm fairly certain that they're not going there, judging from how people in North Poindexter regard Jericho."

"All right," said Brewster. "And how is that?"

"They seem to think that this is a very strange town, that the people here are odd and their ways are old-fashioned or something of the sort." He leaned on the wall beside the pay phone. "That doesn't sound like a lot of people from Jericho work there, does it?"

"Probably not," was all the concession Brewster would make.

"From what I've seen, this place is . . . growing in on itself. It's caught—you know how some of these little places get when the main industry falls through? Remember that town in West Virginia that sort of dried up when the factory that made chairs went under?"

"You do not need to remind me," said Brewster stiffly. "And you think this is another Lambford, do you?"

"Well," said Morton uncertainly, "I'm not positive, no, but it looks likely. If you could send a formal request for records and the rest of it, the bank president will show me the accounts here, but he won't do it without the paperwork. Which is his right, of course. I need a few more days to get all my facts together, and to see what the bank president can offer me"—unbidden, the image of Ilona Wainwright came to his mind, a vision so intense that he was not able to speak for three or four seconds, and he covered this up with a cough—"and . . . take some time to . . . assess what I find."

"What's wrong? You get yourself attended to before you get any worse," demanded Brewster.

"Allergies, I think. It's probably allergies," Morton improvised. "I guess I should take another pill."

"Don't neglect it. We don't want to have to pay hospital bills for you," said Brewster as if he were speaking to a fractious six-year-old.

"I don't want to be any trouble," Morton assured him at once. "Pollen does it, and there's pollen in the fall."

"Yes," said Brewster in a tone that indicated he had heard more than enough about all of Morton's problems. "I will see that the proper documents are sent to the bank by express, or courier, if that's necessary. That should be sufficient for your purposes."

Morton nodded to himself. "I don't think that Mr. Wainwright will refuse any request if it's made properly and officially, but he has the interests of his depositors to defend, and it's proper for him to do it."

"If that's all, Symes?" His tone implied that he did not need Morton Symes to teach him his job.

"For the time being," said Morton, one hand to his head. "I'll call again day after tomorrow. And you'll have my written reports when I get back." His head was ringing now, and every word he spoke crashed through his skull.

"Keep your medical records separate from the rest. We'll have to review them for reimbursement." He paused, then bade Morton a stiff farewell and hung up without further ado.

After his phone call, and sitting in the empty lobby for almost half an hour, Morton was barely able to walk the short distance from the Inn to the diner, and when he got there, he sat for some time staring at the menu, its offerings of corned beef and cabbage so uninteresting to him that he actually felt slightly sick as he read it. Corned beef and cabbage, and doubtless it had been boiled to the point of falling apart, the cabbage nothing more than taste-less vegetable goo. Finally, when the waitress came to take his order, he turned bleary eyes on her. "Is there any chance you could get me a steak, a rare one?"

"Steak?" said the waitress, a fleeting, ferocious look at the back of her eyes.

"Yes; you know, a slice of cow, singed but bloody." He put his elbows on the table, astonished at his own dreadful manners. "I'd like it soon, if you can arrange that."

"What about hamburger, singed but bloody?" asked the wait-ress, not quite mocking him.

"Fine," said Morton, but with a touch of regret; he had antic-ipated the satisfaction of tearing into the meat; that was not pos-sible with hamburger. He waited for nearly fifteen minutes before the waitress came back with a plate of raw chopped beef and all the makings of steak tartare.

"I thought you might like this a little better," said the waitress with an expression that just missed being a leer. "I'll bring you some French bread to—"

"Never mind," said Morton, whose hunger grew painfully

intense as he looked at the mound of raw beef. "I'll manage." It shocked him to listen to his harsh words; he never treated people the way he was treating the waitress. He could not imagine what had come over him, and decided that it had to be the effect of his allergies, or whatever was making him so abominably weak. "I don't suppose that you suffer from allergies."

"Allergies? Not me." The waitress laughed nastily. "So you got allergies?" She did not wait for him to answer her question, but turned on her heel and left him with his steak tartare.

◊◊◊

By morning, Morton was feeling quite restored. His sight no longer blurred if he moved quickly, and his headache had decreased to bearable levels. He almost passed up the two hard-boiled eggs that were delivered to his room by the sullen clerk, then forced them down so that he would not have another episode like the last. He had decided today he would have to inspect the bank records; he hoped that Hewlett Wainwright would not be too difficult about his requests. At the memory of his illicit meeting with Ilona, he cringed and wondered how he would be able to face her husband. He tried to direct his concentration back to the job he was entrusted to do, but Ilona intruded on all of it, her elegant, sensuous presence insinuating into the world of figures. Finally Morton set his reports aside and decided to pay a visit to the post office. If the documents he requested were there, he could get on with the work; he wanted to believe that his infatuation would diminish as he gave himself over to his task. Romance and tax forms rarely mixed, he decided, and thought of the many times he had found his affections waning as his enthusiasm for tracking down tax inconsistencies waxed. How he longed for his computer screen and the safe haven of dependable, sensible, bloodless figures. The impression of Ilona Wainwright's curving mouth and brilliant eyes could be exorcised by columns of numbers.

There was a single, aged clerk at the post office, a man of a uniform gray color, from his hair and eyes and skin to the sweater and trousers he wore. He monosyllabically refused to say whether the documents had come from the IRS for Hewlett Wainwright, and when pressed, closed the shutter in front of his counter.

Reluctantly, Morton started toward the bank, his eagerness fading with each step. He did not know how he could face Hewlett Wainwright with his guilt; Ilona was his wife, his wife. Morton had never allowed himself to be drawn into associating with a married woman before, and the realization that in a town as small as Jericho, secrets were impossible to keep gave him more dread than the possibility of Brewster's wrath.

"Good day, Mr. Symes. Morton!" Hewlett Wainwright came out of his private office effusively. He gestured to the one teller on duty. "How good of you to have those letters sent. I can't tell you how it relieves me. This way I have not compromised my depositors, have I?" His voice boomed through the vaulted room. "Come back to my office, and we can go over the records."

Morton was nonplussed by this exuberance, and he hesitated as he took the bank president's hand. "Why, thank you."

"You're looking a trifle less robust today. You don't mind my mentioning it, do you?" He guided Morton into his office. "You're the only game in town, and so you—" He broke off as Morton stared at him.

"The only game in town?" Morton said, appalled at his conflicting emotions.

Hewlett folded his arms. "A joke, a kind of pun, Morton. You . . . you're in demand because of it."

To his chagrin, Morton blushed. "Mr. Wainwright, I don't know what to say to you. I never intended to do anything incorrect, and you must believe that—"

Hewlett clapped Morton on the back. "We don't worry about incorrect here, not now." He indicated his visitor's chair. "Do sit down. And let me get the records you want. They're very old-fashioned. We don't have many computers in town these days."

"Since the mill closed," Morton supplied.

"No, not that," Hewlett said, frowning. "What did you used to do on Saturday afternoons when you were young, Morton?"

This abrupt change of subject made Morton blink. "Uh . . . I was a Boy Scout. We did nature walks and things like that."

Hewlett cocked his head. "Around here we went to the movies. Our mothers would take us over to the theater in North Poindexter and leave us while they went shopping and out to lunch and to the hairdresser and all the rest of it." He folded his hands. "Didn't you ever go see *Godzilla* or *Firemaidens from Outer Space?* Or *Dracula?*"

"No," Morton admitted, wondering what Hewlett Wainwright was attempting to tell him. "Sometimes we went roller-skating, but my family believed that children should be outside, doing wholesome things when we weren't in school."

"A-ha," said Hewlett seriously. "And you never sneaked off on your own?"

"Not for that, no," said Morton, more puzzled than ever.

Hewlett drummed his fingers on the table. "What do you think of Ilona's . . . appetites?"

Morton felt his face grow hot. "I . . . I never meant to do anything that you—"

"It doesn't matter what you meant," said Hewlett grandly. "It matters what we want."

"I didn't intend for—" He stopped, staring at Hewlett and noticing for the first time that the bank president was really quite an impressive figure of a man. "I'll leave at once, if you find me an embarrassment. I'll arrange for another investigator to come."

"You'll do that in any case," said Hewlett with calm certainty. "Because it is what we want."

"And. . . ." He let the single word trail off. "I'll leave," he offered, starting to get to his feet.

"I'm not through with you yet, Morton, and neither is Ilona. We can still have something from you, and we intend to get it. We're so very hungry." He leaned forward over his desk.

"Hungry?" Morton repeated, having trouble following Hewlett once again.

For the first time, Hewlett became impatient. "Damn it, man, are you really as ignorant as you appear? Are you really unaware of what has happened to you?"

"I . . . don't know what you're talking about. And if," he went on, suddenly certain that all these peculiar side steps were intended to keep him from his investigation, "it's your plan to withhold the figures the IRS has requested, you're going to be very disappointed."

Hewlett shook his head. "There is no point to this investigation. It doesn't apply to us, not now."

"The rules of the IRS apply to everyone, Mr. Wainwright," said Morton with a sudden assumption of dignity he had not been able to find until that moment. "You understand that even when a town is in difficulties, we cannot make an exception of the people. It's not to their benefit. Everyone has to file income tax. Those are the rules."

Hewlett laughed, and this time there was no trace of joviality in the tone. "Death and taxes, death and taxes. It appears we are not allowed to have the release of death."

"When you die, your heirs will have to file for you in order to let us know that you are dead. Until then, I'm afraid you're all in the same situation as the rest of the country." Morton rose unsteadily. "If you don't mind, I have records to examine. I'm willing to do it at the Inn, if you'd rather."

"Morton, come to your senses," Hewlett ordered, his manner becoming very grand. "Don't you know what's happened to you? Haven't you guessed what you've stumbled upon?"

"I wish you'd stop these melodramatic ploys," said Morton, his face becoming set. If he had felt a little better, he might have taken some satisfaction in setting Hewlett straight. "Your town could be in a lot of trouble, and there's no way you can get out of the consequences now. You can't decide not to file income taxes, Wainwright. That's not your decision to make."

"Isn't it?" Hewlett rose to his feet, his face darkening. "We're vampires here, Morton."

Morton stared; he had never heard so bizarre an excuse for failure to file. "What? Nonsense!"

"At first," said Hewlett resonantly, "there was just Ilona and me, but here in Jericho, we had our pick, and those we chose, chose others. Recently we've had to get by on . . . windfalls. Like you, Morton."

"Like me?" Morton laughed nervously. "Don't make your case any worse than it is. Just give me the records, and let me do my job. And don't try that kind of a farndiddle on—"

Hewlett shook his head, anger changing his expression to something more distressing than it had been. "You think I am lying to you, Morton? You believe that I've made this up?"

"It's ridiculous," said Morton flatly. "You'll have to come up with something better than that. And if you persist with so absurd a story, you will not find the IRS at all sympathetic. We try to be responsive to the predicaments of those taxpayers who are experiencing financial setbacks, but you're mocking our policy, and that will not work to your benefit." He touched his forehead, wishing he did not have a headache.

"And what will you think when you start desiring blood?" Hewlett asked, his tone jeering now. "How do you plan to explain that?"

"Your threats mean nothing to me," said Morton.

"Wait until the next full moon," said Hewlett. "You'll be in for a shock then." He smacked his desk with the flat of his hand once. "For your own benefit, Symes, don't be too hasty. You're at risk now, and once you join our number—"

"Oh come off it!" Morton said, heading toward the door. "I am not going to indulge you in this travesty of yours, Wainwright. If you had been candid with me, I might have been willing to extend myself on behalf of this town, but under the circumstances—circumstances that you have created, Mr. Wainwright—there is no reason for me to do anything more than file my report and let the law take its course." Without waiting for any response, he strode through the office door and across the lobby.

From his place behind the desk, Hewlett Wainwright called out, "Wait for Ilona tonight, Symes. There is still a little wine left in your veins. Then wait for the full moon."

◊◊◊

Morton considered leaving Jericho that very afternoon, but his fatigue was so great that he did not trust himself to drive on the winding, narrow roads as daylight faded. He occupied himself for the remainder of the day updating his reports and adding his own observations to the facts he had discovered. For the most part, he dealt very indirectly with his discoveries, but when it came to Wainwright's ludicrous claims, Morton hesitated. Matters would go badly enough in Jericho without the additional condemnation of the bank president's sarcasm. Morton decided that it was not proper for the entire town to suffer because the bank president was making insulting and outlandish claims. There would be other ways to deal with Hewlett Wainwright; the townspeople had more than enough to contend with.

Dusk turned the Ivy Room dark, and Morton finally set his work aside. He knew he ought to go out for a meal, but his headache was worse, and it appeared to have killed his appetite. He went down to the lobby and asked for a pot of tea to be sent up along with some rolls. Then he tottered back up the stairs and promptly collapsed on his bed. His thoughts began to drift, and soon he was in that strange half-dreaming, half-waking state where his perceptions were pliant as Silly Putty.

In this state, it seemed to him that he got up once again and went down onto the street, where he saw dozens of townspeople waiting in silence as he went toward the Wainwright house. He recognized the chief of police and the waitress who had served him his supper, but the rest meant nothing to him, almost having no faces. Morton sensed they were watching him, though only a few were bold enough to do it openly. There was a brazen hunger in their faces that might have petrified him had this not been a dream. He kept moving.

Ilona Wainwright was in the overrun garden, standing beside a shapeless bush Morton did not recognize. There were a few long flowers hanging on its branches, giving off a sensuous, sickly smell, cloying as overly sweet candies. Ilona, in a trailing lavender dress, smiled and held out her arm to him—part of Morton's mind wanted to laugh at Ilona for not wearing black—beckoning to him.

With the townspeople so near, Morton could hardly bring himself to move. He was compromising himself, his investigation, and the IRS by this infatuation with a married woman. It was one thing when their relationship was a matter of conjecture, for then he had recourse to plausible deniability. Once their trysts were known and seen, there would be no such means to refute any accusations made against him. He trembled as he looked at her; when she called his name, he succumbed.

How cold her arms were, and how she held him! The only thing lacking in the passion of her embrace was warmth. By the time they broke apart, Morton was shivering.

"You must come inside; let me warm you," said Ilona in her lowest, most seductive tone.

"I. . . ." Morton could not break away from her.

"Come inside," she coaxed, going toward the open door that led from the garden into what had once been called the morning room.

Morton went with her, and passed into deeper sleep, to wake in the morning pale and ill, feeling as if he had spent the whole night in an endless fistfight, which he had lost. It took more than five minutes for him to get up, and when at last he did, he was more disoriented than he had been previously. He blinked stupidly, and stared at the atrocious wallpaper as if it might be ancient undeciphered writing rather than a bad representation of ivy leaves. Gradually his thoughts began to piece themselves together, each one adding to the sensation of vertigo building in him, and making him feel queasy.

"Got to get up," he said to himself, then fell silent as he heard the thready noise he made. God! he thought. This is more than allergies. I must have some kind of flu.

That was it, he decided as he pulled himself out of bed and felt his way along the wall. He had picked up some kind of virus, and it had distorted his perceptions. Yes, that explained it. The town was in trouble, no doubt of that, but because of the disease, he was making more out of their troubles than existed. In the bathroom he stared in the mirror at his haggard features, then opened his mouth very wide in the hope that he might be able to see if his throat was red. The angle was wrong, and he could see nothing, though his throat was sore, and his head was full of thunder. He started to shave, doing his best to handle the razor with his customary care.

This time he managed not to nick himself, but his hands were shaking visibly by the time he put the razor away. His bones seemed without form, as if they were made of Jell-O instead of bone. He lowered his head and reached for his toothbrush. Another hour, he said to himself. Another hour, and I'll be gone from here, gone away. I'll make an appointment to see the doctor tomorrow. He considered that, then decided that he had better choose a different doctor, one who was not connected to the Service, so that if he had anything seriously wrong, it would not get back to Brewster. As he finished with his teeth, he began to feel the first stirrings of satisfaction.

The sour-faced clerk was not at the desk, and it took Morton some little time to find him.

"I have work to do," the clerk announced, holding up the handle of his broom to make the point.

"I'd like to check out." He held up the key. "My bags are in the lobby."

The clerk sighed as if he were being asked to undertake all the labors of Hercules. "So you're going," he said as he started toward the hallway.

"Yes," said Morton, doing his best to be pleasant.

"Going to tell them Infernal Revenuers that Jericho's down the drain, is that it?" His rancor was more for show than any strong feeling. "What'll they do to us?"

"I don't know," said Morton seriously. "My job is to investigate. There are others who make those decisions." He wiped his hands on his handkerchief before he looked over the bill that the clerk presented to him, all entries in a crabbed little hand.

"But you got to make recommendations?" said the clerk.

"I have to make reports. Others will do the evaluations." He nodded as he checked the math. "It looks fine. How much more do I owe you?"

The clerk named the figure, and Morton presented him with the an appropriate amount, then looked around the lobby. "This could be such a pretty place. I can't understand why you don't do something with it. Towns like this one can be real tourist attractions if you go about development the right way." It was only a friendly observation, but the clerk looked at him, much struck.

"Mr. Symes," he said as Morton struggled to lift his bags. "What did you mean by that?"

Morton was starting to sweat; it embarrassed him that he could not do so little a thing as lift his bag without coming near faint-ing. "I meant . . . this place . . . is authentic. The setting . . . is beautiful." He put the suitcase down. "If you handled it right, you could develop some seasonal income, anyway."

The clerk nodded several times. "And there'd be a lot of peo-ple through here, you say?"

"In time." Morton had another go at hoisting his suitcase, and did rather better now.

"I'll take your things out to your car," said the clerk in an offhanded way. "No need for you to be puffing like that." Though a young man like you—" He left the rest of his remark to speculation.

"Thanks," said Morton, and turned his luggage over to the clerk. "You know where my car is."

"Sure do," said the clerk. "Look, when you get back to wher-ever your office is, can you find out what they'd do to us, I mean the IRS, if we wanted to turn this village into a tourist place?"

"I'll try. Who knows," he added with more encouragement than sincerity, "I might want to come back myself one of these days." He winced as the bright sunlight stabbed at his eyes; his dark glasses were taken from their case at once and clapped over his face.

"Shows good sense," said the clerk, nodding toward the glass-es. "Light can be hard on a fella."

As Morton opened the trunk, he observed, "I had the impres-sion that . . . pardon me if I'm wrong . . . that the people in Jericho aren't interested in change, and they wouldn't like turn-ing this place into a tourist town."

The clerk shrugged. "Well, the mill's gone, and we're pretty damn stuck. I can't say I want to make it all quaint, but we got to eat, like everyone else." He finished stowing the luggage and slammed the trunk closed for Morton.

Morton offered a five-dollar bill, which was refused. "You find a way to make sure we get some new blood in here—that'll be more than enough." He stood back as Morton got into the car.

Morton started the engine and felt a touch of satisfaction in the muffled roar. "Someone else from our office will be contacting you soon."

"We'll be waiting," said the clerk, and to Morton's amazement, the man licked his lips. "Make sure you save a few for yourself."

Because he could think of no appropriate reply, Morton put the car in gear and started away, waving once to the clerk before he rolled his window up. Perhaps, he thought, Jericho would not be as difficult a place as he had feared. Perhaps there were things that they would accept as necessary and reasonable change in order to continue their town. He rubbed the little raised welts on his neck as he swung into the first big bend in the road. At least he had broken the ice; he could provide some explanation of what had happened—other than the ridiculous tale Wainwright had told— that would make it possible for the townspeople not to be encumbered with an unpayable tax burden. On the whole, he was satisfied with his job, though the episodes, real and imagined, with Ilona Wainwright made his conscience smart. But with a beautiful woman like that, one so irresistible, he supposed many men had fallen under her spell at one time or another. How ludicrous to call her a vampire. If he had remained there much longer, he might have started to believe it. Hell, he might be persuaded that he was one, too. "Absurd," he said out loud. The welts continued to itch, and he scratched them without thinking as he started down the lazy decline toward North Poindexter.

Chelsea Quinn Yarbro is the author of more than fifty books, including the historical novels in the Chronicles of Saint-Germain, which are among the most popular vampire series.

True love is a virtue that conquers all boundaries
It is to be pursued at all costs.

The Brotherhood of Blood

BY HUGH B. CAVE

*I*t is midnight as I write this. Listen! Even now the doleful chimes of the Old North Church, buried in the heart of this enormous city of mine, are tolling the funeral hour.

In a little while, when the city thinks itself immune in sleep, deep-cradled in the somber hours of night—I shall go forth from here on my horrible mission of blood.

Every night it is the same. Every night the same ghoulish orgy. Every night the same mad thirst. And in a little while—

But first, while there is yet time, let me tell you of my agony. Then you will understand, and sympathize, and suffer with me.

I was twenty-six years old then. God alone knows how old I am now. The years frighten me, and I have deliberately forgotten them. But I was twenty-six when she came.

They call me an author. Perhaps I was; and yet the words which I gave to the world were not, and could not be, the true thoughts which hovered in my mind. I had studied—studied things which the average man dares not even to consider. The occult—life after death—spiritualism—call it what you will.

I had written about such things, but in guarded phrases, calculated to divulge only those elementary truths which laymen should be told. My name was well known, perhaps too well known. I can see it now as it used to appear in the pages of the leading medical journals and magazines devoted to psychic investigation.

"By—Paul Munn—Authority on the Supernatural."

In those days I had few friends; none, in fact, who were in harmony with my work. One man I did know well—a medical student at Harvard University, in Cambridge. His name was Rojer Threng.

I can remember him now as he used to sit bolt upright in the huge chair in my lonely Back Bay apartment. He filled the chair with his enormous, loosely constructed frame. His face was angular, pointed to gaunt extremes. His eyes—ah, you will have cause to consider those eyes before I have finished!—his eyes were eternally afire with a peculiar glittering life which I could never fully comprehend.

"And you can honestly sit there, spilling your mad theories to the world?" He used to accuse me in his rasping, deep-throated voice. "Good Lord, Munn, this is the Twentieth century—a scientific era of careful thought—not the time of werewolves and vampires! You are mad!"

And yet, for all his open condemnation, he did not dare to stand erect with his face lifted, and *deny* the things I told him. That sinister gleam of his eyes; there was no denying the thoughts lurking behind it. On the surface he was a sneering, indifferent doubter; but beneath the surface, where no man's eyes penetrated, he *knew*.

He was there in my apartment when she came. That night is vivid even now. There we sat, enveloped in a haze of gray cigarette smoke. I was bent over the desk in the corner, hammering a typewriter. He lay sprawled in the great over-stuffed chair, watching me critically, intently, as if he would have liked to continue the heated argument which had passed between us during the past hour.

He had come in his usual unannounced manner, bringing with him an ancient newspaper clipping from some forgotten file in the university. Thrusting the thing into my hand, he had ordered me to read it.

That clipping was of singular interest. It was a half-hearted account of the infamous vampire horror of the little half-buried village of West Surrey. You recall it? It was known, luridly, as the "crime of eleven terrors." Eleven pitiful victims, each with the same significant blood marks, were one after the other the prey of the unknown vampire who haunted that little village in the heart of an English moor. And then, when the eleventh victim had succumbed, Scotland Yard—with the assistance of the famous psychic investigator, Sir Edmund Friel—discovered the vampire to be the same aged, seemingly innocent old woman who had acted as *attendant nurse* to the unfortunate victims. A ghastly affair.

But Threng held the newspaper clipping up to me as a mere "trick" of journalism. He denounced it bitterly.

"What is a vampire, Munn?" he sneered.

I did not answer him. I saw no use in continuing a futile debate on a subject in which we had nothing in common.

"Well?" he insisted.

I swung around, facing him deliberately.

"A vampire," I said thoughtfully, choosing my words with extreme care, "is a creature of living death, dependent upon human blood for its existence. From sunset to sunrise, during the hours of darkness, it is free to pursue its horrible blood-quest. During the day it must remain within the confines of its grave— dead, and yet alive."

"And how does it appear?" he bantered. "As the usual skeletonic intruder, cowled in black, or perhaps as a mystic wraith without substance?"

"In either of two forms," I said coldly, angered by his twisted smile. "As a bat—or in its natural human substance. In either shape it leaves the grave each night and seeks blood. It obtains its blood from the throats of its victims, leaving two significant wounds in the neck from which it has drawn life. Its victims, after such a death, inherit the powers of their persecutor—and become vampires."

"Rot!" Threng exclaimed. "Utter sentimentality and imagination."

I turned back to my typewriter, ignoring him. His words were not pleasant. I would have been glad to be rid of him.

But he was persistent. He leaned forward in his chair and said critically:

"Suppose I wished to become a vampire, Munn. How could I go about it? How *does* a man obtain life after death, or life *in* death?"

"By study," I answered crisply. "By delving into thoughts which men like you sneer at. By going so deeply into such things that he becomes possessed of inhuman powers."

That ended our discussion. He could not conceive of such possibilities; and he laughed aloud at my statement. Bitterly resentful, I forced myself to continue the work before me. He, in turn, thrust a cigarette into his mouth and leaned back in his chair like a great lazy animal. And then, *she* came.

The soft knock on the door panel—so suggestive that it seemed from the world beyond—startled me. I swung about, frowning at the intrusion. Visitors at this hour of night were not the kind of guests I wished to face.

I went to the door slowly, hesitantly. My hand touched the latch nervously. Then I forced back the foolish fear that gripped me and drew the barrier wide. And there I saw her for the first time—tall, slender, radiantly lovely as she stood in the half-light of the outer passage.

"You—are Mr. Paul Munn?" she inquired quietly.

"I am," I admitted.

"I am Margot Vernee. It is unconventional, I suppose, calling upon you at this hour; but I have come because of your reputation. You are the one man in this great city who may be able to—help me."

I would have answered her, but she caught sight, then, of Rojer Threng. Her face whitened. She stepped back very abruptly, fearful—or at least so I thought—that he might have overheard her.

"I—I am sorry," she said quickly. "I thought that you were alone, Mr. Munn. I—may I return later? Tomorrow, perhaps—when you are not occupied?"

I nodded. At that particular moment I could not find a voice to answer her; for she had inadvertently stepped directly beneath the bracket lamp in the wall and her utter beauty fascinated me, choking the words back into my throat.

Then she went; and as I closed the door reluctantly, Rojer Threng glanced quizzically into my face and said dryly:

"Wants you to help her, eh? I didn't know you went in for that sort of thing, Munn. Better be careful!"

And he laughed. God, how I remember that laugh—and the cruel, derisive hatred that was inherent in it! But I did not answer him. In fact, his words were driven mechanically into my mind, and I hardly heard them. Returning to the typewriter, I attempted to force myself once more into the work that confronted me, but the face of that girl blurred the lines of my manuscript.She seemed to be still in the room, still standing near me. Imagination, of course; and yet, in view of what has happened since that night, I do not know.

◊◊◊

She did not return as she had promised. All during the following day I awaited her coming—restless, nervous, unable to work. At eleven in the evening I was still pacing automatically back and forth across the floor when the door-bell rang. It was Rojer Threng who stepped over the threshold.

At first he did not mention the peculiar affair of the previous night. He took his customary place in the big chair and talked idly about medical topics of casual interest. Then, bending forward suddenly, he demanded:

"Did she return, Munn?"

"No," I said.

"I thought not," he muttered harshly. "Not after she saw me here. I—used to know her."

It was not so much the thing he said, as the complete bitterness with which he spoke, that brought me about with a jerk, confronting him.

"You—knew her?" I said slowly.

"I knew her," be scowled. "Think of the name, man. Margot Vernee. Have I never mentioned it to you?"

"No." And then I knew that he had. At least, the inflection of it was vaguely familiar.

"Her story would interest you," he shrugged. "Peculiar, Munn—very peculiar, in view of what you were telling me last night, before she came."

He looked up at me oddly. I did not realize the significance of that crafty look then, but now I know.

"The Vernee family," he said, "is as old as France."

"Yes?" I tried to mask my eagerness.

"The Château Vernee is still standing—abandoned—forty miles south of Paris. A hundred years before the Revolution it was occupied by Armand Vernee, noted for his occult research and communications with the spirit world. He was dragged from the château by the peasants of the surrounding district when he was twenty-eight years old and burned at the stake—for witchcraft."

I stared straight into Threng's angular face. If ever I noticed that unholy gleam in his strange eyes, it was at that moment. His eyes were wide open, staring, burning with a dead, phosphorescent glow. Never once did they flicker as he continued his story in that sibilant, half-hissing voice of his.

"After Armand Vernee's execution, his daughter Regine lived alone in the château. She married a young count, gave birth to a son. In her twenty-eighth year she was prostrated with a strange disease. The best physicians in the country could not cure her. She—"

"What—kind of disease?" I said very slowly.

"The symptoms," he said, sucking in his breath audibly, "baffled all those who examined her. Two small red marks at the throat, Munn—and a continual loss of blood *while she slept*. She confessed to horrible dreams. She told of a great bat which possessed her father's face, clawing at the window of her chamber every night—gaining admittance by forcing the shutters open with its claws—hovering over her."

"And—she died?"

"She died. In her twenty-eighth year."

"And then?" I shuddered.

"Her son, François Vernee Leroux, lived alone in the château. The count would not remain. The horror of her death drove him away—drove him mad. The son, François, lived—alone."

Threng looked steadily at me. At least, his *eyes* looked. The rest of his face was contorted with passion, malignant.

"François Vernee died when he was twenty-eight years of age," he said meaningly. "He, too, left a son—and *that* son died at the age of twenty-eight. Each death was the same. The same crimson marks at the throat. The same loss of blood. The same—madness."

Threng reached for a cigarette and held a match triumphantly to the end of it. His face, behind the sudden glare of that stick of wood, was horrible with exultation.

"Margot Vernee is the last of her line," he shrugged. "Every direct descendant of Armand Vernee has died in the same ghastly way, at twenty-eight years of age. *That* is why the girl came here for help, Munn. She knows the inevitable end that awaits her! She knows that she can not escape the judgment which Armand Vernee has inflicted upon the family of Vernee!"

◊◊◊

Rojer Threng was right. Three weeks after those significant words had passed his lips, the girl came to my apartment. She repeated, almost word for word, the very fundamental facts that Threng had disclosed to me. Other things she told me, too—but I see no need to repeat them here.

"You are the only man who knows the significance of my fate," she said to me; and her face was ghastly white as she said it. "Is there no way to avert it, Mr. Munn? Is there no alternative?"

I talked with her for an eternity. The following night, and every night for the next four weeks, she came to me. During the hours of daylight I delved frantically into research work, in an attempt to find an outlet from the dilemma which faced her. At night, alone with her, I learned bit by bit the details of her mad story, and listened to her pleas for assistance.

Then came that fatal night. She sat close to me, talking in her habitually soft, persuasive voice.

"I have formed a plan," I said quietly.

"A plan, Paul?"

"When the time comes, I shall prepare a sleeping-chamber for you with but one window. I shall seal that window with the mark of the cross. It is the only way."

She looked at me for a long while without speaking. Then she said, slowly:

"You had better prepare the room, Paul—soon."

The Brotherhood of Blood   57

"You mean—" I said suddenly. But I knew what she meant. "I shall be twenty-eight tonight—at midnight."

◊◊◊

God forgive me that I did not keep her with me that night! I was already half in love with her. No—do not smile at that. You, too, after looking into her face continually for four long weeks— sitting close to her—listening to the soft whisper of her voice— you, too, would have loved her. I would have given my work, my reputation, my very life for her; and yet I permitted her to walk out of my apartment that night, to the horror that awaited her!

She came to me the next evening. One glance at her and I knew the terrible truth. I need not have asked the question that I did, but it came mechanically from my lips, like a dead voice.

"It—came?"

"Yes," she said quietly. "It came."

She stood before me and untied the scarf from her neck. And there, in the center of her white throat, I saw those infernal marks—two parallel slits of crimson, an eighth of an inch in length, horrible in their evil.

"It was a dream," she said, "and yet I know that it was no dream, but vivid reality. A gigantic bat with a woman's face—my mother's face—appeared suddenly at the window of my room. Its claws lifted the window. It circled over my bed as I lay there, star- ing at it in mute horror. Then it descended upon me, and I felt warm lips on my neck. A languid, wonderfully contented feeling came over me. I relaxed—and slept."

"And—when you awoke?" I said heavily.

"The mark of the vampire was here on my throat."

I stared at her for a very long time, without speaking. She did not move. She stood there by my desk; and a pitiful, yearning look came into her deep eyes.

Then, of a sudden, I was gripped with the helplessness of the whole evil affair. I stormed about the room, screaming my curses to the walls, my face livid with hopeless rage, my hands clawing at anything within reach of them. I tore at my face. I seized the wooden smoking-stand and broke it in my fingers, hurling the shattered pieces into a grinning, maddening picture of the Creator that hung beside the door. Then I tripped, fell, sprawled headlong—and groped again to my feet, quivering as if some tropic fever had laid its cold hands upon me.

There were tears in Margot's eyes as she came toward me and placed her hands on my arm. She would have spoken, to comfort me. I crushed her against me, holding her until she cried out in pain.

"Merciful Christ!" I cried. And the same words spurted from my lips, over and over again, until the room echoed with the intensity of them.

"You—love me, Paul?" she said softly.

"Love you!" I said hoarsely. *"Love* you! God, Margot—is there no way—"

"I love you, too," she whispered wearily. "But it is too late, Paul. The thing has visited me. I am a part of it. I—"

"I can keep you away from it!" I shouted. "I can hide you—protect you—where the thing will never find you!"

She shook her head, smiling heavily.

"It is too late, Paul."

"It is never too late!"

God! The words sounded brave enough then. Since then I have learned better. The creature that was preying on her possessed the infernal powers of life-in-death—powers that no mortal could deny. I knew it well enough, even when I made that rash promise. I had studied those things long enough to know my own limitations against them.

And yet I made the attempt. Before I left her that night, I hung the sign of the cross about her lovely throat, over the crimson stain of the vampire. I locked and sealed the windows of my apartment, breathing a prayer of supplication at each barrier as I made it secure. And then, holding her in my arms for a single unforgettable moment, I left her.

The apartment above mine was occupied by a singular fellow who had more than once called upon me to discuss my work. He, too, was a writer of sorts, and we had a meager something in common because of that. Therefore, when I climbed the stairs at a quarter to twelve that night and requested that he allow me to remain with him until morning, he was not unwilling to accede to my request, though he glanced at me most curiously as I made it.

However, he asked no questions, and I refrained from supplying any casual information to set his curiosity at rest. He would not have understood.

All that night I remained awake, listening for signs of disturbance in the rooms below me. But I heard nothing—not so much as a whisper. And when daylight came I descended the stairs with false hope in my heart.

There was no answer to my knock. I waited a moment, thinking that she might be yet asleep; then I rapped again on the panels. Then, when the silence persisted in haunting me, I fumbled frantically in my pockets for my spare key. I was afraid—terribly afraid.

And she was lying there when I stumbled into the room. Like a creature already dead she lay upon the bed, one white arm drooping to the floor. The silken comforter was thrown back. The breast of her gown was torn open. Fresh blood gleamed upon those dread marks in her throat.

I thought that she was dead. A sob choked in my throat as I dropped down beside her, peering into her colorless face. I clutched at her hand, and it was cold—stark cold. And then, unashamed of the tears that coursed down my cheeks, I lay across her still body, kissing her lips—kissing them as if it were the last time that I should ever see them.

She opened her eyes.

Her fingers tightened a little on my hand. She smiled—a pathetic, tired smile.

"It—came," she whispered. "I—knew it would."

◊◊◊

I will not dwell longer on the death of the girl I loved. Enough to recount the simple facts.

I brought doctors to her. No less than seven expert physicians attended her and consulted among themselves about her affliction. I told them my fears; but these were men of the world, not in sympathy with what I had to tell them.

"Loss of blood," was their diagnosis—but they looked upon me as a man gone mad when I attempted to *explain* the loss of blood.

There was a transfusion. My own blood went into her veins, to keep her alive. For three nights she lived. Each of those nights I stood guard over her, never closing my eyes while darkness was upon us. And each night the thing came, clawing at the windows, slithering its horrible shape into the room where she lay. I did not know, then, how it gained admittance. Now—God help me—I know all the powers of that unholy clan. Its nocturnal creatures know no limits of space or confinement.

And this thing that preyed upon the girl I loved—I refuse to describe it. You will know *why* I make such a refusal when I have finished.

Twice I fought it, and found myself smothered by a ghastly shape of fog that left me helpless. Once I lay across her limp body with my hands covering her throat to keep the thing away from her—and I was hurled unmercifully to the floor, with an unearthly, long-dead stench of decayed flesh in my nostrils. When I regained consciousness, the wounds in her throat were newly opened, and my own wrists were marked with the ragged stripes of raking claws.

I realized, after that, that I could do nothing. The horror had gone beyond human power of prevention.

The mark of the cross which I had given her—that was worse than useless. I *knew* that it was useless. Had she worn it on that very first night of all, before the thing had claimed her for its own, it might have protected her. But now that this infernal mark was upon her throat, even the questionable strength of the cross was nullified by its evil powers. There was nothing left—nothing that could be done.

As a last resort I called upon Rojer Threng. He came. He examined her. He turned to rise and said in a voice that was pregnant with unutterable malice: "I can do nothing. If I could, I *would* not."

And so he left me—alone with the girl who lay there, pale as a ghost, upon the bed.

I knelt beside her. It was eight o'clock in the evening. Dusk was beginning to creep into the room. And she took my hand in hers, drawing me close so that she might speak to me.

"Promise me, Paul—" she whispered.

"Anything." I said.

"In two years you will be twenty-eight," she said wearily. "I shall be forced to return to you. It is not a thing that I can help; it is the curse of my family. I have no descendants—I am the last of my line. You are the one dearest to me. It is *you* to whom I must return. Promise me—"

She drew me very close to her, staring into my face with a look of supplication that made me cold, fearful.

"Promise me—that when I return—you will fight against me," she entreated. "You must wear the sign of the cross—always—Paul. No matter how much I plead with you—to remove it—promise me that you will not!"

"I would rather join you, even in such a condition," I said bitterly, "than remain here alone without you."

"No, Paul. Forget me. Promise!"

"I—promise."

"And you will wear the cross always, and never remove it?"

"I will—fight against you," I said sadly.

Then I lost control. I flung myself beside her and embraced her. For hours we lay there together in utter silence.

She died—in my arms.

◊◊◊

It is hard to find words for the rest of this. It was hard, then, to find any reason for living. I did no work for months on end. The typewriter remained impassive upon its desk, forgotten, dusty, mocking me night after night as I paced the floor of my room.

In time I began to receive letters from editors, from prominent medical men, demanding to know why my articles had so suddenly ceased to appear in current periodicals. What could I say to them? Could I explain to them that when I sat down at the typewriter, *her* face held my fingers stiff? No; they would not have understood; they would have dubbed me a rank sentimentalist. I could not reply to their requests. I could only read their letters over and over again, in desperation, and hurl the missives to the floor, as a symbol of my defeat.

I wanted to talk. God, how I wanted to! But I had no one to listen to me. Casual acquaintances I did not dare take into my confidence. Rojer Threng did not return. Even the fellow in the rooms above me, who shared his apartment with me that night, did not come near me. He sensed that something peculiar, something beyond his scope of reason, enveloped me.

Six months passed and I began, slowly at first, to return to my regular routine. That first return to work was agony. More than one thesis I started in the proper editorial manner, only to find myself, after the first half-dozen pages, writing about *her—her* words, *her* thoughts. More than once I wrenched pages from the roll of the typewriter, ripped them to shreds and dashed them to the floor—only to gather them together again and read them a hundred times more,because they spoke of her.

And so a year passed. A year of my allotted time of loneliness, before she should return.

Three months more, and I was offered an instructorship at the university, to lecture on philosophy. I accepted the position. There I learned that Rojer Threng had graduated from the medical school, had hung out his private shingle, and was well along the road to medical fame. Once, by sheer accident, I encountered him in the corridors of the university. He shook my hand, spoke to me for a few minutes regarding his success, and excused himself at the first opportunity. He did not mention *her.*

Then, months later, came the night of my twenty-eighth birthday.

That night I did a strange thing. When darkness had crept into my room, I drew the great chair close to one of the windows, flung the aperture open wide, and waited. Waited—and *hoped.* I *wanted* her to come.

Yet I remembered my promise to her. Even as I lowered myself into the chair, I hung a crucifix about my throat and made the sign of the cross. Then I sat stiff, rigid, staring into the black void before me.

The hours dragged. My body became stiff, sore from lack of motion. My eyes were glued open, rimmed with black circles of anxiety. My hands clutched the arms of the chair, and never relaxed their intense grip.

I heard the distant bell of the Old North Church tolling eleven o'clock; and later—hours and hours and hours later—it struck a single note to indicate the half-hour before midnight.

Then, very suddenly, a black, bat-like shape was fluttering in the open window. It had substance, for I heard the dead impact of its great wings as they struck the ledge in front of me; and yet it had *no* substance, for I could discern the definite, unbroken shape of the window frame *through* its massive body! And I sat motionless, transfixed—staring.

The thing swooped past me. I saw it strike the floor—heard it struggling erratically between the legs of the table. Then, in front of my eyes, it dissolved into a creature of mist; and another shape took form. I saw it rise out of the floor—saw it become tall and lithe and slender. And then—then *she* stood before me, radiantly beautiful.

In that moment of amazement I forgot my danger. I lurched up from the chair and took a sudden step toward her. My arms went out. Her arms were already out; and she was standing there waiting for me to take her.

But even as I would have clasped her slender body, she fell away from me, staring in horror at the crucifix that hung from my throat. I stopped short. I spoke to her, calling her by name. But she retreated from me, circling around me until she stood before the open window. Then, with uncanny quickness, she was gone— and a great black-winged bat swirled through the opening into the outer darkness.

For an eternity I stood absolutely still, with my arms still outstretched. Then, with a dry, helpless sob, I turned away.

◊◊◊

Need I repeat what must already be obvious? She returned. Night after night she returned to me, taking form before me with her lovely, pleading arms outstretched to enfold me. I could not bring myself to believe that this utterly lovely, supplicating figure could wish to do me harm. For that matter, I could not believe that she was dead—that she had ever died. I wanted her. God, how I wanted her! I would have given my life to take her beautiful body once more in my arms and hold her close to me.

But I remembered my promise to her. The crucifix remained about my throat. Never once did she touch it—or touch me. In fact, never once did I see her for more than a single fleeting instant. She took birth before my eyes—stood motionless while I stumbled out of the chair and groped toward her—and then the awful power of the sign of the cross thrust her back. Always the same. One maddening moment—and hours upon hours of abject, empty loneliness that followed.

I did no work. All day, every day, I waited in agony for the hour of her coming. Then one day I sat by myself and thought. I reasoned with myself. I argued my personal desires against the truths which I knew to be insurmountable.

And that night, when she stood before me, I tore the crucifix from my throat and hurled it through the open window. I took her in my arms. I embraced her; and I was glad, wonderfully glad, for the first time in more than two years.

We clung to each other. She, too, was glad. I could see it in her face, in her eyes. Her lips trembled as they pressed mine. They were warm, hot—alive.

I am not sure of all that happened. I do not want to be sure. Even as her slender body quivered in my arms, a slow stupor came over me. It was like sleep, but more—oh, so much more desirous than mere slumber. I moved back—I was forced back—to the great chair. I relaxed. Something warm and soft touched my throat. There was no pain, no agony. Life was drawn out of me.

It was daylight when I awoke. The room was empty. The sunlight streamed through the open window. Something wet and sticky lay upon my throat. I reached up, touched it. and stared at my fingers dispassionately. They were stained with blood.

I did not need to seize upon a mirror. The two telltale marks of the vampire were upon my neck. I knew it.

◊◊◊

She came the next night. Again we lay together, deliriously happy. I had no regrets. I felt her lips at my throat . . .

Next morning I lay helpless in the big chair, unable to move. My strength had been drawn from me. I had no power to rise. Far into the day I remained in the same posture. When a knock came at my door, I could not stand up to admit the visitor. I could only turn my head listlessly and murmur: "Come in."

It was the manager of the house who entered. He scuffed toward me half apologetically and stood there, looking down at me.

"I've been 'avin' complaints, sor," he scowled, as if he did not like to deliver his message. "The chap up above yer 'as been kickin' about the noise yer makes down 'ere o' nights. It'll 'ave ter stop, sor. I don't like to be tellin' yer—but the chap says as 'ow 'e's seen yer sittin' all night long in front o' yer winder, with the winder wide open. 'E say's 'e 'ears yer talkin' ter some 'un down 'ere late at night, sor."

"I'm—very ill, Mr. Robell," I said weakly. "Will you—call a doctor?"

He blinked at me. Then he must have seen that significant thing on my throat, for he bent suddenly over me and said harshly:

"My Gawd, sor. You *are* sick!"

He hurried out. Fifteen minutes later he returned with a medical man whom I did not recognize.The fellow examined me, ordered me to bed, spent a long while peering at the mark on my neck, and finally went out—perplexed and scowling. When he came back, in an hour or so, be brought a more experienced physician with him.

They did what they could for me; but they did not understand, nor did I undertake to supply them with information. They could not prevent the inevitable; that I knew. I did not want them to prevent it.

And that night, as I lay alone, *she* came as usual. Ten minutes before the luminous hands of the clock on the table beside me registered eleven o'clock, she came to my bed and leaned over me. She did not leave until daylight was but an hour distant.

The next day was my last; and that day brought a man I had never expected to see again. It brought Rojer Threng!

I can see his face even now, as he paced across the room and stood beside my bed. It was repulsive with hate, masked with terrible triumph. His lips curled over his teeth as he spoke; and his eyes—those boring. glittering, living eyes—drilled their way into my tired brain as he glared into my face.

"You wonder why I have come, Munn?"

"Why—" I replied wearily. I was already close to eternity; and having him there beside me, feeling the hideous dynamic quality of his gaunt body, drew the last tongue of life out of me.

"She has been here, eh?" he grinned evilly.

I did not answer. Even the word *she*, coming from his lips, was profanity.

"I came here to tell you something, Munn," he rasped. "Something that will comfort you on the journey you are about to take. Listen—"

He lowered himself into the great chair and hunched himself close. And I was forced to listen to his savage threat, because I could not lift my hand to silence him.

"I used to love Margot Vernee, Munn," he said. "I loved her as much as you do—but in a different way. She'd have none of me. Do you understand? She would have none of me! She despised me. She *told* me that she despised me! *She!*"

His massive hands clenched and unclenched, as if they would have twisted about my throat. His eyes flamed.

"Then she loved *you! You*—with your thin, common body and hoary brain. She refused me, with all I had to offer her, and accepted you! Now do you know why I've come here?"

"You can do nothing—now," I said heavily. "It is too late. She is beyond your power."

Then he laughed. God, that laugh! It echoed and re-echoed across the room, vibrating with fearful intensity. It lashed into my brain like fire—left me weak and limp upon the bed. And there I lay, staring after him as he strode out of the room.

I never saw Rojer Threng again.

◊◊◊

I wonder if you know the meaning of death? Listen . . .

They carried me that evening to a strange place. I say *they*, but perhaps I should say *he*, for Rojer Threng was the man who ordered the change of surroundings. As for myself, I was too close to unconsciousness to offer resistance. I know only that I was lifted from my bed by four strong arms, and placed upon a stretcher, and then I was carried out of my apartment to a private car which waited at the curb below.

I bear no malice toward the two subordinates who performed this act. They were doing as they had been told to do. They were pawns of Rojer Threng's evil mind.

They made me as comfortable as possible in the rear section of the car. I heard the gears clash into place; then the leather cushion beneath me jerked abruptly, and the car droned away from the curb.

I could discern my surroundings, and I took mental note of the route we followed, though I do not know that it matters particularly. I remembered crossing the Harvard Bridge above the Charles River, with innumerable twinkling lights showing their reflections in the quiet water below. Then we followed one of the central thoroughfares, through a great square where the noise and harsh glare beat into my mind. And later—a long time later—the car came to a stop in the yards of the university.

Once again I was placed upon a stretcher. Where they took me I do not know; except that we passed through a maze of endless corridors in the heart of one of the university's many buildings. But the end of my journey lay in a small, dimly lighted room on one of the upper floors; and there I was lifted from the stretcher and placed upon a comfortable brocaded divan.

It was dusk then, and my two attendants set about making my comfort more complete. They spooned broth between my lips. They turned the light out of my eyes. They covered my prostrate body with a silken robe of some deep red color.

"Why," I murmured, "have you—brought me here?"

"It is Doctor Threng's order, sir," one of them said quietly.

"But I don't want—"

"Doctor Threng fully understands the nature of your malady, sir," the attendant replied, silencing my protest. "He has prepared this room to protect you."

I studied the room, then. Had he not spoken in such a significant tone. I should probably never have given a thought to the enclosure; but the soft inflection of his words was enough to remove my indifference.

As I have said, it was a small room. That in itself was not peculiar; but when I say that the walls were broken by only *one* window, you too will realize something sinister. The walls were low, forming a perfect square with the divan precisely in the center.

No hangings, no pictures or portraits of any kind, adorned the walls themselves; they were utterly bare. I know now that they were *not* bare; but the infernal wires that extended across them were so nearly invisible that my blurred sight did not notice.

One thing I shall never forget. When the attendants left me, after preparing me for the night, one of them said deliberately, as if to console me:

"You will be guarded every moment of this night, sir. The wall facing you has been bored through with a spy-hole. Doctor Threng, in the next room, asked me to inform you that he will remain at the spy-hole all night—and will allow nothing to come near you."

And then they left me alone.

I knew that she would come. It was my last night on earth, and I was positive that she would see it through by my side, to give me courage. The strange room would not keep her away. She would be able to find me, no matter where they secreted me.

I waited, lying limp on the divan with my face toward the window. The window was open. I thought then that the attendants had left it open by mistake; that they had overlooked it. I know now that it was left wide because of Rojer Threng's command.

An hour must have passed after they left me to myself. An hour of despair and emptiness for me. She did not come. I began to doubt—to be afraid. I knew that I should die soon—very soon—and I dreaded to enter the great unknown without her guidance. And so I waited and waited and waited, and never once took my eyes from the window, which was my only hope of relief.

Then—it must have been nearly midnight—I heard the doleful howling of a dog, somewhere down in the yard below. I knew what it meant. I struggled up, propping myself on one elbow, staring eagerly.

A moment later the faint square of moonlight that marked the window-frame was suddenly blotted out. I saw a massive, winged shape silhouetted in the opening. For an instant it hovered there, flapping its great body. Then it swooped into the room where I lay.

I saw again that uncanny transformation of spirit. The nocturnal specter dissolved before my eyes and assumed shape again, rising into a tall, languid, divinely beautiful woman. And *she* stood there, smiling at me.

All that night she remained by my side. She talked to me, in a voice that was no more than a faint whisper, comforting me for the ordeal which I must soon undergo. She told me secrets of the grave—secrets which I may not repeat here, nor ever wish to repeat. Ah, but it was a relief from the loneliness and restlessness of my heart to have her there beside me, sitting so quietly, confidently, in the depths of the divan. I no longer dreaded the fate in store for me. It meant that I would be with her always. You who love or ever have loved with an all-consuming tenderness—you will understand.

The hours passed all too quickly. I did not take account of them. I knew that she would leave when it was necessary for her to go. I knew the unfair limits that were imposed upon her very existence. Hers was a life of darkness, from sunset to sunrise. Unless she returned to the secrets of the grave before daylight crept upon us, her life would be consumed.

The hour of parting drew near. I feared to think of it. With her eyes close to me, holding my hand, I was at peace; but I knew that without her I should lapse again into an agony of doubt and fear. If I could have died then, with her near me, I think I should have been contented.

But it was not to be. She bent over to kiss me tenderly, and then rose from the divan.

"I—must go back, beloved," she whispered.

"Stay a moment more," I begged. "One moment—"

"I dare not, Paul."

She turned away. I watched her as if she were taking my very soul with her. She walked very softly, slowly, to the window. I saw her look back at me, and she smiled. God, how I remember that last smile! It was meant to give me courage—to put strength into my heart.

And then she stepped to the window.

Even as she moved that last step, the horrible thing happened. A monstrous, livid streamer of white light seared across the space in front of her. It blazed in her face like a rigid snake, hurling her back. There, engraved upon the wall, hung the sign of the cross, burning like a thing possessed of life!

She staggered away from it. I saw the terror in her face as she ran to the opposite wall. Ten steps she took; and then that wall too shone livid with the cross. Two horrible wires, transformed into writhing reality by some tremendous charge of electricity, glowed before her.

She sought frantically for a means of escape. Back and forth she turned. The sign of the cross confronted her on every side, hemming her in. There *was* no escape. The room was a veritable trap—a trap designed and executed by the infernally cunning mind of Rojer Threng.

I watched her in mute madness. Back and forth she went., screaming, sobbing her helplessness. I have watched a mouse in a wire cage do the same thing, but this—this was a thousand times more terrible.

I called out to her. I attempted to rise from the divan and go to her; but weakness came over me and I fell back quivering.

She realized then that it was the end. She fought to control herself, and she walked to the divan where I lay, and knelt beside me.

She did not speak. I think she had no voice at that moment. I held her close against me, my lips pressed into her hair. Like a very small, pitiful leaf she trembled in my arms.

And then—even as I held her—the first gleam of dawn slid across the floor of that ghastly room. She raised her head and looked into my face.

"Good-bye—Paul—"

I could not answer her. Something else answered. From the spy-hole in the opposite wall of the room came a hoarse, triumphant cackle—in Rojer Threng's malignant voice.

The girl was dead—dead in my arms. And that uncouth voice from the wall, screaming its derision, brought madness to my heart.

I lunged to my feet, fighting against the torture that drove through my body. I stumbled across the room. I reached the wall—found the spy-hole with my frozen fingers—clawed at it—raged against it—

And there, fighting to reach the man who had condemned me to an eternity of horror—I died.

My story is finished. The chimes of the Old North Church have just tolled a single funereal note to usher in the hour. One o'clock . . .

It is many, many years since that fateful night when I became a creature of the blood. I do not dare to remember the number of them. Between the hours of sunrise and sunset I cling to the earth of my grave—where I refuse to stay, until I have avenged her. Then I shall write more, perhaps, pleading for your assistance that I may join her in the true death. A spike through the heart will do it. . . .

From sunset until sunrise, throughout the hours of night, I am as one of you. I breathe, I drink; occasionally, as at this moment, I write—so that I may speak her name again and see it before me. I have attended social functions, mingled with people. Only one precaution must I take, and that to avoid mirrors, since my deathless body casts no reflection.

Every night—*every night*—I have visited the great house where Rojer Threng lives. No, I have not yet avenged her. The monster is too cunning, too clever. The sign of the cross is always upon him, to keep me from his throat. But sometime—*sometime*—he will forget. And then—ah, *then!*

When it is done, I shall find a way to quit this horrible brotherhood. I shall die the real death, as she did—and I shall find her.

Hugh B. Cave, a prolific writer for the fantasy, weird menace, detective, and adventure pulps, is the author of many books, including *Death Stalks the Night, Lucifer's Eye, Legion of the Dead,* and the collection *Murgunstrumm and Others,* which won a World Fantasy Award.

*Would a vampire find it amusing to participate
in a stage version of* Dracula?

Chastel

BY MANLY WADE WELLMAN

hen you won't let Count Dracula rest in his tomb?"
inquired Lee Cobbett, his square face creasing with a grin.
Five of them sat in the parlor of Judge Keith Hilary
Pursuivant's hotel suite on Central Park West. The Judge
lounged in an armchair, a wineglass in his big old hand. On this,
his eighty-seventh birthday, his blue eyes were clear, penetrating.
His once tawny hair and mustache had gone blizzard-white, but
both grew thick, and his square face showed rosy. In his tailored
blue leisure suit, he still looked powerfully deep-chested and
broad-shouldered.

Blocky Lee Cobbett wore jacket and slacks almost as brown as
his face. Next to him sat Laurel Parcher, small and young and cin-
namon-haired. The others were natty Phil Drumm the summer
theater producer, and Isobel Arrington from a wire press service.
She was blonde, expensively dressed, she smoked a dark cigarette
with a white tip. Her pen scribbled swiftly.

"Dracula's as much alive as Sherlock Holmes," argued Drumm.
"All the revivals of the play, all the films—"

"Your musical should wake the dead, anyway," said Cobbett,
drinking. "What's your main number, Phil? *Garlic Time? Gory,
Gory Hallelujah?*"

"Let's have Christian charity here, Lee," Pursuivant came to Drumm's rescue. "Anyway, Miss Arrington came to interview me. Pour her some wine and let me try to answer her questions."

"I'm interested in Mr. Cobbett's remarks," said Isobel Arrington, her voice deliberately throaty. "He's an authority on the supernatural."

"Well, perhaps," admitted Cobbett, "and Miss Parcher has had some experiences. But Judge Pursuivant is the true authority, the author of *Vampiricon*."

"I've read it, in paperback," said Isobel Arrington. "Phil, it mentions a vampire belief up in Connecticut, where you're having your show. What's that town again?"

"Deslow," he told her. "We're making a wonderful old stone barn into a theater. I've invited Lee and Miss Parcher to visit."

She looked at Drumm. "Is Deslow a resort town?"

"Not yet, but maybe the show will bring tourists. In Deslow, up to now, peace and quiet is the chief business. If you drop your shoe, everybody in town will think somebody's blowing the safe."

"Deslow's not far from Jewett City," observed Pursuivant. "There were vampires there about a century and a quarter ago. A family named Ray was afflicted. And to the east, in Rhode Island, there was a lively vampire folklore in recent years."

"Let's leave Rhode Island to H. P. Lovecraft's imitators," suggested Cobbett. "What do you call your show, Phil?"

"The Land Beyond the Forest," said Drumm. "We're casting it now. Using locals in bit parts. But we have Gonda Chastel to play Dracula's countess."

"I never knew that Dracula had a countess," said Laurel Parcher.

"There was a stage star named Chastel, long ago when I was young," said Pursuivant. "Just the one name—Chastel."

"Gonda's her daughter, and a year or so ago Gonda came to live in Deslow," Drumm told them. "Her mother's buried there. Gonda has invested in our production."

"Is that why she has a part in it?" asked Isobel Arrington.

"She has a part in it because she's beautiful and gifted," replied Drumm, rather stuffily. "Old people say she's the very picture of her mother. Speaking of pictures, here are some to prove it."

He offered two glossy prints to Isobel Arrington, who murmured "Very sweet," and passed them to Laurel Parcher. Cobbett leaned to see.

One picture seemed copied from an older one. It showed a woman who stood with unconscious stateliness, in a gracefully draped robe with a tiara binding her rich flow of dark hair. The other picture was of a woman in fashionable evening dress, her hair ordered in modern fashion, with a face strikingly like that of the woman in the other photograph.

"Oh, she's lovely," said Laurel. "Isn't she, Lee?"

"Isn't she?" echoed Drumm.

"Magnificent," said Cobbett, handing the pictures to Pursuivant, who studied them gravely.

"Chastel was in Richmond, just after the first World War," he said slowly, "A dazzling Lady Macbeth. I was in love with her. Everyone was."

"Did you tell her you loved her?" asked Laurel.

"Yes. We had supper together, twice. Then she went ahead with her tour, and I sailed to England and studied at Oxford. I never saw her again, but she's more or less why I never married."

Silence a moment. Then: *"The Land Beyond the Forest,"* Laurel repeated. "Isn't there a book called that?"

"There is indeed, my child," said the Judge. "By Emily de Laszowska Gerard. About Transylvania, where Dracula came from."

"That's why we use the title, that's what Transylvania means," put in Drumm. "It's all right, the book's out of copyright. But I'm surprised to find someone who's heard of it."

"I'll protect your guilty secret, Phil," promised Isobel Arrington. "What's over there in your window, Judge?"

Pursuivant turned to look. "Whatever it is," he said, "it's not Peter Pan."

Cobbett sprang up and ran toward the half-draped window. A silhouette with head and shoulders hung in the June night. He had a glimpse of a face, rich-mouthed, with bright eyes. Then it was gone. Laurel had hurried up behind him. He hoisted the window sash and leaned out.

Nothing. The street was fourteen stories down. The lights of moving cars crawled distantly. The wall below was course after course of dull brick, with recesses of other windows to right and left, below, above. Cobbett studied the wall, his hands braced on the sill.

"Be careful, Lee," Laurel's voice besought him.

He came back to face the others. "Nobody out there," he said evenly. "Nobody could have been. It's just a wall—nothing to hang to. Even that sill would be tricky to stand on."

"But I saw something, and so did Judge Pursuivant," said Isobel Arrington, the cigarette trembling in her fingers.

"So did I," said Cobbett. "Didn't you, Laurel?"

"Only a face."

Isobel Arrington was calm again. "If it's a trick, Phil, you played a good one. But don't expect me to put it in my story."

Drumm shook his head nervously. "I didn't play any trick, I swear."

"Don't try this on old friends," she jabbed at him. "First those pictures, then whatever was up against the glass. I'll use the pictures, but I won't write that a weird vision presided over this birthday party."

"How about a drink all around?" suggested Pursuivant.

He poured for them. Isobel Arrington wrote down answers to more questions, then said she must go. Drumm rose to escort her. "You'll be at Deslow tomorrow, Lee?" he asked.

"And Laurel, too. You said we could find quarters there."

"The Mapletree's a good auto court," said Drumm. "I've already reserved cabins for the two of you."

"On the spur of the moment," said Pursuivant suddenly, "I think I'll come along, if there's space for me."

"I'll check it out for you, Judge," said Drumm.

He departed with Isobel Arrington. Cobbett spoke to Pursuivant. "Isn't that rather offhand?" he asked. "Deciding to come with us?.'

"I was thinking about Chastel." Pursuivant smiled gently. "About making a pilgrimage to her grave."

"We'll drive up about nine tomorrow morning."

"I'll be ready, Lee."

Cobbett and Laurel, too, went out. They walked down a flight of stairs to the floor below, where both their rooms were located. "Do you think Phil Drumm rigged up that illusion for us?" asked Cobbett.

"If he did, he used the face of that actress. Chastel."

He glanced keenly at her. "You saw that."

"I thought I did, and so did you."

They kissed goodnight at the door to her room.

◊◊◊

Pursuivant was ready next morning when Cobbett knocked. He had only one suitcase and a thick, brown-blotched malacca cane, banded with silver below its curved handle.

"I'm taking only a few necessaries, I'll buy socks and such things in Deslow if we stay more than a couple of days," he said. "No, don't carry it for me, I'm quite capable."

When they reached the hotel garage, Laurel was putting her luggage in the trunk of Cobbett's black sedan. Judge Pursuivant declined the front seat beside Cobbett, held the door for Laurel to get in, and sat in the rear. They rolled out into bright June sunlight.

Cobbett drove them east on Interstate 95, mile after mile along the Connecticut shore, past service stations, markets, sandwich shops. Now and then they glimpsed Long Island Sound to the right. At toll gates, Cobbett threw quarters into hoppers and drove on.

"New Rochelle to Port Chester," Laurel half chanted. "Norwalk, Bridgeport, Stratford—"

"Where, in 1851, devils plagued a minister's home," put in Pursuivant.

"The names make a poem," said Laurel.

"You can get that effect by reading any timetable," said Cobbett. "We miss a couple of good names—Mystic and Giants Neck, though they aren't far off from our route. And Griswold— that means Gray Woods—where the Judge's book says Horace Ray was born."

"There's no Griswold on the Connecticut map any more," said the Judge.

"Vanished?" said Laurel. "Maybe it appears at just a certain time of the day, along about sundown."

She laughed, but the Judge was grave.

"Here we'll pass by New Haven," he said. "I was at Yale here, seventy years ago."

They rolled across the Connecticut River between Old Saybrook and Old Lyme. Outside New London, Cobbett turned them north on State Highway 82 and, near Jewett City, took a two-lane road that brought them into Deslow, not long afternoon.

There were pleasant clapboard cottages among elm trees and flower beds. Main Street had bright shops with, farther along, the belfry of a sturdy old church. Cobbett drove them to a sign saying MAPLETREE COURT. A row of cabins faced along a cement-floored colonnade, their fronts painted white with blue doors and window frames. In the office, Phil Drumm stood at the desk, talking to the plump proprietress.

"Welcome home," he greeted them. "Judge, I was asking Mrs. Simpson here to reserve you a cabin."

"At the far end of the row, sir," the lady said. "I'd have put you next to your two friends, but so many theater folks have already moved in."

"Long ago I learned to be happy with any shelter," the Judge assured her.

They saw Laurel to her cabin and put her suitcases inside, then walked to the farthest cabin where Pursuivant would stay. Finally Drumm followed Cobbett to the space next to Laurel's. Inside, Cobbett produced a fifth of bourbon from his briefcase. Drumm trotted away to fetch ice. Pursuivant came to join them.

"It's good of you to look after us," Cobbett said to Drumm above his glass.

"Oh, I'll get my own back," Drumm assured him. "The Judge and you, distinguished folklore experts—I'll have you in all the papers."

"Whatever you like," said Cobbett. "Let's have lunch, as soon as Laurel is freshened up."

The four ate crab cakes and flounder at a little restaurant while Drumm talked about *The Land Beyond the Forest*. He had signed the minor film star Caspar Merrick to play Dracula. "He has a fine baritone singing voice," said Drumm. "He'll be at afternoon rehearsal."

"And Gonda Chastel?" inquired Pursuivant, buttering a roll.

"She'll be there tonight." Drumm sounded happy about that. "This afternoon's mostly for bits and chorus numbers. I'm directing as well as producing." They finished their lunch, and Drumm rose. "If you're not tired, come see our theater."

It was only a short walk through town to the converted barn. Cobbett judged it had been built in Colonial times, with a recent roof of composition tile, but with walls of stubborn, brown-gray New England stone. Across a narrow side street stood the old white church, with a hedge-bordered cemetery.

"Quaint, that old burying ground," commented Drumm. "Nobody's spaded under there now, there's a modern cemetery on the far side, but Chastel's tomb is there. Quite a picturesque one."

"I'd like to see it," said Pursuivant, leaning on his silver-banded cane.

The barn's interior was set with rows of folding chairs, enough for several hundred spectators. On a stage at the far end, workmen moved here and there under lights. Drumm led his guests up steps at the side.

High in the loft, catwalks zigzagged and a dark curtain hung like a broad guillotine blade. Drumm pointed out canvas flats, painted to resemble grim castle walls. Pursuivant nodded and questioned.

"I'm no authority on what you might find in Transylvania," he said, "but this looks convincing."

A man walked from the wings toward them. "Hello, Caspar," Drumm greeted him. "I want you to meet Judge Pursuivant and Lee Cobbett. And Miss Laurel Parcher, of course." He gestured the introductions. "This is Mr. Caspar Merrick, our Count Dracula."

Merrick was elegantly tall, handsome, with carefully groomed black hair. Sweepingly he bowed above Laurel's hand and smiled at them all. "Judge Pursuivant's writings I know, of course," he said richly. "I read what I can about vampires, inasmuch as I'm to be one."

"Places for the Delusion number!" called a stage manager.

Cobbett, Pursuivant, and Laura went down the steps and sat on chairs. Eight men and eight girls hurried into view, dressed in knockabout summer clothes. Someone struck chords on a piano,

Drumm gestured importantly, and the chorus sang. Merrick, coming downstage, took solo on a verse. All joined in the refrain. Then Drumm made them sing it over again.

After that, two comedians made much of confusing the words vampire and empire. Cobbett found it tedious. He excused himself to his companions and strolled out and across to the old, tree-crowded churchyard.

The gravestones bore interesting epitaphs: not only the familiar *Pause O Stranger Passing By! As You Are Now So Once Was I,* and *A Bud on Earth to Bloom in Heaven,* but several of more originality. One bewailed a man who, since he had been lost at sea, could hardly have been there at all. Another bore, beneath a bat-winged face, the declaration *Death Pays All Debts* and the date *1907,* which Cobbett associated with a financial panic.

Toward the center of the graveyard, under a drooping willow, stood a shedlike structure of heavy granite blocks. Cobbett picked his way to the door of heavy grillwork, which was fastened with a rusty padlock the size of a sardine can. On the lintel were strongly carved letters, CHASTEL.

Here, then, was the tomb of the stage beauty Pursuivant remembered so romantically. Cobbett peered through the bars.

It was murkily dusty in there. The floor was coarsely flagged, and among sooty shadows at the rear stood a sort of stone chest that must contain the body. Cobbett turned and went back to the theater. Inside, piano music rang wildly and the people of the chorus desperately rehearsed what must be meant for a folk dance.

"Oh, it's exciting," said Laurel as Cobbett sat down beside her. "Where have you been?"

"Visiting the tomb of Chastel."

"Chastel?" echoed Pursuivant. "I must see that tomb."

Songs and dance ensembles went on. In the midst of them, a brisk reporter from Hartford appeared, to interview Pursuivant and Cobbett. At last Drumm resoundingly dismissed the players on stage and joined his guests.

"Principals rehearse at eight o'clock," he announced. "Gonda Chastel will be here; she'll want to meet you. Could I count on you then?"

"Count on me, at least," said Pursuivant. "Just now, I feel like resting before dinner, and so, I think, does Laurel here."

"Yes, I'd like to lie down for a little," said Laurel.

"Why don't we all meet for dinner at the place where we had lunch?" said Cobbett. "You come too, Phil."

"Thanks, I have a date with some backers from New London."

It was half-past five when they went out.

Cobbett went to his quarters, stretched out on the bed, and gave himself to thought.

He hadn't come to Deslow because of this musical interpretation of the Dracula legend. Laurel had come because he was coming, and Pursuivant on a sudden impulse that might have been more than a wish to visit the grave of Chastel. But Cobbett was here because this, he knew, had been vampire country, maybe still was vampire country.

He remembered the story in Pursuivant's book about vampires at Jewett City, as reported in the Norwich *Courier* for 1854. Horace Ray, from the now vanished town of Griswold, had died of a "wasting disease." Thereafter his oldest son, then his second son, had also gone to their graves. When a third son sickened, friends and relatives dug up Horace Ray and the two dead brothers and burned the bodies in a roaring fire. The surviving son got well. And something like that had happened in Exeter, near Providence in Rhode Island. Very well, why organize and present the Dracula musical here in Deslow, so near those places?

Cobbett had met Phil Drumm in the South the year before, knew him for a brilliant if erratic producer, who relished tales of devils and the dead who walk by night. Drumm might have known enough stage magic to have rigged that seeming appearance at Pursuivant's window in New York. That is, if indeed it was only a seeming appearance, not a real face. Might it have been real, a manifestation of the unreal? Cobbett had seen enough of what people dismissed as unreal, impossible, to wonder.

◊◊◊

A soft knock came at the door. It was Laurel. She wore green slacks, a green jacket, and she smiled, as always, at sight of

Cobbett's face. They sought Pursuivant's cabin. A note on the door said, *Meet me at the cafe.*

When they entered there, Pursuivant hailed them from the kitchen door. "Dinner's ready," he hailed them. "I've been supervising in person, and I paid well for the privilege."

A waiter brought a laden tray. He arranged platters of red-drenched spaghetti and bowls of salad on a table. Pursuivant himself sprinkled Parmesan cheese. "No salt or pepper," he warned. "I seasoned it myself, and you can take my word it's exactly right."

Cobbett poured red wine into glasses. Laurel took a forkful of spaghetti. "Delicious," she cried. "What's in it, Judge?"

"Not only ground beef and tomatoes and onions and garlic," replied Pursuivant. "I added marjoram and green pepper and chile and thyme and bay leaf and oregano and parsley and a couple of other important ingredients. And I also minced in some Italian sausage."

Cobbett, too, ate with enthusiastic appetite. "I won't order any dessert"' he declared. "I want to keep the taste of this in my mouth."

There's more in the kitchen for dessert if you want it," the Judge assured him. "But here, I have a couple of keepsakes for you."

He handed each of them a small, silvery object. Cobbett examined his. It was smoothly wrapped in foil. He wondered if it was a nutmeat.

"You have pockets, I perceive," the Judge said. "Put those into them. And don't open them, or my wish for you won't come true."

When they had finished eating, a full moon had begun to rise in the darkening sky. They headed for the theater.

A number of visitors sat in the chairs and the stage lights looked bright. Drumm stood beside the piano, talking to two plump men in summer business suits. As Pursuivant and the others came down the aisle, Drumm eagerly beckoned them and introduced them to his companions, the financial backers with whom he had taken dinner.

"We're very much interested," said one. "This vampire legend intrigues anyone, if you forget that a vampire's motivation is simply nourishment."

"No, something more than that," offered Pursuivant. "A social motivation."

"Social motivation," repeated the other backer.

"A vampire wants company of its own kind. A victim infected becomes a vampire, too, and an associate. Otherwise the original vampire would be a disconsolate loner."

"There's a lot in what you say," said Drumm, impressed.

After that there was financial talk, something in which Cobbett could not intelligently join. Then someone else approached, and both the backers stared.

It was a tall, supremely graceful woman with red-lighted black hair in a bun at her nape, a woman of impressive figure and assurance. She wore a sweeping blue dress, fitted to her slim waist, with a frill-edged neckline. Her arms were bare and white and sweetly turned, with jewelled bracelets on them. Drumm almost ran to bring her close to the group.

"Gonda Chastel," he said, half-prayerfully. "Gonda, you'll want to meet these people."

"The two backers stuttered admiringly at her. Pursuivant bowed and Laurel smiled. Gonda Chastel gave Cobbett her slim, cool hand. "You know so much about this thing we're trying to do here," she said, in a voice like cream.

Drumm watched them. His face looked plaintive.

"Judge Pursuivant has taught me a lot, Miss Chastel," said. Cobbett. "He'll tell you that once he knew your mother."

"I remember her, not very clearly," said Gonda Chastel. "She died when I was just a little thing, thirty years ago. And I followed her here, now I make my home here."

"You look very like her," said Pursuivant.

"I'm proud to be like my mother in any way," she smiled at them. She could be overwhelming, Cobbett told himself.

"And Miss Parcher," went on Gonda Chastel, turning toward Laurel. "What a little presence she is. She should be in our show—I don't know what part, but she should." She smiled dazzlingly. "Now then, Phil wants me on stage."

"Knock-at-the-door number, Gonda," said Drumm.

Gracefully she mounted the steps. The piano sounded, and she sang. It was the best song, felt Cobbett, that he had heard so far in the rehearsals. "Are they seeking for a shelter from the night?" Gonda Chastel sang richly. Caspar Merritt entered, to join in a recitative. Then the chorus streamed on, singing somewhat shrilly.

Pursuivant and Laurel had sat down. Cobbett strode back up the aisle and out under a moon that rained silver-blue light.

He found his way to the churchyard. The trees that had offered pleasant afternoon shade now made a dubious darkness. He walked underneath branches that seemed to lower like hovering wings as he approached the tomb structure at the center.

The barred door that had been massively locked now stood open. He peered into the gloom within. After a moment he stepped across the threshold upon the flagged floor.

He had to grope, with one hand upon the rough wall. At last he almost stumbled upon the great stone chest at the rear.

It, too, was flung open, its lid heaved back against the wall.

There was, of course, complete darkness within it. He flicked on his cigar lighter. The flame showed him the inside of the stone coffer, solidly made and about ten feet long. Its sides of gray marble were snugly fitted. Inside lay a coffin of rich dark wood with silver fittings and here, yet again, was an open lid.

Bending close to the smudged silk lining, Cobbett seemed to catch an odor of stuffy sharpness, like dried herbs. He snapped off his light and frowned in the dark. Then he groped back to the door, emerged into the open, and headed for the theater again.

"Mr. Cobbett," said the beautiful voice of Gonda Chastel.

She stood at the graveyard's edge, beside a sagging willow. She was almost as tall as he. Her eyes glowed in the moonlight.

"You came to find the truth about my mother," she half-accused.

"I was bound to try," he replied. "Ever since I saw a certain face at a certain window of a certain New York hotel."

She stepped back from him. "You know that she's a—"

"A vampire," Cobbett finished for her. "Yes."

"I beg you to be helpful—merciful." But there was no supplication in her voice. "I already realized, long ago. That's why I live in little Deslow. I want to find a way to give her rest. Night after night, I wonder how."

"I understand that," said Cobbett.

B L O O D   L I N E S

Gonda Chastel breathed deeply. "You know all about these things. I think there's something about you that could daunt a vampire."

"If so, I don't know what it is," said Cobbett truthfully.

"Make me a solemn promise. That you won't return to her tomb, that you won't tell others what you and I know about her. I—I want to think how we two together can do something for her."

"If you wish, I'll say nothing," he promised.

Her hand clutched his.

"The cast took a five-minute break, it must be time to go to work again," she said, suddenly bright. "Let's go back and help the thing along."

They went.

Inside, the performers were gathering on stage. Drumm stared unhappily as Gonda Chastel and Cobbett came down the aisle. Cobbett sat with Laurel and Pursuivant and listened to the rehearsal.

Adaptation from Bram Stoker's novel was free, to say the least. Dracula's eerie plottings were much hampered by his having a countess, a walking dead beauty who strove to become a spirit of good. There were some songs, in interesting minor keys. There was a dance, in which men and women leaped like kangaroos. Finally Drumm called a halt, and the performers trooped wearily to the wings.

Gonda Chastel lingered, talking to Laurel. "I wonder, my dear, if you haven't had acting experience," she said.

"Only in school entertainments down south, when I was little."

"Phil," said Gonda Chastel, "Miss Parcher is a good type, has good presence. There ought to he something for her in the show."

"You're very kind, but I'm afraid that's impossible," said Laurel, smiling.

"You may change your mind, Miss Parcher. Will you and your friends come to my house for a nightcap?"

"Thank you," said Pursuivant. "We have some notes to make, and we must make them together."

"Until tomorrow evening, then. Mr. Cobbett, we'll remember our agreement."

She went away toward the back of the stage. Pursuivant and Laurel walked out. Drumm hurried up the aisle and caught Cobbett's elbow.

"I saw you," he said harshly. "Saw you both as you came in."

"And we saw you, Phil. What's this about?"

"She likes you." It was half an accusation, "Fawns on you, almost."

Cobbett grinned and twitched his arm free. "What's the matter, Phil, are you in love with her?"

"Yes, God damn it. I am. I'm in love with her. She knows it but she won't let me come to her house. And you—the first time she meets you, she invites you."

"Easy does it, Phil," said Cobbett. "If it'll do you any good, I'm in love with someone else, and that takes just about all my spare time."

He hurried out to overtake his companions.

Pursuivant swung his cane almost jauntily as they returned through the moonlight to the auto court.

"What notes are you talking about, Judge?" asked Cobbett.

"I'll tell you at my quarters. What do you think of the show?"

"Perhaps I'll like it better after they've rehearsed more," said Laurel. "I don't follow it at present."

"Here and there, it strikes me as limp," added Cobbett.

They sat down in the Judge's cabin. He poured them drinks. "Now," he said, "there are certain things to recognize here. Things I more or less expected to find."

"A mystery, Judge?" asked Laurel.

"Not so much that, if I expected to find them. How far are we from Jewett City?"

"Twelve or fifteen miles as the crow flies," estimated Cobbett. "And Jewett City is where that vampire family, the Rays, lived and died."

"Died twice, you might say," nodded Pursuivant, stroking his white mustache. "Back about a century and a quarter ago. And here's what might be a matter of Ray family history. I've been thinking about Chastel, whom once I greatly admired. About her full name."

"But she had only one name, didn't she?" asked Laurel.

"On the stage she used one name, yes. So did Bernhardt, so did Duse, so later did Garbo. But all of them had full names. Now, before we went to dinner, I made two telephone calls to theatrical historians I know. To learn Chastel's full name."

"And she had a full name," prompted Cobbett.

"Indeed she did. Her full name was Chastel Ray."

Cobbett and Laurel looked at him in deep silence.

"Not apt to be just coincidence," elaborated Pursuivant. "Now then, I gave you some keepsakes today."

"Here's mine," said Cobbett, pulling the foil-wrapped bit from his shirt pocket.

"And I have mine here," said Laurel, her hand at her throat. "In a little locket I have on this chain."

"Keep it there," Pursuivant urged her. "Wear it around your neck at all times. Lee, have yours always on your person. Those are garlic cloves, and you know what they're good for. You can also guess why I cut up a lot of garlic in our spaghetti for dinner."

"You think there's a vampire here," offered Laurel.

"A specific vampire." The Judge took a deep breath into his broad chest. "Chastel. Chastel Ray."

"I believe it, too," declared Cobbett tonelessly, and Laurel nodded. Cobbett looked at the watch on his wrist.

"It's past one in the morning," he said. "Perhaps we'd all be better off if we had some sleep."

◊◊◊

They said their good nights and Laurel and Cobbett walked to where their two doors stood side by side. Laurel put her key into the lock, but did not turn it at once. She peered across the moonlit street.

"Who's that over there?" she whispered; "Maybe I ought to say, what's that?"

Cobbett looked. "Nothing, you're just nervous. Good night, dear."

She went in and shut the door. Cobbett quickly crossed the street.

"Mr. Cobbett," said the voice of Gonda Chastel.

"I wondered what you wanted, so late at night," he said, walking close to her.

She had undone her dark hair and let it flow to her shoulders. She was, Cobbett thought, as beautiful a woman as he had ever seen."

"I wanted to be sure about you," she said. "That you'd respect your promise to me, not to go into the churchyard."

"I keep my promises, Miss Chastel."

He felt deep, hushed silence all around them. Not even the leaves rustled in the trees.

"I had hoped you wouldn't venture even this far," she went on. "You and your friends are new in town, you might tempt her specially." Her eyes burned at him. "You know I don't mean that as a compliment."

She turned to walk away. He fell into step beside, her. "But you're not afraid of her," he said.

"Of my own mother?"

"She was a Ray," said Cobbett. "Each Ray sapped the blood of his kinsmen. Judge Pursuivant told me all about it."

Again the gaze of her dark, brilliant eyes. "Nothing like that has ever happened between my mother and me." She stopped, and so did he. Her slim, strong hand took him by the wrist.

"You're wise and brave," she said. "I think you may have come here for a good purpose, not just about the show."

"I try to have good purposes."

The light of the moon soaked through the overhead branches as they walked on. "Will you come to my house?" she invited.

"I'll walk to the churchyard," replied Cobbett. "I said I wouldn't go into it, but I can stand at the edge."

"Don't go in."

"I've promised that I wouldn't, Miss Chastel."

She walked back the way they had come. He followed the street on under silent elms until he reached the border of the churchyard. Moonlight flecked and spattered the tombstones. Deep shadows lay like pools. He had a sense of being watched from within.

As he gazed, he saw movement among the graves. He could not define it, but it was there. He glimpsed, or fancied he glimpsed, a head, indistinct in outline as though swathed in dark fabric. Then another. Another. They huddled in a group, as though to gaze at him.

"I wish you'd go back to your quarters," said Gonda Chastel beside him. She had drifted after him, silent as a shadow herself.

"Miss Chastel," he said, "tell me something if you can. Whatever happened to the town or village of Griswold?"

"Griswold?" she echoed. "What's Griswold? That means gray woods."

"Your ancestor, or your relative, Horace Ray, came from Griswold to die in Jewett City. And I've told you that I knew your mother was born a Ray."

Her shining eyes seemed to flood upon him. "I didn't know that," she said.

He gazed into the churchyard, at those hints of furtive movement.

"The hands of the dead reach out for the living," murmured Gonda Chastel.

"Reach out for me?" he asked.

"Perhaps for both of us. Just now, we may be the only living souls awake in Deslow." She gazed at him again. "But you're able to defend yourself, somehow."

"What makes you think that?" he inquired, aware of the clove of garlic in his shirt pocket.

"Because they—in the churchyard there—they watch, but they hold away from you. You don't invite them."

"Nor do you, apparently," said Cobbett.

"I hope you're not trying to make fun of me," she said, her voice barely audible.

"On my soul, I'm not."

"On your soul," she repeated. "Good night, Mr. Cobbett."

Again she moved away, tall and proud and graceful. He watched her out of sight. Then he headed back toward the motor court.

Nothing moved in the empty street. Only one or two lights shone here and there in closed shops. He thought he heard a soft rustle behind him, but did not look back.

As he reached his own door, he heard Laurel scream behind hers.

◇◇◇

Judge Pursuivant sat in his cubicle, his jacket off, studying a worn little brown book. Skinner, said letters on the spine, and *Myths and Legends of Our Own Land*. He had read the passage so often that he could almost repeat it from memory:

> To slay this monster he must be taken up and burned; at least his heart must be; and he must be disinterred in the daytime when he is asleep and unaware.

There were other ways, reflected Pursuivant.

It must be very late by now, rather it must be early. But he had no intention of going to sleep. Not when stirs of motion sounded outside, along the concrete walkway in front of his cabin. Did motion stand still, just beyond the door there? Pursuivant's great, veined hand touched the front of his shirt, beneath which a bag of garlic hung like an amulet. Garlic—was that enough? He himself was fond of garlic, judiciously employed in sauces and salads. But then, he could see himself in the mirror of the bureau yonder; could see his broad old face with its white sweep of mustache like a wreath of snow on a sill. It was a clear image of a face, not a calm face just then, but a determined one. Pursuivant smiled at it, with a glimpse of even teeth that were still his own.

He flicked up his shirt cuff and looked at his watch. Half past one, about. In June, even with daylight savings time, dawn would come early. Dawn sent vampires back to the tombs that were their melancholy refuges, "asleep and unaware," as Skinner had specified.

Putting the book aside, he poured himself a small drink of bourbon, dropped in cubes of ice and a trickle of water, and sipped. He had drunk several times during that day, when on most days he partook of only a single highball, by advice of his doctor; but just now he was grateful for the pungent, walnutty taste of the liquor. It was one of Earth's natural things, a good companion when not abused. From the table he took a folder of scribbled notes. He looked at jottings from the works of Montague Summers.

These offered the proposition that a plague of vampires usually

90   B L O O D   L I N E S

stemmed from a single source of infection, a king or queen vampire whose feasts of blood drove victims to their graves, to rise in their turn. If the original vampires were found and destroyed, the others relaxed to rest as normally dead bodies. Bram Stoker had followed the same gospel when he wrote *Dracula,* and doubtless Bram Stoker had known. Pursuivant looked at another page, this time a poem copied from James Grant's curious *Mysteries of All Nations.* It was a ballad in archaic language, that dealt with baleful happenings in "The Towne of Peste"—Budapest?

> It was the Corses that our Churchyardes filled
> That did at midnight lumberr up our Stayres;
> They suck'd our Bloud, the gorie Banquet swilled,
> And harried everie Soule with hydeous Feares.

Several verses down:

> They barr'd with Boltes of Iron the Churchyard-pale
> To keep them out; but all this wold not doe;
> For when a Dead-Man has learn'd to draw a naile,
> He can also burst an iron Bolte in two.

Many times Pursuivant had tried to trace the author of that verse. He wondered if it was not something quaintly confected not long before 1880, when Grant published his work. At any rate, the Judge felt that he knew what it meant, the experience that it remembered.

He put aside the notes, too, and picked up his spotted walking stick. Clamping the balance of it firmly in his left hand, he twisted the handle with his right and pulled. Out of the hollow shank slid a pale, bright blade, keen and lean and edged on both front and back.

Pursuivant permitted himself a smile above it. This was one of his most cherished possessions, this silver weapon said to have been forged a thousand years ago by Saint Dunstan. Bending, he spelled out the runic writing upon it: *Sic pereant omnes inimici tui, Domine.*

That was the end of the fiercely triumphant song of Deborah in the Book of Judges: So perish all thine enemies, O Lord. Whether the work of Saint Dunstan or not, the metal was silver, the writing was a warrior's prayer. Silver and writing had proved their strength against evil in the past.

Then, outside, a loud, tremulous cry of mortal terror.

Pursuivant sprang out of his chair on the instant. Blade in hand, he fairly ripped his door open and ran out. He saw Cobbett in front of Laurel's door, wrenching at the knob, and hurried there like a man half his age.

"Open up, Laurel," he heard Cobbett call. "It's Lee out here!"

The door gave inward as Pursuivant reached it, and he and Cobbett pressed into the lighted room.

Laurel half-crouched in the middle of the floor. Her trembling hand pointed to a rear window. "She tried to come in," Laurel stammered.

"There's nothing at that window," said Cobbett, but even as he spoke, there was. A face, pale as tallow, crowded against the glass. They saw wide, staring eyes, a mouth that opened and squirmed. Teeth twinkled sharply.

Cobbett started forward, but Pursuivant caught him by the shoulder. "Let me," he said, advancing toward the window, the point of his blade lifted.

The face at the window writhed convulsively as the silver weapon came against the pane with a clink. The mouth opened as though to shout, but no sound came. The face fell back and vanished from their sight.

"I've seen that face before," said Cobbett hoarsely.

"Yes," said Pursuivant. "At my hotel window. And since."

He dropped the point of the blade to the floor. Outside came a whirring rush of sound, like feet, many of them.

"We ought to wake up the people at the office," said Cobbett

"I doubt if anyone in this little town could be wakened," Pursuivant told him evenly. "I have it in mind that every living soul, except the three of us, is sound asleep. Entranced."

"But out there—" Laurel gestured at the door, where something seemed to be pressing.

"I said, every living soul," Pursuivant looked from her to Cobbett. "Living," he repeated.

He paced across the floor, and with his point scratched a perpendicular line upon it. Across this he carefully drove a horizontal line, making a cross. The pushing abruptly ceased. "There it is, at the window again," breathed Laurel.

Pursuivant took long steps back to where the face hovered, with black hair streaming about it. He scraped the glass with his silver blade, up and down, then across, making lines upon it. The face drew away. He moved to mark similar crosses on the other windows.

"You see," he said, quietly triumphant, "the force of old, old charms."

He sat down in a chair, heavily. His face was weary, but he looked at Laurel and smiled.

"It might help if we managed to pity those poor things out there," he said.

"Pity?" she almost cried out.

"Yes," he said, and quoted:

. . . Think how sad it must be
To thirst always for a scorned elixir,
The salt of quotidian blood.

"I know that," volunteered Cobbett. "It's from a poem by Richard Wilbur, a damned unhappy poet."

"Quotidian," repeated Laurel to herself.

"That means something that keeps coming back, that returns daily," Cobbett said.

"It's a term used to refer to a recurrent fever," added Pursuivant.

Laurel and Cobbett sat down together on the bed.

"I would say that for the time being we're safe here," declared Pursuivant. "Not at ease, but at least safe. At dawn, danger will go to sleep and we can open the door."

"But why are we safe, and nobody else?" Laurel cried out. "Why are we awake, with everyone else in this town asleep and helpless?"

"Apparently because we all of us wear garlic," replied Pursuivant patiently, "and because we ate garlic, plenty of it, at dinner time. And because there are crosses—crude, but unmistakable—wherever something might try to come in. I won't ask you to be calm, but I'll ask you to be resolute."

"I'm resolute," said Cobbett between clenched teeth. "I'm ready to go out there and face them."

"If you did that, even with the garlic," said Pursuivant, "you'd last about as long as a pint of whiskey in a five-handed poker game. No, Lee, relax as much as you can, and let's talk."

They talked, while outside strange presences could be felt rather than heard. Their talk was of anything and everything but where they were and why. Cobbett remembered strange things he had encountered, in towns, among mountains, along desolate roads, and what he had been able to do about them. Pursuivant told of a vampire he had known and defeated in upstate New York, of a werewolf in his own Southern countryside. Laurel, at Cobbett's urging, sang songs, old songs, from her own rustic home place. Her voice was sweet. When she sang "Round is the Ring," faces came and hung like smudges outside the cross—scored windows. She saw, and sang again, an old Appalachian carol called "Mary She Heared a Knock in the Night." The faces drifted away again. And the hours, too, drifted away, one by one.

"There's a horde of vampires on the night street here then." Cobbett at last brought up the subject of their problem.

"And they lull the people of Deslow to sleep, to be helpless victims," agreed Pursuivant. "About this show, *The Land Beyond the Forest*, mightn't it be welcomed as a chance to spread the infection? Even a townful of sleepers couldn't feed a growing community of blood drinkers."

"If we could deal with the source, the original infection—" began Cobbett.

"The mistress of them, the queen," said Pursuivant. "Yes. The one whose walking by night rouses them all. If she could be destroyed, they'd all die properly."

He glanced at the front window. The moonlight had a touch of slaty gray.

"Almost morning," he pronounced. "Time for a visit to her tomb."

"I gave my promise I wouldn't go there," said Cobbett.

"But I didn't promise," said Pursuivant, rising. "You stay here with Laurel."

His silver blade in hand, he stepped out into darkness from which the moon had all but dropped away. Overhead, stars were fading out. Dawn was at hand.

He sensed a flutter of movement on the far side of the street, an almost inaudible gibbering of sound. Steadily he walked across. He saw nothing along the sidewalk there, heard nothing. Resolutely he tramped to the churchyard, his weapon poised. More grayness had come to dilute the dark.

He pushed his way through the hedge of shrubs, stepped in upon the grass, and paused at the side of a grave. Above it hung an eddy of soft mist, no larger than the swirl of water draining from a sink. As he watched, it seemed to soak into the earth and disappear. That, he said to himself, is what a soul looks like when it seeks to regain its coffin.

On he walked, step by weary, purposeful step, toward the central crypt. A ray of the early sun, stealing between heavily leafed boughs, made his way more visible. In this dawn, he would find what he would find. He knew that.

The crypt's door of open bars was held shut by its heavy padlock. He examined that lock closely. After a moment, he slid the point of his blade into the rusted keyhole and judiciously pressed this way, then that, and back again the first way. The spring creakily relaxed and he dragged the door open. Holding his breath, he entered.

The lid of the great stone vault was closed down. He took hold of the edge and heaved. The lid was heavy, but rose with a complaining grate of the hinges. Inside he saw a dark, closed coffin. He lifted the lid of that, too.

She lay there, calm-faced, the eyes half shut as though dozing. "Chastel," said Pursuivant to her. "Not Gonda. Chastel."

The eyelids fluttered. That was all, but he knew that she heard what he said.

"Now you can rest," he said. "Rest in peace, really in peace."

He set the point of his silver blade at the swell of her left breast. Leaning both his broad hands upon the curved handle, he drove downward with all his strength.

She made a faint squeak of sound.

Blood sprang up as he cleared his weapon. More light shone in. He could see a dark moisture fading from the blade, like evaporating dew.

In the coffin, Chastel's proud shape shrivelled, darkened. Quickly he slammed the coffin shut, then lowered the lid of the vault into place and went quickly out. He pushed the door shut again and fastened the stubborn old lock. As he walked back through the churchyard among the graves, a bird twittered over his head. More distantly, he heard the hum of a car's motor. The town was waking up.

In the growing radiance, he walked back across the street. By now, his steps were the steps of an old man, old and very tired.

◊◊◊

Inside Laurel's cabin, Laurel and Cobbett were stirring instant coffee into hot water in plastic cups. They questioned the judge with their tired eyes.

"She's finished," he said shortly.

"What will you tell Gonda?" asked Cobbett.

"Chastel was Gonda."

"But—"

"She was Gonda," said Pursuivant again, sitting down. "Chastel died. The infection wakened her out of her tomb, and she told people she was Gonda, and naturally they believed her." He sagged wearily. "Now that she's finished and at rest, those others—the ones she had bled, who also rose at night—will rest, too."

Laurel took a sip of coffee. Above the cup, her face was pale.

"Why do you say Chastel was Gonda?" she asked the Judge. "How can you know that?"

"I wondered from the very beginning. I was utterly sure just now."

"Sure?" said Laurel. "How can you be sure?"

Pursuivant smiled at her, the very faintest of smiles.

"My dear, don't you think a man always recognizes a woman he has loved?"

He seemed to recover his characteristic defiant vigor. He rose and went to the door and put his hand on the knob. "Now, if you'll just excuse me for awhile."

"Don't you think we'd better hurry and leave?" Cobbett asked him. "Before people miss her and ask questions?"

"Not at all," said Pursuivant, his voice strong again. "If we're gone, they'll ask questions about us, too, possibly embarrassing questions. No, we'll stay. We'll eat a good breakfast, or at least pretend to eat it. And we'll be as surprised as the rest of them about the disappearance of their leading lady."

"I'll do my best," vowed Laurel.

"I know you will, my child," said Pursuivant, and went out the door.

Manly Wade Wellman was one of the main writers for *Weird Tales* magazine in the 1930s and 1940s, where he created several popular series characters, including the psychic sleuth Judge Pursuivant who appears here in "Chastel." He is the author of numerous books and won a World Fantasy award for his collection *Worse Things Waiting*. "Chastel" draws on and references true historical accounts of vampires in Connecticut; the story of the Ray family of Griswold, for instance, was reported in the *Norwich Courier* of May 20, 1854.

What if vampirism were a curse—
a family curse passed down through the ages?
What if you knew you were next?

The Doom of
the House of Duryea

BY EARL PIERCE JR.

1

Arthur Duryea a young, handsome man, came to meet his father for the first time in twenty years. As he strode into the hotel lobby—long strides which had the spring of elastic in them—idle eyes lifted to appraise him, for he was an impressive figure, somehow grim with exaltation

The desk clerk looked up with his habitual smile of expectation—how-do-you-do-Mr. So-and-So—and his fingers strayed to the green fountain pen which stood in a holder on the desk.

Arthur Duryea cleared his throat, but still his voice was clogged and unsteady. To the clerk he said:

"I'm looking for my father, Doctor Henry Duryea. I understand he is registered here. He has recently arrived from Paris."

The clerk lowered his glance to a list of names. "Doctor Duryea is in suite 600, sixth floor." He looked up, his eyebrows arched questioningly. "Are you staying too, sir, Mr. Duryea?"

Arthur took the pen and scribbled his name rapidly. Without a further word, neglecting even to get his key and own room number, he turned and walked to the elevators. Not until he reached his father's suite on the sixth floor did he make an audible noise, and this was a mere sigh which fell from his lips like a prayer.

The man who opened the door was unusually tall, his slender frame clothed in tight-fitting black. He hardly dared to smile. His clean-shaven face was pale, an almost livid whiteness against the sparkle in his eyes. His jaw had a bluish luster.

"Arthur!" The word was scarcely a whisper. It seemed choked up quietly, as if it had been repeated time and again on his thin lips.

Arthur Duryea felt the kindliness of those eyes go through him, and then he was in his father's embrace.

Later, when these two grown men had regained their outer calm, they closed the door and went into the drawing room. The elder Duryea held out a humidor of fine cigars, and his hand shook so hard when he held the match that his son was forced to cup his own hands about the flame. They both had tears in their eyes, but their eyes were smiling.

Henry Duryea placed a hand on his son's shoulder. "This is the happiest day of my life," he said. "You can never know how much I have longed for this moment."

Arthur, looking into that glance, realized, with growing pride, that he had loved his father all his life, despite any of those things which had been cursed against him. He sat down on the edge of a chair.

"I—I don't know how to act," he confessed. "You surprised me, Dad. You're so different from what I had expected."

A cloud came over Doctor Duryea's features. "What *did* you expect, Arthur?" he demanded quickly. "An evil eye? A shaved head and knotted jowls?"

"Please, Dad—no!" Arthur's words clipped short. "I don't think I ever really visualized you. I knew you would be a splendid man. But I thought you'd look older, more like a man who has really suffered."

"I have suffered, more than I can ever describe. But seeing you again, and the prospect of spending the rest of my life with you, has more than compensated for my sorrows. Even during the twenty years we were apart I found an ironic joy in learning of your progress in college, and in your American game of football."

"Then you've been following my work?"

"Yes, Arthur; I've received monthly reports ever since you left me. From my study in Paris I've been really close to you, working out your problems as if they were my own. And now that the twenty years are completed, the ban which kept us apart is lifted forever. From now on, son, we shall be the closest of companions—unless your Aunt Cecilia has succeeded in her terrible mission."

The mention of that name caused an unfamiliar chill to come between the two men. It stood for something, in each of them, which gnawed their minds like a malignancy. But to the younger Duryea, in his intense effort to forget the awful past, her name as well as her madness must he forgotten.

He had no wish to carry on this subject of conversation, for it betrayed an internal weakness which he hated. With forced determination, and a ludicrous lift of his eyebrows, he said,

"Cecilia is dead, and her silly superstition is dead also. From now on, Dad, we're going to enjoy life as we should. Bygones are really bygones in this case."

Doctor Duryea closed his eyes slowly, as though an exquisite pain had gone through him.

"Then you have no indignation?" he questioned. "You have none of your aunt's hatred?"

"Indignation? Hatred?" Arthur laughed aloud. "Ever since I was twelve years old I have disbelieved Cecilia's stories. I have known that those horrible things were impossible, that they belonged to the ancient category of mythology and tradition. How, then, can I be indignant, and how can I hate you? How can I do anything but recognize Cecilia for what she was—a mean, frustrated woman, cursed with an insane grudge against you and your family? I tell you, Dad, that nothing she has ever said can possibly come between us again."

Henry Duryea nodded his head. His lips were tight together, and the muscles in his throat held back a cry. In that same soft tone of defense he spoke further, doubting words.

"Are you so sure of your subconscious mind, Arthur? Can you be so certain that you are free from all suspicion, however vague? Is there not a lingering premonition—a premonition which warns of peril?"

"No, Dad—no!" Arthur shot to his feet. "I don't believe it. I've never believed it. I know, as any sane man would know, that you are neither a vampire nor a murderer. You know it, too; and Cecilia knew it, only she was mad.

"That family rot is dispelled, Father. This is a civilized century. Belief in vampirism is sheer lunacy. Wh-why, it's too absurd even to think about!"

"You have the enthusiasm of youth," said his father, in a rather tired voice. "But have you not heard the legend?"

Arthur stepped back instinctively. He moistened his lips, for their dryness might crack them. "The—legend?"

He said the word in a curious hush of awed softness, as he had heard his Aunt Cecilia say it many times.

"That awful legend that you—"

"That I *eat* my children?"

"Oh, God, Father!" Arthur went to his knees as a cry burst through his lips. "Dad, that—that's ghastly! We must forget Cecilia's ravings."

"You are affected, then?" asked Doctor Duryea bitterly.

"Affected? Certainly I'm affected, but only as I should be at such an accusation. Cecilia was mad, I tell you. Those books she showed me years ago, and those folktales of vampires and ghouls—they burned into my infantile mind like acid. They haunted me day and night in my youth, and caused me to hate you worse than death itself."

"But in Heaven's name, Father, I've outgrown those things as I have outgrown my clothes. I'm a man now; do you understand that? A man, with a man's sense of logic."

"Yes, I understand." Henry Duryea threw his cigar into the fireplace, and placed a hand on his son's shoulder.

"We shall forget Cecilia," he said. "As I told you in my letter, I have rented a lodge in Maine where we can go to be alone for the rest of the summer. We'll get in some fishing and hiking and perhaps some hunting. But first, Arthur, I must be sure in my own mind that you are sure in yours. I must be sure you won't bar your door against me at night, and sleep with a loaded revolver at your elbow. I must be sure that you're not afraid of going up there alone with me, and dying—"

His voice ended abruptly, as if an age-long dread had taken hold of it. His son's face was waxen, with sweat standing out like pearls on his brow. He said nothing, but his eyes were filled with questions which his lips could not put into words. His own hand touched his father's and tightened over it.

Henry Duryea drew his hand away.

"I'm sorry," he said, and his eyes looked straight over Arthur's lowered head. "This thing must be thrashed out now. I believe you when you say that you discredit Cecilia's stories, but for a sake greater than sanity I must tell you the truth behind the legend—and believe me, Arthur; there is a truth!"

He climbed to his feet and walked to the window which looked out over the street below. For a moment he gazed into space, silent. Then he turned and looked down at his son.

"You have heard only your aunt's version of the legend, Arthur. Doubtless it was warped into a thing far more hideous than it actually was—if that is possible! Doubtless she spoke to you of the Inquisitorial stake in Carcassonne where one of my ancestors perished. Also she may have mentioned that book, *Vampyrs*, which a former Duryea is supposed to have written. Then certainly she told you about your two younger brothers—my own poor, motherless children—who were sucked bloodless in their cradles. . . ."

Arthur Duryea passed a hand across his aching eyes. Those words, so often repeated by that witch of an aunt, stirred up the same visions which had made his childhood nights sleepless with terror. He could hardly bear to hear them again—and from the very man to whom they were accredited.

"Listen, Arthur," the elder Duryea went on quickly, his voice low with the pain it gave him. "You must know that true basis of your aunt's hatred. You must know of that curse—that curse of vampirism which is supposed to have followed the Duryeas through five centuries of French history, but which we can dispel as pure superstition, so often connected with ancient families. But I must tell you that this part of the legend is true:

"Your two young brothers actually died in their cradles, bloodless. And I stood trial in France for their murder, and my name was smirched throughout all of Europe with such an inhuman damnation that it drove your aunt and you to America, and has left me childless, hated, and ostracized from society the world over.

"I must tell you that on that terrible night in Duryea Castle I had been working late on historic volumes of Crespet and Prinn, and on that loathsome tome, *Vampyrs*. I must tell you of the soreness that was in my throat and of the heaviness of the blood which coursed through my veins. . . . And of that *presence*, which was neither man nor animal, but which I knew was some place near me, yet neither within the castle nor outside of it, and which was closer to me than my heart and more terrible to me than the touch of the grave. . . .

"I was at the desk in my library, my head swimming in delirium which left me senseless until dawn. There were nightmares that frightened me—frightened me, Arthur, a grown man who had dissected countless cadavers in morgues and medical schools. I know that my tongue was swollen in my mouth and that brine moistened my lips, and that a rottenness pervaded my body like a fever.

"I can make no recollection of sanity or of consciousness. That night remains vivid, unforgettable, yet somehow completely in shadows. When I had fallen asleep—if in God's name it *was* sleep—I was slumped across my desk. But when I awoke in the morning I was lying face down on my couch. So you see, Arthur, I *had* moved during that night, *and I had never known it!*

"What I'd done and where I'd gone during those dark hours will always remain an impenetrable mystery. But I do know this. On the morrow I was torn from my sleep by the shrieks of maids and butlers, and by that mad wailing of your aunt. I stumbled through the open door of my study, and in the nursery I saw those two babies there—lifeless, white and dry like mummies, and with twin holes in their necks that were caked black with their own blood. . . .

"Oh, I don't blame you for your incredulousness, Arthur. I cannot believe it yet myself, nor shall I ever believe it. The belief of it would drive me to suicide; and still the doubting of it drives me mad with horror.

"All of France was doubtful, and even the savants who defended my name at the trial found that they could not explain it nor disbelieve it. The case was quieted by the Republic, for it might have shaken science to its very foundation and split the pedestals of religion and logic. I was released from the charge of murder; but the actual murder has hung about me like a stench.

"The coroners who examined those tiny cadavers found them both dry of all their blood, but could find no blood on the floor of the nursery nor in the cradles. Something from hell stalked the halls of Duryea that night—and I should blow my brains out if I dared to think deeply of who that was. You, too, my son, would have been dead and bloodless if you hadn't been sleeping in a separate room with your door barred on the inside.

"You were a timid child, Arthur. You were only seven years old, but you were filled with the folklore of those mad Lombards and the decadent poetry of your aunt. On that same night, while I was some place between heaven and hell, you, also, heard the padded footsteps on the stone corridor and heard the tugging at your door handle, for in the morning you complained of a chill and of terrible nightmares which frightened you in your sleep. . . . I only thank God that your door was barred!"

Henry Duryea's voice choked into a sob which brought the stinging tears back into his eyes. He paused to wipe his face, and to dig his fingers into his palm.

"You understand, Arthur, that for twenty years, under my sworn oath at the Palace of Justice, I could neither see you nor write to you. Twenty years, my son, while all of that time you had grown to hate me and to spit at my name. Not until your aunt's death have you called yourself a Duryea. . . . And now you come to me at my bidding, and say you love me as a son should love his father.

"Perhaps it is God's forgiveness for everything. Now, at last, we shall be together, and that terrible, unexplainable past will be buried forever. . . ."

He put his handkerchief back into his pocket and walked slowly to his son. He dropped to one knee, and his hands gripped Arthur's arms.

"My son, I can say no more to you. I have told the truth as I alone know it. I may be, by all accounts, some ghoulish creation of Satan on earth. I may be a child-killer, a vampire, some morbidly diseased specimen of *vrykolakas*—things which science cannot explain.

"Perhaps the dreaded legend of the Duryeas is true. Autiel Duryea was convicted of murdering his brother in that same monstrous fashion in the year 1576, and he died in flames at the stake. François Duryea, in 1802, blew his head apart with a blunderbuss on the morning after his youngest son was found dead, apparently from anemia. And there are others, of whom I cannot bear to speak, that would chill your soul if you were to hear them.

"So you see, Arthur, there is a hellish tradition behind our family. There is a heritage which no sane God would ever have allowed. The future of the Duryeas lies in you, for you are the last of the race. I pray with all of my heart that providence will permit you to live your full share of years, and to leave other Duryeas behind you. And so if ever again I feel that presence as I did in Duryea Castle, I am going to die as François Duryea died, over a hundred years ago. . . ."

He stood up, and his son stood up at his side.

"If you are willing to forget, Arthur, we shall go up to that lodge in Maine. There is a life we've never known awaiting us. We must find that life, and we must find the happiness which a curious fate snatched from us on those Lombard sourlands, twenty years ago. . . ."

2

Henry Duryea's tall stature, coupled with a slenderness of frame and a sleekness of muscle, gave him an appearance that was unusually *gaunt*. His son couldn't help thinking of that word as he sat on the rustic porch of the lodge, watching his father sunning himself at the lake's edge.

Henry Duryea had a kindliness in his face, at times an almost sublime kindliness which great prophets often possess. But when his face was partly in shadows, particularly about his brow, there was a frightening tone which came into his features; for it was a tone of farness, of mysticism and conjuration. Somehow, in the late evenings, he assumed the unapproachable mantle of a dreamer and sat silently before the fire, his mind ever off in unknown places.

In that little lodge there was no electricity, and the glow of the oil lamps played curious tricks with the human expression which frequently resulted in something unhuman. It may have been the dusk of night, the flickering of the lamps, but Arthur Duryea had certainly noticed how his father's eyes had sunken further into his head, and how his cheeks were tighter, and the outline of his teeth pressed into the skin about his lips.

◊◊◊

It was nearing sundown on the second day of their stay at Timber Lake. Six miles away the dirt road wound on toward Houtlon, near the Canadian border. So it was lonely there, on a solitary little lake hemmed in closely with dark evergreens and a sky which drooped low over dusty-summitted mountains.

Within the lodge was a homey fireplace, and a glossy elk's head which peered out above the mantel. There were guns and fishing tackle on the walls, shelves of reliable American fiction—Mark Twain, Melville, Stockton, and a well-worn edition of Bret Harte.

A fully supplied kitchen and a wood stove furnished them with hearty meals which were welcome after a whole day's tramp in the woods. On that evening Henry Duryea prepared a select French stew out of every available vegetable, and a can of soup. They ate well, then stretched out before the fire for a smoke. They were outlining a trip to the Orient together, when the back door blew open with a terrific bang, and a wind swept into the lodge with a coldness which chilled them both.

"A storm," Henry Duryea said, rising to his feet. "Sometimes they have them up here, and they're pretty bad. The roof might leak over your bedroom. Perhaps you'd like to sleep down here with me." His finger strayed playfully over his son's head as he went out into the kitchen to bar the swinging door.

Arthur's room was upstairs, next to a spare room filled with extra furniture. He'd chosen it because he liked the altitude, and because the only other bedroom was occupied. . . .

He went upstairs swiftly and silently. His roof didn't leak; it was absurd even to think it might. It had been his father again, suggesting that they sleep together. He had done it before, in a jesting, whispering way—as if to challenge them both if they *dared* to sleep together.

Arthur came back downstairs dressed in his bathrobe and slippers. He stood on the fifth stair, rubbing a two-day's growth of beard. "I think I'll shave tonight," he said to his father. "May I use your razor?"

Henry Duryea, draped in a black raincoat and with his face haloed in the brim of a rain hat, looked up from the hall. A frown glided obscurely from his features. "Not at all, son. Sleeping upstairs?"

Arthur nodded, and quickly said, "Are you—going out?"

"Yes, I'm going to tie the boats up tighter. I'm afraid the lake will rough it up a bit."

Duryea jerked back the door and stepped outside. The door slammed shut, and his footsteps sounded on the wood flooring of the porch.

Arthur came slowly down the remaining steps. He saw his father's figure pass across the dark rectangle of a window, saw the flash of lightning that suddenly printed his grim silhouette against the glass.

He sighed deeply, a sigh which burned in his throat, for his throat was sore and aching. Then he went into the bedroom, found the razor lying in plain view on a birch table-top.

As he reached for it, his glance fell upon his father's open Gladstone bag which rested at the foot of the bed. There was a book resting there, half hidden by a gray flannel shirt. It was a narrow, yellow-bound book, oddly out of place.

Frowning, he bent down and lifted it from the bag. It was surprisingly heavy in his hands, and he noticed a faintly sickening odor of decay which drifted from it like a perfume. The title of the volume had been thumbed away into an indecipherable blur of gold letters. But pasted across the front cover was a white strip of paper, on which was typewritten the word—INFANTIPHAGI.

He flipped back the cover and ran his eyes over the title page. The book was printed in French—an early French—yet to him wholly comprehensible. The publication date was 1580, in Caen.

Breathlessly he turned back a second page, saw a chapter headed, *Vampires.*

He slumped to one elbow across the bed. His eyes were four inches from those mildewed pages, his nostrils reeked with the stench of them.

He skipped long paragraphs of pedantic jargon on theology, he scanned brief accounts of strange, blood-eating monsters, *vryko-lakas,* and leprechauns. He read of Jeanne d'Arc, of Ludvig Prinn, and muttered aloud the Latin snatches from *Episcopi.*

He passed pages in quick succession, his fingers shaking with the fear of it and his eyes hanging heavily in their sockets. He saw vague reference to "Enoch," and saw the terrible drawings by an ancient Dominican of Rome. . . .

Paragraph after paragraph he read: the horror-striking testimony of Nider's *Ant-Hill,* the testimony of people who died shrieking at the stake; the recitals of grave-tenders, of jurists and hangmen. Then unexpectedly, among all of this monumental vestige, there appeared before his eyes the name of—*Autiel Duryea;* and he stopped reading as though invisibly struck.

Thunder clapped near the lodge and rattled the windowpanes. The deep rolling of bursting clouds echoed over the valley. But he heard none of it. His eyes were on those two short sentences which his father—someone—had underlined with dark red crayon.

. . . The execution, four years ago, of Autiel Duryea does not end the Duryea controversy. Time alone can decide whether the Demon has claimed that family from its beginning to its end. . . .

Arthur read on about the trial of Autiel Duryea before Veniti, the Carcassonnean Inquisitor-General; read, with mounting horror, the evidence which had sent that far-gone Duryea to the pillar—the evidence of a bloodless corpse who had been Autiel Duryea's young brother.

Unmindful now of the tremendous storm which had centered over Timber Lake, unheeding the clatter of windows and the swish of pines on the roof—even of his father who worked down on the lake's edge in a drenching rain—Arthur fastened his glance to the blurred print of those pages, sinking deeper and deeper into the garbled legends of a dark age. . . .

On the last page of the chapter he again saw the name of his ancestor, Autiel Duryea. He traced a shaking finger over the narrow lines of words, and when he finished reading them he rolled sideways on

the bed, and from his lips came a sobbing, mumbling prayer. "God, oh God in Heaven protect me. . . ."
For he had read:

As in the case of Autiel Duryea we observe that this specimen of *vrykolakas* preys only upon the blood of its own family. It possesses none of the characteristics of the undead vampire, being usually a living male person of otherwise normal appearance, unsuspecting its inherent demonism.

But this *vrykolakas* cannot act according to its demoniacal possession unless it is in the presence of a second member of the same family, who acts as a medium between the man and its demon. This medium has none of the traits of the vampire, but it senses the being of this creature (when the metamorphosis is about to occur) by reason of intense pains in the head and throat. Both the vampire and the medium undergo similar reactions, involving nausea, nocturnal visions, and physical disquietude.

When these two outcasts are within a certain distance of each other, the coalescence of inherent demonism is completed, and the vampire is subject to its attacks, demanding blood for its sustenance. No member of the family is safe at these times, for the *vrykolakas,* acting in its true agency on earth, will unerringly seek out the blood. In rare cases, where other victims are unavailable, *the vampire will even take the blood from the very medium which made it possible.*

This vampire is born into certain aged families, and naught but death can destroy it. It is not conscious of its blood-madness, and acts only in a psychic state. The medium, also, is unaware of its terrible role; and when these two are together, despite any lapse of years, the fusion of inheritance is so violent that no power known on earth can turn it back.

3

The lodge door slammed shut with a sudden, interrupting bang. The lock grated, and Henry Duryea's footsteps sounded on the planked floor.

Arthur shook himself from the bed. He had only time to fling that haunting book into the Gladstone bag before he sensed his father standing in the doorway.

"You—you're not shaving, Arthur." Duryea's words, spliced hesitantly, were toneless. He glanced from the table-top to the Gladstone, and to his son. He said nothing for a moment, his glance inscrutable.

Then, "It's blowing up quite a storm outside."

Arthur swallowed the first words which had come into his throat, nodded quickly. "Yes, isn't it? Quite a storm." He met his father's gaze, his face burning. "I—I don't think I'll shave, Dad. My head aches."

Duryea came swiftly into the room and pinned Arthur's arms in his grasp. "What do you mean—your head aches? How? Does your throat—"

"No!" Arthur jerked himself away. He laughed. "It's that French stew of yours! It's hit me in the stomach!" He stepped past his father and started up the stairs.

"The stew?" Duryea pivoted on his heel. "Possibly. I think I feel it myself."

Arthur stopped, his face suddenly white. "You—too?"

The words were hardly audible. Their glances met—clashed like dueling swords.

For ten seconds neither of them said a word or moved a muscle: Arthur, from the stairs, looking down; his father below, gazing up at him. In Henry Duryea the blood drained slowly from his face and left a purple etching across the bridge of his nose and above his eyes. He looked like a death's head.

Arthur winced at the sight and twisted his eyes away. He turned to go up the remaining stairs.

"Son!"

He stopped again; his hand tightening on the banister.

"Yes, Dad?"

Duryea put his foot on the first stair. "I want you to lock your door tonight. The wind would keep it banging!"

"Yes," breathed Arthur, and pushed up the stairs to his room.

◊◊◊

The Doom of the House of Duryea   111

Doctor Duryea's hollow footsteps sounded in steady, unhesitant beats across the floor of Timber Lake Lodge. Sometimes they stopped, and the crackling hiss of a sulfur match took their place, then perhaps a distended sigh, and, again, footsteps. . . .

Arthur crouched at the open door of his room. His head was cocked for those noises from below. In his hands was a double-barrel shotgun of violent gage.

. . . Thud . . . thud . . . thud . . .

Then a pause, the clinking of a glass and the gurgling of liquid. The sigh, the tread of his feet over the floor.

He's thirsty, Arthur thought—*Thirsty!*

Outside, the storm had grown into fury. Lightning zigzagged between the mountains, filling the valley with weird phosphorescence. Thunder, like drums, rolled incessantly.

Within the lodge the heat of the fireplace piled the atmosphere thick with stagnation. All the doors and windows were locked shut, the oil-lamps glowed weakly—a pale, anemic light.

Henry Duryea walked to the foot of the stairs and stood looking up.

Arthur sensed his movements and ducked back into his room, the gun gripped in his shaking fingers.

Then Henry Duryea's footstep sounded on the first stair.

Arthur slumped to one knee. He buckled a fist against his teeth as a prayer tumbled through them.

Duryea climbed a second step . . . and another . . . and still one more. On the fourth stair he stopped.

"Arthur!" His voice cut into the silence like the crack of a whip. "Arthur! Will you come down here?"

"Yes, Dad." Bedraggled, his body hanging like cloth, young Duryea took five steps to the landing.

"We can't be zanies!" cried Henry Duryea. "My soul is sick with dread. Tomorrow we're going back to New York. I'm going to get the first boat to open sea. . . . Please come down here." He turned about and descended the stairs to his room.

Arthur choked back the words which had lumped in his mouth. Half dazed, he followed. . . .

In the bedroom he saw his father stretched face-up along the bed. He saw a pile of rope at his father's feet.

"Tie me to the bedposts, Arthur," came the command. "Tie both my hands and both my feet."

Arthur stood gaping.

"Do as I tell you!"

"Dad, what hor—"

"Don't be a fool! You read that book! You know what relation you are to me! I'd always hoped it was Cecilia, but now I know it's you. I should have known it on that night twenty years ago when you complained of a headache and nightmares. . . . Quickly, my head rocks with pain. Tie me!"

Speechless, his own pain piercing him with agony, Arthur fell to that grisly task. Both hands he tied—and both feet . . . tied them so firmly to the iron posts that his father could not lift himself an inch off the bed.

Then he blew out the lamps, and without a further glance at that Prometheus, he reascended the stairs to his room, and slammed and locked his door behind him.

He looked once at the breech of his gun, and set it against a chair by his bed. He flung off his robe and slippers, and within five minutes he was senseless in slumber.

4

He slept late, and when he awakened his muscles were as stiff as boards, and the lingering visions of a nightmare clung before his eyes. He pushed his way out of bed, stood dazedly on the floor.

A dull, numbing cruciation circulated through his head. He felt bloated . . . coarse and running with internal mucus. His mouth was dry, his gums sore and stinging.

He tightened his hands as he lunged for the door. "Dad," he cried, and he heard his voice breaking in his throat.

Sunlight filtered through the window at the top of the stairs. The air was hot and dry, and carried in it a mild odor of decay.

Arthur suddenly drew back at that odor—drew back with a gasp of awful fear. For he recognized it—that stench, the heaviness of his blood, the rawness of his tongue and gums. . . . Age-long it seemed, yet rising like a spirit in his memory. All of these things he had known and felt before.

He leaned against the banister, and half slid, half stumbled down the stairs. . . .

His father had died during the night. He lay like a waxen figure tied to his bed, his face done up in knots.

Arthur stood dumbly at the foot of the bed for only a few seconds; then he went back upstairs to his room.

Almost immediately he emptied both barrels of the shotgun into his head.

◇◇◇

The tragedy at Timber Lake was discovered accidentally three days later. A party of fishermen, upon finding the two bodies, notified state authorities, and an investigation was directly under way.

Arthur Duryea had undoubtedly met death at his own hands. The condition of his wounds, and the manner with which he held the lethal weapon, at once foreclosed the suspicion of any foul play.

But the death of Doctor Henry Duryea confronted the police with an inexplicable mystery; for his trussed-up body, unscathed except for two jagged holes over the jugular vein, *had been drained of all its blood.*

The autopsy protocol of Henry Duryea laid death to "undetermined causes," and it was not until the yellowish tabloids commenced an investigation into the Duryea family history that the incredible and fantastic explanations were offered to the public.

Obviously such talk was held in popular contempt; yet in view of the controversial war which followed, the authorities considered it expedient to consign both Duryeas to the crematory. . . .

At the encouragement of his friend Robert Bloch, Earl Pierce Jr. wrote seven stories for *Weird Tales* published between 1936 and 1940. He also appeared in *Startling Mystery Stories, Dime Mystery,* and *Detective Tales.*

BLOOD LINES

Some towns would rather entertain a family of vampires than cityfolk—
at least vampires have a sense of history.

Moonlight in Vermont

BY ESTHER FRIESNER

knew that city kid was wise to us that morning when my sister Louisa's husband, George, welcomed some new-come guests to their bed-and-breakfast and he snarfed his Cheerios so hard the milk come out his nose. Lord, it was ugly enough to stop a freight train, 'specially when some of the cereal bits got stuck on that gold chain he had running from his nose-ring to his earring and just hung there like clothes on a washline.

Not so ugly as what he said next, though, out loud: "Bed and breakfast! Yeah, right. And once you're in your bed, you get to be their breakfast."

The newcomers stood there in the doorway, trading weird looks. The city kid wiped the milk off his face and grinned like a hound that's just caught a fat rabbit. That's what George told me, anyhow. I wasn't there to actually *see* any of this firsthand. I was down the cellar over to our own place, laid out comfy in my good ol' pine box. I don't know about you, but turning into a heap of ancestral dust at the touch of the sun's first rays ain't never been my idea of a good time.

"So what'd they say when he said that, Georgie dear?" Mama asked. (Mama's the only one can call Louisa's husband Georgie without him pitching a fit. I did that once, real sassy like dumb kids get, you know, and next evening when I tried to rise out of my box, I found out that the rascally creep had phoned down to one of his old high school buddies who works in the Brattleboro Domino's Pizza place and there was an extra-large, extra-cheese, extra-*garlic* pie flopped down on my lid.)

"Pass the potatoes," said George. The whole family was gathered over to our place for dinner, like we always do Sundays. Louisa passed him the big yellow bowl and gave him a poke in the ribs. Louisa's the only one who can find old George's ribs these days, he's so fat.

"He did *not* say 'pass the potatoes,' you big lummox," she sniped. Louisa's so pretty, with them long goldy curls and them china-doll blue eyes, that she can get away with saying 'bout most anything she likes to George or God or anyone.

"Sorry." He looked real sheepish. "They didn't say much of anything, truth to tell. Just looked at each other, then at him. You seen him: Tall, so skinny he's gotta stand twice in the same place to make a shadow, half his hair shaved off, the other half spiked up and striped pink and green—"

"The preppie-punk-skunk look," Louisa said sourly.

"I don't know nothing 'bout that," George replied. "His folks are okay people, quiet guests, just trying to enjoy the fall foliage up here. They take his little sis with them for drives every day, but *he* won't go. Yeah, he's a tough cud to chew, all right. Kinda reminds me of Albert." He gave me one of his shit-eatingest grins. I gave him the finger real quick, so's Pa wouldn't catch me at it.

"Anyway," George went on, "the new guests sorta shrugged it off, what he said. I guess they figured either he was on drugs and had a few cracked cups in the cupboard, or else he was just trying to say stuff that'd shock 'em, so it'd go with the way he was dressed. When you're that ugly, you gotta make folks look at you some way."

"So they just dismissed him," Pa remarked. His carving knife sliced into the nice roast Mama'd set down for us like the meat was butter. Beautiful red juices oozed out over the blade. "Just as well. In all probability he knows nothing and was merely extemporizing for effect."

"But Pa," I said, hating how my voice cracked when I got worried, "what if he's not?"

"Nonsense, Albert. How could he know anything?"

Mama was quick to back up Pa. "He hasn't been up here to our place, and Louisa and Georgie do not give their guests the run of the house, and I am certain that Georgie takes the strictest care of locking up the basement daytimes. I don't care if that child's so nosy he can hear grass grow, if he hasn't seen the coffins, how could he think we're vampires? Children today have no imagination. It's all that television, you know." Mighty pleased with herself, she urged me to eat up my turnips and have some more meat if I wanted to be done with my dinner before it was time for *The Simpsons*.

Pa forked over my third helping and asked, "How long are his people going to stay, did you say, George?"

"They're leaving next Monday."

"A boy his age should be in school," Mama commented. She sounded bitter. Before Pa came creeping in at her bedroom window to suck her blood and make her one of the undead, she'd been a schoolteacher. She managed to smack him once or twice with her old *McGuffey's Reader* before he did for her—something about how men like 'em hard to get but easy to hold, she told Louisa. Mama always was a great believer in education.

(You can still see the one-room schoolhouse where she used to work. The municipal council here in Wintersend, Vermont, offered up a motion to keep it up as a historic monument, in Mama's honor, and it passed unanimously at the town meeting. Mama says it's on account of how she had one of her "little talks" with the council chairman's son, Joey Cassidy, when that no-neck fool was thinking 'bout dropping out of school and running off to California to start a rock band. Some nights she still goes up there to the schoolhouse to get in a few practice licks with the birch switches and the teacher's ferule, just to keep up her what she calls "interpersonal pedagogic skills." Louisa says the night Mama had that "little talk" with Joey, you could hear the yowls clear to White River Junction.)

So I guess you can imagine what color Mama's face turned when George told her, "He don't go to school anymore."

"What? Why, the child's no more than fifteen years old! The last I heard, public school attendance was still mandatory at that age."

"Still is," George affirmed. "Only this brat's parents got more money than sense. He got himself booted out of every public school down where they come from—and that's New York City, mind!—and near every private school they tried, too. I know, 'cause his little sister told me all about it while she was watching me work on my old Corvette last Tuesday. So now his parents got him and her both in one of these 'experimental' schools and the girl don't much like it. The teachers there, they don't give no tests, no grades, attendance is optional, and if there's any way they can say that something the kid does out of school is—shoot, what'd she call it?—oh, yeah, *whole-life-experience enrichment,* they say go for it!"

"No grades," Mama repeated, scandalized. "No tests. Whole-life-experience hogwash. Mercy on us." Her long, slim fingers kept curling, like they was closing around the business end of a good, flexible length of hickory wood.

"Now, now, Maude," said Pa, tucking into his third slice of blood-rare beef. "It's none of our business how other people raise their children. We've got enough to do looking after our own. Which reminds me: Albert, when I went out to the barn this evening, Elvira was bawling as if her heart would break. You know that cow is your responsibility. You forgot to milk her before sunup again, didn't you?"

I hung my head. No use lying to Pa; he's been lied to by the best, and it never cut no ice with him. Ethan Allen himself tried to sweet-talk him out of a mess of supplies for the Green Mountain Boys back when Pa was just fresh come up to Wintersend from Boston—that's why he talks the fanciest of us all, you know, Boston. Old Ethan, he got sent on his way short and sweet, with a flea in his ear. Not a lick of his bullying or threats would move Pa, not even when they called him a Tory.

Tory, sir? he yelled at 'em. *Tory, is it? By heaven and all the hills, I may be an unnatural blood-drinking, virtually immortal member of the living dead, but no one has ever dared impugn my patriotism!* That's when he tore the throats out of a couple of the Boys to make his point. The rest grabbed Ethan and moved on lickety-split. Pa kept on the two he'd killed for hired hands, but being mountain men, they were heedless and it didn't take but ninety years before both of 'em got caught by the dawn. Still, they made pretty good fertilizer for Mama's vegetable patch. You should've seen them pumpkins that year!

But all that's older than the devil's grandfather. I was in trouble up to the minute, and I knew it. "I'm sorry, Pa," I said. "I thought I took care of her. See, there was this light in the east and I thought dawn was coming on mighty fast and I didn't want to be—"

"Idleness always makes excuses." Pa shook his head and turned to Mama. "Either you've got to bring us in another son, Maude, or else I'd better look to taking on more daily hands."

That did it; the fight was on. Every time Pa suggested getting some more salaried hands to help run the farm, Mama hit the roof and stayed there. See, Pa always fancied himself the gentleman farmer, even if he did wear L. L. Bean overalls these days. He doesn't like to talk about it much, but we all know how he was educated for the ministry, original, at Harvard. (I know just the trunk to look in up attic, if you want proof. It's got his raggedy Greek and Hebrew texts in it, and it's something scandalous, the things he wrote in the margins about his old schoolmate, Mr. Mather, and hooved animals.)

Mama, on the other hand, was an orphan like me, who'd had to make her own way and valued a penny earned a sliver *too* much, if you get my drift. Some of the almost-Christian ladies in town went so far as to say that she'd skin a mouse for the hide and fat. So whenever she and Pa got to arguing over money, the rest of the world went away. Louisa and I exchanged a look and went back to our dinner plates. George never had looked up from his. It was like that miserable city kid and his smartmouth talk had vanished with last year's snow.

Too bad that wasn't the way of it.

Next evening I made it my business to get my chores done quick and take me a ride down to town on my bike. Pa always talks about how it used to be, our place was nice and isolated, where a man could breathe and a vampire could stretch his wings some, only time went by and the town grew and now a body couldn't roll over in his own coffin without rubbing elbows with them damned snowmobilers from New York. Me, I'm just glad the town grew enough so I could reach it by bike.

Wintersend ain't no big town; small as a chicken's sneeze, I'd call it. Friday nights, most of the young people meet in the Shop-Mor parking lot and drive over to Brattleboro for the movies. Some of my friends from school waved to me and shouted I should come along, but I had other fish to fry. Besides, sometimes I wonder if they really like me or just the fact that I been in the eleventh grade so long I got all the final exam answers memorized by heart.

The city kid was right where I expected to find him, sitting on the front porch of Louisa's bed-and-breakfast, with his feet up on the rail. I leaned my bike up against the big sign that said this was the Maple Sugar Inne (formerly the Maple Tree Inn, formerly the Green Tree Inn, formerly the Green Mountain Guest House, and any further back than that I lose track of Louisa's husbands and what they named the place) and sauntered up the walk, real casual.

"Hi," I said, like I was sixteen and bored.

"They're glowing," he said back.

"Huh?"

"Your eyes, dork. If you stand with your back to the porch light I can really see 'em glow. You oughta see it—they're awesome. Only I guess you'll hafta take my word for it. Can't see yourself in mirrors, right?" And the son of a bitch laughed.

I pulled one of the porch rocking chairs up next to him and had myself a seat. He was still laughing like a jackass, pushing himself back and forth with them clunky sneakers he had on, only I bet they cost upwards of a hundred dollars easy and had their bottoms full of air or water or gel.

All I knew was they had a thick layer of wet, dirty leaves trampled into the treads, presently filthying up the nice, white, fresh—painted railing, and Louisa'd have a hissy when she saw it.

"You talk crazy, you know?" I said, still trying to keep it calm. "All you New Yorkers nuts or just you?"

He only chuckled, a hollow sound like a milk bucket full of acorns. Then he stuck out a hand at me, big as life and twice as natural. "Evan Tyler. My friends call me Venom."

I was raised too polite not to shake a man's hand when he offers. "Albert Miller Harriman."

"No shit." His palm was damp, and he had a grip as weak as city coffee. "Mind if I call you Bela?" Henry David Thoreau be damned, if this brat kept on riding me like a prize mule, I was gonna nail down his loose shingles good and proper.

"You sure do have a peculiar notion 'bout my family," I said, acting like nothing much was amiss, rocking real slow. "You know, we ain't half the shitkickers up here you take us for." I stopped rocking and leaned over to him, real confidential. "You brought any good stuff up here with you from New York, I got what to buy it off you with. Fair price for the goods."

He frowned. "What the fuck are you—? Drugs? You mean *drugs*, batboy? You think I'm—!" He brayed, long and loud, then latched onto my near arm. "I got some tough news for you, dipshit: You can't do a line when you're hangin' upside down from the ceiling, okay?"

"You're nuts." I said it with as much conviction as I could. It wasn't easy. I'll be first to admit, this city brat had me scared halfway to next Thursday. When I looked into his eyes, I saw that everything he was saying about me and my family wasn't on account of any stuff he'd been smoking or snorting or shooting. He *knew*. Somehow—I was gonna find out how—he'd found out about us.

"Nice fake," Venom said, showing off his teeth. They looked yellow and slimy by the porch buglight. "You want me to prove what I know? Okay. What'll it take? Hey, I know. How about I wait until tomorrow morning, after the sun comes up, and I go down into the cellar of this stupid hole, and I tiptoe behind that rack of jelly jars that's about as real as rubber dogshit—Oh, don't worry about me getting caught. I'll wait until your sister's asshole husband's out of the house first; he'll never know I'm there. Dumb fuck's so drunk half the time that he don't know *nothing!*"

I stiffened. "George drinks?"

"Like a freakin' fish, man." Venom was having a good old time. "Goes into that toolshed behind the house right after breakfast."

"Lotsa folks go into their toolsheds, mornings," I said drily. "It's called work."

"The hell it is. Not when you keep looking over your shoulder every two steps, like you're doing something you wanna hide. I saw it all from my room upstairs. I got to sleep in the other day while Mom and Dad dragged Lindsay off to gawk at the leaves, bee-eff-dee. They know better than to try making me come along." Someday I may hear a more obnoxious laugh, but I doubt it.

"So when he doesn't come out right away, I go follow him, peek in the little window on the side. I think maybe, y'know, the old fart's got some stash or something he'll share real generous, to keep my mouth shut. Only thing he's got out there's liquor, though, lots of it. He gets loaded, then he starts talkin' to himself about how he's got the most gorgeous little wife in Vermont, only she's always gonna *be* the most gorgeous piece of ass around long after *he's* a bundle of bones in the grave."

He was still laughing about that one when I jumped up, grabbed his feet off the porch rail, and tipped him over backward on his pointy head. "Don't you *never* talk that way about my sister," I told him.

He picked himself up, not laughing anymore. "Listen, fuckhead, I'll talk about your sister any way I want, got it? Because if you try any of that macho shit on me again, next time I go down the cellar here, I'll take my old man along for the ride. Whadda you think he'll do when he sees your sis laid out like that?" He showed me them ugly teeth again. "Take it from me, even if old Iron Ass freaks, he'll get over it fast and then—*ciao, chicky.*"

I looked him in the eye. "That's if you get to *see* your pa again." No way he could miss my meaning.

Wish I could say that rattled him, but he stayed cooler than a toad with a muddy tail. "What're you gonna do? Make me one of *you?* Hey, sucker, that'd suit me fine. Live forever, stay fifteen forever, what's the big scare? That's what I want."

All the more reason not to give it to him. We was squared off like a pair of stray dogs in an alley, my turn to growl, "You like to think you know what there is to know about my family, Genesis to Revelation, don't you?"

He nodded, looking modest; "Believe it or not, I read, dickbreath. And I watch movies. I figure some of that stuff's bullshit, but the part about where if a vampire kills you, you become a vampire, that's in too many of the stories for it not to be true."

"Only if he kills you by drinking your blood," I reminded him, and closed my right hand around the porch railing. The solid wood splintered before I even got half a good grip going. Louisa'd tan my hide for it, but I had a point to make.

Venom lost a little color under the gills there for a bit. Still he had the balls to come back at me with, "So you break my neck, asshole. And maybe you got the brains to make it look like an accident. And then, when my folks are packing up my stuff to take home, they find this note saying 'In the event of my death,' and it tells them where to look and what to look for. Oh, and before you start burning out your gray cells, figuring you'll get your sister's box moved and search my stuff for the note yourself, let me save you the hassle. Even on the move, I got hiding places you couldn't find in a zillion years. My folks could, though. I gave 'em plenty of practice. Every week is stash-search week at our house; sometimes they even find my shit. Sometimes I leave them little notes to find, and a coupla gold stickum stars for being such good narcs. They'll find the note, okay. And when they see it says 'In the event of my death,' and they know I'm dead, they won't just toss it like it was a bad joke. Nothing like being a corpse to make your parents take you seriously."

Venom. He sure did choose the right name for himself. The poison was deep in him, flowing like an April river. I bet he was even one of those snot-noses who only thinks about his own death as then-they'll-be-sorry-time. Like he could kill himself for the kick of coming back, and watching all the folks who'd cared about him suffer, and gloating over their helplessness and misery until he swelled up on it like a tick on a deerhound.

And he wanted to be a vampire. Like he wasn't one already.

I had to admit, though, he had me. For the time being, anyhow. I let the chunk of railing in my hand fall to the porch. "What do you want?"

Now he wasn't just showing teeth, but gums. The sight would turn a tax collector's stomach. "What you already offered, dumbass: I wanna be one of you."

◊◊◊

Next Sunday dinner was like black and white compared to last week's. George sat with his hands in his lap and his head down the whole time, not eating a bite. Mama tried and tried to get him to take some of her delicious ham, so pink and tender it melted in your mouth, but he wasn't having any.

"Look here, George, it isn't your fault," Pa said. "No one is angry with you."

"Honey, listen to Papa," Louisa coaxed her husband. No one can coax prettier than Louisa.

(She was raised by a maiden aunt in Amherst to be a regular little New England bluestocking—one of them females who puts it all into brains and figures that looking fetching means you got cotton between the ears. I got a look at that aunt of hers when they first come up here and if I was that ugly, I'd shout louder'n anyone that looks ain't everything. Anyhow, Mama wanted a daughter, and Pa always does like to please Mama, and Louisa was sick of visiting distant cousins in Wintersend with Aunt Troll, so she was bored half to death already and agreeable to going the rest of the way, and the rest is history. First thing Louisa did when she rose from the grave was to burn her copy of Emerson's *Literary Ethics* and buy her some curling irons, orange flower water, frilly petticoats, and a lace-trimmed corset.)

Louisa could've been an old shoe for all the mind George paid her. "It's all my fault," he kept repeating. "I'm to blame."

"We must share at least some measure of your culpability, George," Pa said. "Certainly I do not mean to discount or disavow your own meed of responsibility for our present situation, yet take comfort justly earned in the fact that you are not alone. We should have foreseen it."

"What, Ven—I mean, Evan?" I asked. Mama had already told me I was not to refer to our nose-ringed nemesis by "that barbaric nickname." It wasn't refined.

Pa shook his head. "Nonsense, Albert; who could predict that six thousand years of civilization would disgorge such an end-

124   BLOOD LINES

product? No, I refer to poor George's emotional state, which in turn led him to the bibulous excess that so sadly abridged his ordinarily excellent vigilance over Louisa's resting place."

"I'll never touch another drop, I swear," George said to his lap. Now, dear." Mama leaned over and patted his hand.

"Nihil nimis. Nothing to excess; not even abstinence. We've gone through this before, you know. With Louisa's"—I could tell she was searching for a way to mention Louisa's previous husbands without hurting George's feeling—"with prior managers of the inn."

George finally raised his head. There were tears in his eyes. It was scary. You don't expect to see a real man cry, just them wimps like Donahue or Alan Alda. Or Geraldo, if there was a buck in it. But not George. "Why does it have to be this way?" he asked, real pitiful. "Why can't you change me so's I'm just like you?" He turned to Louisa, and just about whined, "How come we can't be together forever? Don't you love me enough for that?"

I gotta hand it to my sister, every time they pose the same old questions she acts like it's the absolute first time on God's green earth she ever heard a man ask why he can't become a vampire, too. Mama says that's her good breeding coming through. Bet it gets pretty boring, though.

"Darling, it's *because* I love you that I won't do that," she told him. "Whenever a vampire brings a human over, there's a certain bond formed. The older vampire has power and authority over the newer one."

"So?" Now there was fire back in George's eye. "That's not so bad. Look at your own ma and dad!"

Mama pursed her lips. "Georgie, William and I get along well *in spite* of the fact that he has but to exert his natural dominion over me to win any and all domestic differences of opinion. His Puritan upbringing may be regarded as repressive by some, yet it has given him a wonderful measure of self-discipline and restraint, together with a love for the rational processes. Where some vampires in want of a wife would have bitten first and asked second, William talked it over with me beforehand."

Mama gave Pa one of those drippy fond looks and continued, "I will always cherish those days of courtship. He would come by the schoolhouse a little after sundown, while I was correcting papers, and engage me in conversation about eternity, existence, and the nature of the soul. He made sure to establish my amenity towards a radically different style of living before pressing his suit with any amount of ardor."

"If you liked me so much then, Maude, why did you throw the *McGuffey's* at me?" Pa chaffed, a twinkle in his eye.

Mama ignored him and turned her attention back to George. "That was William. However, bear in mind that you and William and Louisa were raised in different times. You would not be undead two days before you began to resent the knowledge that your wife owned total control over your will."

"I would not!" George objected. But he sounded more loud than sincere.

"I don't criticize you, dear, it's simply a cultural thing, Women's Liberation notwithstanding. And I also fear that our Louisa would not be so benevolent an autocrat as her father. You *do* have the tendency to be a shade too willful, my angel," Mama said, looking right at Louisa.

"You would, too, if you'd been raised by Aunt Jane!" Louisa exclaimed, hot under the collar. "If you never got to make any decisions about your own life, and the few petty choices she did let you make—'What color dress material do you fancy, Louisa?'—always got twisted around back to her way of thinking—'Oh, surely you can't mean *blue,* child! Blue makes you look so wan. Look, here's this lovely green gingham, and such a good price, too!'"

"You'd boss me around like that, Louisa?" George asked, sad-eyed.

"I wouldn't mean to," Louisa replied, gently taking one of his big hands between her two small ones. "But you know how things sometimes happen, even when we don't mean for them to turn out that way."

"But—but you still love me?"

"If I didn't love you, why would I risk the breaking of my heart having you now, knowing I can't have you forever?"

"Love is often thus," Pa opined. "Those who merely seek its pleasures without embracing its pains do not love deeply or truly."

"They're wimps," I agreed, and Mama boxed my ears for using common slang at the dinner table.

Well, we brought George around to where he'd have a piece of ham. "After I went to all the trouble of biting the pig, it's the least you can do, Georgie," Mama reminded him. Then Louisa piped up about how biting the food first so's it gets all imbued with our peculiar nature—*imbued;* now there's a two-dollar word for you!—isn't half the chore that driving in the wooden stake is, after, so's we can actually eat the stuff.

"Pigs and cows and such aren't so bad," she said. "But you're not the one who spent all last night in the kitchen staking down the Brussels sprouts with toothpicks."

"Don't like Brussels sprouts," George said.

"If I turned you into a vampire, I'd be able to make you eat Brussels sprouts," Louisa shot back. "Like them or not." Well, that last argument really got George to see reason and he was happily shoveling in the food while we went back to discussing the next step for solving the crisis.

In the long run, Pa decided that he'd best make a trip down to Boston to ask the opinion of his old friend and mentor, Resolution Green.

(Old Greenie's the king-vampire of Boston, and most of New England excepting Maine. Ain't no vampires in Maine 'cause Greenie don't much like Stephen King books and he'd sooner try for a suntan than give that uppity human any free ideas. Pa's got all kinds of status points among our kind for having been brought into the deadlife by Resolution himself personally.)

Pa got up from the table to change into his flying clothes. "I'll set off at once and be back tomorrow night unless Resolution insists on a visit, Lord help me."

"William, it is our duty to pay our respects to our elders." Mama can get stuffier than a room full of Bull Moosers.

"I can bear with his crotchets, Maude, but if I have to play one more round of Super Mario Brothers with him, I shall scream. You'd think that a man of his age would be able to get past level two by this time! Well, what can't be cured must be endured. Meanwhile, the rest of you must take some stopgap measures in my absence. George, I fear that moving Louisa's coffin would be useless. From what Albert tells us, the Tyler boy is a past master of ferreting out hideaways. Too, there is not a better place for Louisa than her own home."

"I could move back up here with you, Papa," Louisa suggested. "You could give me back my old spot down cellar."

"Not since we got the new washer and drier installed," Mama said. "There's no room. In any case, this child would only direct his attention here, since he has accused us all, and I will not tolerate such a ruffian's presence in my home, thank you."

"Louisa will stay where she is and George will return to his post. He can effectively bar entrance to the cellar."

"What if he tells his folks about Louisa's coffin?" I asked.

"So long as the boy lives, I doubt his parents will take that as other than an hallucination on their son's part. And should they insist, to humor him, George will be within his rights to ask them to leave."

"Leave, yeah." I thought about it. "You don't need to go to Boston, Pa. They're supposed to check out tomorrow, anyhow. Can't we wait 'em out, 'til they go back to New York and take their brat with 'em?"

Pa gave me one of those when-you're-older-you'll-understand looks. I hate those worse than sour apples. With worms. "Persistence is a virtue, Albert. Unfortunately, it is often found in the less than virtuous. Your . . . friend Evan is the only son of affluent though morally irresolute parents who coddle and spoil the boy shamefully. You have only conversed with him once, yet in the course of that exchange he readily—nay, proudly!—admitted to spying, trespassing, disrespect for his elders, sneakery, and the repeated use of illegal intoxicants. What, then, would hold him back from stealing money from his own parents to finance an independent return to Wintersend, the better to further his own twisted desires? Leaving behind, no doubt, a similar telltale letter should we deal with him in any terminal way."

In other words, the little cowpat had us by the short ones.

Mama rose from her place. "William, go ahead with your departure preparations. We shall do what we can while you are away." She gave him a quick peck on the neck, then got back to us. "Louisa, to the telephone, if you please. I think we all know what we must do."

◊◊◊

"No, no, Albert, don't eat that!" Mrs. Peterman squeaked, snatching the plate of chocolate cake out from under my fork. "That's Mary Vincent's, and she never once had your mother up to tea, so not a lick of her pantry supplies have been made over properly for your eating." She slipped a different plate into my hand. "Here, I baked this, so you know it's safe. Lord knows what would happen to you if you ate Mary Vincent's." She flounced back into the church kitchen, still clucking.

I looked down at the cake she'd given me: carrot with cream-cheese frosting. Yuck. Worst that could've happened to me eating Mrs. Vincent's cake would be a bout of the stomach cramps and maybe throwing up after, but it would've been worth it. I don't know but what Mrs. Peterman thought that if I ate the unprocessed chocolate cake, I'd turn into a handful of dust and dry bones right in front of the Ladies' Aid.

(Anyhow, someone ought to tell Mrs. Peterman that it doesn't matter whether we *imbue* the raw materials or the finished product. Nothing at all would happen if I bit the cake itself first before I actually ate it.)

Yeah, the Ladies' Aid: Mama had called out the big guns. Every folding chair in the basement social hall of the First Congregational Church of Wintersend had been deployed on the black linoleum, every Tupperware cake-keeper and pie-toter in town had been mobilized. It didn't take but five phone calls to get this "extraordinary circumstances emergency meeting" together for Monday night. We could've had it going the same Sunday night we called, only Rachel Tolliver, who's the Ladies' Aid president, got the keys to the closet where they keep the ten-gallon coffeemaker, and she was visiting her daughter out on Cape Cod for the weekend.

So, anyway.

"Ladies, ladies, please take your seats." Mrs. Tolliver stood up at the president's card table and banged on it with the cardboard core from a roll of paper towels. (She left the president's official gavel out in Truro; her grandson's teething.) Everybody settled down, gavel or no. Mrs. Tolliver's got a voice louder than a sow with one tit caught in a wringer. "As you are aware, we have been called together to help one of our most valuable and long-standing members in her time of need. Considering all that Maude Harriman and her family have done for our town over the years, asking precious little in return, can we do less than pledge them our full support now?"

A murmur of agreement passed over the assembly, broken only by the sound of Mrs. MacLennan choking on a mouthful of meringue. Mrs. Peterman gave her one solid newfangled-Heimlich-nonsense-be damned thwack on the back and they got back to business.

Louisa raised her hand and stood up when Mrs. Tolliver recognized her. "We've had further bad news, ladies," she announced. "Today the Tylers said they'll be staying an extra week. I'm sure it was Evan's request."

"Why didn't you just tell them you were full up?" Mrs. Kemmer wanted to know. "It's a perfectly logical excuse at the height of the foliage season."

Louisa sighed. "George tried that. Mr. Tyler offered us double the usual room rate, then triple when George still said no."

Triple the going rate. No one had to ask what George had done. If he'd turned down those pickings from a New Yorker, they'd have run him out of Wintersend on a rail.

"My, my," said Mrs. Tolliver. "Someone is spoiled."

"Someone is dangerous," Mama spoke up.

"Maude, dear, if all the child wants is to become a vampire, why don't you just do it and be shut of him?" Mrs. Eastman inquired. "The last time you came by for coffee, didn't you tell me that a vampire has some sort of influence over any new vampires he makes? Something to do with your, uh, spit?"

Mama turned a little huffy. If I'd been the one to mention one of the big taboo body juices right out baldfaced to her like that, I'd've got my mouth washed out for me.

"That is a rather—*common* explanation, Edna, dear. In the sense of simplistic." Bullshit. We all knew she meant plain old *common* as in *vulgar*. Mrs. Eastman blushed. "My husband is of the opinion that there may be some chemical substance manufactured in our, pardon the expression, salivary glands which, upon introduction to other organic tissue, causes a specific mutation. The change so effected makes the new tissue's host totally compatible with our own unique metabolism."

"Which is why she has to come around every so often and spit in my flour and sugar and such," I heard Mrs. Kemmer whisper to Mrs. Vincent. "It's the only way she can eat my baking."

"She—she spits in your staples? No! Well, I'd *never* allow anything like that in my house for all the tea in—!"

"Then you're a fool, Mary Vincent. It's not as if she spits in *all* the flour. Or the tea either, come to think of it. The Harrimans have been the backbone of this town from the beginning. Where's your civic spirit? Oh. I forgot. *Your* people have only been in Wintersend since 1903. *Real* Wintersenders stick together."

Mrs. Eastman wasn't satisfied. "I don't pretend to know a thing about any such scientific rigmarole. You still haven't explained why you don't do whatever *uncommon* thing it is you do to vampirize someone and then use your influence to make him do anything you please!"

"Edna," Mama said a little too sweetly, "tell me how you'd like it if you found out that someone had turned your son into a vampire."

"Well, Maude, if it were *you*—"

"Say it were someone you didn't know so well. Certainly we have no ties with the Tylers apart from that of host and paying guest. What if you took your family down to Disneyworld for a lovely vacation and came back to the Holiday Inn to find that the bell captain had turned your Jeremy into one of the undead because you had undertipped?"

"Why, the nerve! I'd—I'd—" She didn't have to say a word. We could all read murder in her eyes.

"Precisely," Mama said softly. "And so would the Tylers. They would take action against us, unless we were prepared to deal with the entire family in similar fashion. Edna, dear .... do *you* want that many New Yorkers living year-round in Wintersend?"

Well, that put *that* idea out of the running. The ladies discussed and moved and seconded and pondered and then moved and seconded some more. The results weren't all we'd hoped for—mostly cosmetic-type remedies to the Venom question were proposed. (What'd we expect from a town where half the women sold Mary Kay *to* and bought Avon *from* the other half?) The best help we got was several offers for Louisa and the rest of us to move our coffins into our neighbors' cellars "until this whole nasty mess blows over."

"That way," said Mrs. Kemmer, "George can relax, and when that loathsome boy does convince his parents to come down cellar with him and see what he found, they will find nothing. He will be shown up as a liar, a fool, and a fraud."

"And he will go home with his parents and do something coarse and rude and possibly illegal," Mama said grimly.

She stood up in her place, her hands closed tightly around the top of the metal folding chair in front of her.

"Deliberately. And they will mop up his mess, taking him to a psychiatrist instead of to the woodshed he so richly deserves. And the results shall be that the doctor, whose salary *they* pay, shall turn right about and tell them that *they* are to blame for their son's criminal behavior. How so? By refusing to believe the child's supposedly fanciful tales of vampires they have created a breach of parental faith, wounded the hapless lad's self-esteem, and forced him to a life of iniquity as surely as if they tilted his head back and poured laudanum down his throat."

"I hardly think that even New Yorkers would be so foolish as to—" Mrs. Tolliver tried to object.

Mama rode roughshod over her. "Oh yes, that will be the way of it! The boy will pipe the very tune to which he wishes the so-called doctor to dance, in just the way he has manipulated his parents all these years. *Ergo,* unless they wish to be tarred with the dysfunctional family brush—and you know as well as I, ladies, that they would sooner forswear sushi for life—they will have to bring the obnoxious beast back up here, as a gesture of parental support. *Do you think he will allow them to give us any forewarning of their return?* He is as sly as a mink and twice as vicious. He will catch us out with his parents as witness, and that shall be the end of us all."

She sat down. The chair in front of her now had a back that

looked like it was made of lace. The only other time I saw Mama's fingers poke clear through solid metal was the time in 1968 when Louisa announced she was going to move out and join a commune in New Hampshire.

That was when I left the social hall. The ladies were okay—down to the last one, they'd rather have vampires than summer people, ski bums, and leaf peepers in Wintersend any old day—but we couldn't depend on 'em to do more than postpone the inevitable showdown with Venom. And I already knew in my heart of hearts that Pa wouldn't bring back any kind of help from Boston.

No, really, I could tell for sure on account of how the last time he went down there to get old Greenie's sage advice and the wisdom of the ages, he took me along. Resolution Green's got this fine old house on Tory Row in Cambridge. Only good thing about that visit was he didn't waste all our time playing Super Mario Brothers 'cause there wasn't any Super Mario Brothers around yet.

I recollect Pa starting off the conversation by telling old Greenie how Louisa wanted to hare off to New Hampshire and paint herself blue, and change her name to Peace Freedom Rainbow. "I suppose it's understandable," he said. "The girl is between husbands, running the inn on her own, and the young man in question is fairly good-looking."

"Him?" I made a face. "Maybe he is and maybe he isn't, but his beard fits him about as well as a bearskin on a woodchuck."

"Have you seen my decals?" old Greenie whined. The king-vampire of all New England (at the time including Maine) was down on his hands and knees under a Hepplewhite table, searching the Turkey rug. "If I can't find the decals, I can't customize the model, and no one will be able to tell that it's the real Starship Enterprise!"

We helped old Greenie find his decals and stick them on. It was like watching a spider at work—a skinny, bald, skim-milk skinned spider. While Pa went on about our troubles with Louisa, that moss-a-back old bloodsucker kept interrupting him with stuff like:

"Do you think Shatner's hair is real?"

or: "If Mr. Spock, who is half Vulcan and half human, were to mate with another hybrid of similar background, would Mendelian genetics let them have a fully human child?"

and: "I received a charming autographed photo of Mr. DeForrest Kelley today, in response to my letter. However, I have reason to believe that the signature was done by machine. I am considering flying out to the Coast and tearing the throats out of those parties responsible for so grave a betrayal of trust towards that gentleman's loyal fans."

Finally Pa got him to pay some mind, but the only solution he could field was, "Tear out the boy's throat and be done with it, William! Must I teach you everything?" Last I heard out of him as we were leaving was this funny little mutter: "Green blood . . . I wonder how it would taste? Ummmmm."

So I pretty much doubted Pa would be coming home with any brainstorms, courtesy of Resolution Green. (Oh, that hippie guy Louisa was gonna run off with? George found out about it and gave him a friendly thump in the head. Instead of fighting back, or even reciting some Joan Baez lyrics at him, the boy took off quicker than hell beating tan bark. Louisa saw, got fed up with the rabbity twerp, married George, and that was that.)

I walked back home from the church. It was a pretty night, balmy for late autumn. All Wintersend was tucked in under a black velvet blanket sewn bright with stars. As I strolled past the inn, I looked up and saw a light burning, in one of the rooms Louisa and George had rented to Evan's folks. Was it his? That'd be just like him, staying up late, planning more mischief against me and mine.

When I was a boy—really a boy, a boy who wouldn't stay a boy forever—most nights I used to look out through the dirt-smeared windows of the orphan asylum and wish I could be free to walk around under a sky so fine. I remember the first harvest they sent a bunch of us bigger boys out to labor on local farms, for a fee we never got to see. I was worked hard, but I didn't mind so much, because after the sun went down, no one much cared where I wandered, and my kingdom of dreams had no limits but what my eyes could see.

And I remember seeing them for the first time one night, that family strolling through the moon-washed fields at midnight.

Her, tall and straight as righteousness, and her pretty daughter, dancing with the starlight, light as song, and him, watching over the both of 'em, his face so warm with joy and tenderness, looking like the love of God they always preached at us up the asylum but never made into more than words.

But most of all, I remember my tears, welling up out of a hungering spirit, and how I longed with all my heart to hold what they all held among them, at any price. I crouched there at the edge of the meadow and wept until the tall shadow fell over me in the moonlight, and his embered eyes read my soul, and his gentle voice called me, "Son . . ."

Maybe when I became a vampire I traded the day for the night, but I also traded loneliness for kin, indifference for caring, sadness for love. And no little shit-tail like Evan "Venom" Tyler was about to take that away from me.

I went home, but not into the empty house. I still don't like to feel alone. I went out to the barn. I do most of my best thinking with the smell of cows around me. I was sitting on a bale of hay, rolling over some half-baked notions in my head, when my thoughts got interrupted by this loud, sorrowful bellowing from the third stall down.

Well, I could've kicked myself. All this fuss Venom stirred up and I'd got so fuddled I couldn't't've found my way out of a wet paper bag. It was Elvira, and this time not only had I forgotten her sundown milking, but I'd left her in her stall when I drove the rest of the herd out to pasture. Now the poor cow was hurting and hungry, and I felt almost bright enough to be an idiot.

Excepting that idiots don't generally have brilliant ideas come over them when they're standing up to their ankles in cowpats.

It wasn't easy to manage; nothing really worthwhile ever is, Mama'd say. Most cows are stupid, but Elvira's dumber than a doorknob. Once I milked her, she didn't want to know nothing except which way to breakfast, but I soon got her to understand that tonight she'd better pay some mind to me first if she ever wanted to eat again. See, I can do just about anything I want with that cow, seeing as how I'm the one who raised her from a calf and won a 4-H ribbon for her and drank her blood. She's *got* to mind me, because I brought her into the family. It just takes a while for her to catch on that I want something more out of her than a tall glass of milk.

The window was open. No wonder, the night so warm and all. It wouldn't matter even did he have it locked. We could've broke it in easy. Everything's relative, Pa says, and relatively speaking, do you *know* how big a bat you get when you start off with a full-grown Guernsey cow?

Venom never knew what hit him. One minute he's lying sprawled out on his bed, sound asleep; the next I'm shaking his arm and saying, "Wake up, asshole, you asked for this," and then he's looking up into two of the biggest, softest, sweetest, reddest eyes in Wintersend just before Elvira moos once and sinks her teeth into his neck.

◊◊◊

The Tylers came to Sunday dinner. They didn't look too happy, but Evan soon set them straight. He pointed out that even if he was dead, he had what he wanted—eternal life, eternal youth—and that if they blew any whistles on my family, they'd be pounding a stake through his heart as well.

"If anyone *believes* you," he sneered. "I mean vampires in Vermont? Here's a dollar, buy a clue! There's not a whole lotta *nouvelle cuisine* in Bellevue."

Mama reached over and whapped him in the back of the head with the soup ladle. *"Evan,"* she said in that skincrawly *meaningful* way she's got. Evan apologized to his folks fast. That was the first time they smiled.

"Fresh air," said Mr. Tyler, having some of Mama's creamy mashed potatoes. "He will get lots of fresh air up here."

"And he'll be kept far away from the wrong element," Mrs. Tyler agreed, spooning up peas. (They're almost as tough to prepare as Brussels sprouts, but at least you can stick the toothpicks through the full pods, not the individual peas.) "It's so difficult to raise a child in the city."

"We can tell people that he's pursuing his studies at an exclusive Vermont academy." Mr. Tyler seemed relieved to have come up with that one.

"For the gifted," Mrs. Tyler added. "The Harriman Academy," she pronounced us. Then she took more turkey.

"Madam, you do us an honor. Feel free to visit him whenever you like," Pa said graciously. "Our home is yours. Or your boy can fly down to the city now and then. Just make sure to take a shoeboxful of our native earth with you when you depart tomorrow and sprinkle it on his bed before his arrival. Little things mean a lot."

Evan's sister, Lindsay, leaned up to him and whispered, "When you come for a visit, I'm gonna wait until it's daytime and you're asleep and I'm gonna open the blinds on you," but Mrs. Tyler announced that two could learn to use a soup ladle as easily as one and she got the message.

Our mamas were trading promises to get together for a big, gut-busting Christmas dinner when the call came. Evan's eyes went blank. He pushed away from his place and stood up. "Coming," he said in a voice about as hollow as a blown eggshell, and he walked out of the dining room without another word, even when his mother called his name.

"Elvira wants to be milked," Mama explained, all apologetic. "I'm afraid that what Elvira wants from Evan now Elvira gets. It's simply the way things are. Once she's milked and pastured, she generally leaves him alone. More squash-and-apple casserole?"

"Oh, dear," Mrs. Tyler sighed. "There's one part of this whole business I don't think I'll ever get used to."

"Now, *cara,* don't let it trouble you," her husband said. "You'll have the Harrimans all upset, and it isn't as if any of what's happened to Evan is their fault." He had more squash-and-apple casserole.

"I know, I know." Mrs. Tyler shook her head. "You can't blame *people* for any mischief their animals get into. That's what I tried to make Mrs. Gaspard understand the time Evan's pet boa got into her apartment and ate her Lhasa Apso, but *she* wouldn't listen. Still—" she turned her eyes after her departed son—"still, it's so difficult to accept the fact that our Evan must be ruled for all eternity by—by—a *cow!*"

"You should talk to *Mr.* Gaspard about how that feels." Her husband chuckled.

So while Pa was telling her how up here in Wintersend there's plenty of folks put their livestock before their families (and plenty more where you can hardly tell the family from the livestock), I got to thinking how we've got us a good life, being undead, but it ain't by any means a perfect one.

Why, I still recall the first time I went joyriding with the gang down to the all-night Dunkin' Donuts in Brattleboro, and I accidentally-on-purpose forgot to stick a toothpick in my donut before I ate it on account of I didn't want to look like a big dweeb in front of my friends, and I couldn't finish it and accidentally-*not*-on-purpose just up and left this half-eaten donut on my plate, and pretty soon we started hearing these reports about how all these Brattleboro policemen were being found dead in their squad cars with two little punctures in their necks and chocolate crumbs all over their uniforms, and when Mama found out I really caught—

But that's another story.

Esther Friesner is the editor of the anthology *Blood Muse*, of vampire stories about the arts, and is the author of numerous fantasy novels, including *Blood of Mary*, *Psalms of Herod*, *The Sherwood Game*, *Druid's Blood*, and *Sphynxes Wild*, among others.

Everyone has wanted at one time or another to "fit in"—to be part of a special group. This fellow is about to be inducted into an organization beyond his wildest dreams.

Secret Societies

BY LAWRENCE SCHIMEL

hile people may not be sure of what, exactly, goes on at meetings, it is rather widely known that there are secret societies at Yale University, cabals that choose the elite of each senior class to join their ranks. Imaginations tend to run rampant, as non-initiates speculate and ponder the activities that go on inside the imposing buildings that house each group, their "tomb" as the largely windowless constructs are commonly called. Usually these fantasies tend toward bacchanalian orgies, for the minds of the excluded often turn toward scandal and debauchery—and sex is never far from the minds of most underclassmen, caught in the first exuberant flush of their libidos, distracting them from pursuit of their studies. Others enviously imagine power meetings with famous and influential alumni, who show favoritism toward and shower opportunities on their clan brethren.

The activities of these secret societies may be a mystery to the world at large, and even to most of campus, but it's not all that secret who's in them, or which ones they're in. It's commonly known, for instance, that our president was in Skull & Bones.

The University keeps an eye on—and occasionally a hand in—their activities, as well, as evidenced by that recent brouhaha when the last of the secret societies, Wolfshead, was forced to go co-ed.

How secret can a society be, when its membership and existence, if not its activities, are so much in the public view?

In my senior year, however, I joined a group that was truly a covert brotherhood, whose existence was unknown to all save its members; its existence was not even a matter for speculation, neither for the University nor its students, alumni, and professors. I joined a secret society that was older than all the rest of them.

A fact about Yale that I've always enjoyed: Yale pays its taxes voluntarily. The university is exempt from paying taxes, because it existed prior to the state of Connecticut, let alone the founding of the United States of America; the state charter therefore acknowledges Yale's prior claim by exempting the University from taxes. I always love contemplating that fact, and how it puts history into such perspective. How recent so much of what we take for granted truly is.

Yale is kind of funny, in that outdated way. Whereas most schools have a healthy Greek Life, with frat houses and sororities, Yale's social structures are a little different. Sure, there are fraternities and sororities on (well, technically off) campus, but they play a minor role in campus life. Of much more importance are the singing groups.

There were thirteen a cappella singing groups when I was on campus—an ominous number?—from the world-famous, all-male Whiffenpoofs, comprised only of seniors, down the hierarchy of single-sex and mixed-gender groups whose popularity (and quality) varied from year to year as older members graduated and new voices were added.

Singing groups gave regular concerts, both official ones in theaters and impromptu ones in courtyards and hallways, as well as hosting lots of parties. They were quite competitive to get into, and the first few months of freshmen year everyone was nervous as frosh (and some sophomores) practiced their scales and auditioned. Even if you were like me and were embarrassed even to sing in the showers lest someone overhear you, this was a time of excitement, because someone you knew was auditioning and all jittery. And it was important to know people in the "right" groups, so you hoped your friends got tapped, and by the groups that were most popular.

All three of my frosh roomates auditioned for groups, but only one of them, Eric, got tapped, by an all-male group called the Baker's Dozen. He went on to become their Business Manager, and in his senior year was tapped for the Whiffenpoofs as "pitch" for the group. He dropped out of school for that year he was in the Whiffs, since it was pretty much a full-time job coordinating and organizing their repertoire, scheduling rehearsals, and so on.

Eric and I had never been close, but there's a bond that comes from being roommates during that most intense freshman year, even if you can't stand each other. And because I knew Eric, I gained entree to some of "the" parties to be at, or learned dish about other groups that got me lots of points and favors with other people.

We got along fine as roommates, we just had nothing in common. But I was so excited to see Eric on *national television,* leading the Whiffs when they sang the National Anthem at the Superbowl! I felt that thrill of a brush with celebrity; I not only knew someone famous, I had lived with him for almost nine months! Even though we'd lost track of each other, or rather, didn't bother to keep up with each other, I still felt that incredible connection to him.

But that excitement paled in comparison to the thrill that was to run through my veins later my senior year. For I was tapped for a group—and I mean that literally. I'll explain in a moment.

One thing I just want to get out of the way is to say that I got into Yale on my own merit. I was not a legacy, who was admitted simply because generations of men in my family had gone to Yale before me and our family gave lots of money to the school's endowment fund. My parents had never even gone to college, and though we were well off enough that I didn't need a scholarship—though my grades and test scores were certainly high enough to merit one. The truth is, I *liked* to study, and that's what got me admitted.

Yes, I am a bit contemptuous of the legacies, who were able to ride their families' coattails into school no matter how dense they were, and who lived their lives with a sense of privilege that infuriated me. I was also very jealous at how easy they had it, and would've probably been able to live with myself had I been in their shoes.

I was sure that one reason I was not tapped for one of the secret societies my senior year was because I wasn't old Yale. I couldn't fill any multicultural quotas, and as far as white males went, I couldn't bring anything special to the group—at least, not in terms of family names or money. So I was especially resentful of legacies for much of my senior year.

I was not above learning, and following, some of the traditions of Yale, like drinking from the enormous chalices down at Mory's until my companions stopped chanting songs of old Yale or I had drained the vat, whichever came soonest. There's a certain power, when tradition becomes almost ritual, that intoxicates almost more than the alcohol we drank those nights; we shared an energy, a history, and it invigorated us all.

And eventually I was able to put aside my envy of those whose parents had gone to Yale before them, when I was given a blood legacy to Yale that was stronger than the ones they had. Like the fact about Yale being grandfathered into the Constitution exempting the University from paying taxes, this put so much into perspective.

I'm procrastinating, aren't I, in getting to the heart of the matter; I feel exactly as I did when I was trying to write my senior essay, and couldn't bring myself to actually begin. I wrote voluminous notes and researched like crazy, but to actually begin, to truly tackle my subject head on, terrified me.

It was as I was procrastinating on my thesis that the momentous event took place. It was early February, and New Haven was a bleak landscape of slushy streets and ice-encased trees. Spring Break seemed an eternity away, and the deadline for my thesis far too soon—I wanted years to be able to research my subject better. I loved the hunt of research, tracking down obscure books mentioned in footnotes, that joy of discovery when I unearthed them on a forgotten shelf of one of the many floors of the Sterling Memorial Library. I lived at the library in those days, hiding from my life—and in some ways, my studies—by roaming the stacks and reading whatever books caught my fancy. I loved to wander among all those old books, to pull down volumes at random and see what fascinating truths (or mistaken ideas) they held. Sterling had eight floors accessible by elevator, but in between each floor was a mezzanine level, to cram even more books into the building. The sheer available knowledge overwhelmed me sometimes, and I'd sit in an aisle and gaze rapturously at all those books.

Wandering the stacks one night in that bleak midwinter, I saw something flutter out of the corner of my eye. I had heard friends of mine talk of pigeons or bats that came in through the windows left open in warmer months, but so far as I knew the building was sealed tight against the icy winds of February. Still, I welcomed the distraction from my pursuit of knowledge, let alone my degree, and I followed the faint sussuration of sound.

I trailed this noise down aisle after aisle, yet it always seemed to elude me, keeping one step ahead. I was dying of curiosity at this point, and determined to arrive at some knowledge of what was making these sounds, so I could set my mind at rest and have some closure. I didn't pay attention to the books I passed, keeping my attention focused entirely on catching up to it, as we raced through aisle after aisle. Eventually, the aisle I was on dead-ended—or so I thought. At the end of the aisle was a door, which stood ajar. I listened for the sussurations I had been trailing, and heard nothing. The bird, or mouse, or whatever it had been, must have gone through the door, I reasoned—there was no place else for it to have disappeared to.

I must confess that I grew curious, as I paused to catch my breath after the chase, as I had never been in this part of the library before, and that surprised me. While I made no pretense to having read more than a fraction of the 16 million volumes the library contained, I had thought that I'd at least visited every section of the library at some point during my three plus years.

I pushed the door open, and walked through into the dimly lit room beyond.

Inside was a small study carrel, like the rows of tiny cubicles that flanked the walls of the Cross Campus Library, where students could study without the distraction of the library's other patrons. For CCL was actually one of the most convenient meeting places on campus, so it was always a terrible social scene. Terrible if you were there to study, that is.

Someone sat at the small desk, his back to me. He appeared to be reading something before him, despite the awful light level in the room.

"Sorry to disturb you," I said, as soon as I realized someone was in there. "I thought I saw a bird fly in here. I was going to try and catch it, I guess—before it left droppings all over my favorite books."

He turned toward me, and smiled as he saw me, or in reaction to my joke, I wasn't quite sure.

"It was a bat," he corrected, and stared at me with that weird smile. His skin was pale, and I couldn't help thinking that he was one of those students who spent too much time indoors studying, to the neglect of all else. Not a well-rounded personality, which was sort of weird, since the stereotypic Yale profile was that of the overachiever—you know, the kind of student who not only maintained a 4.0 average but who also was coach of the volleyball team and had founded a soup kitchen and wrote a column for one of the campus magazines.

"Shouldn't a bat be hibernating?" I asked.

"It was . . . awakened," the guy answered cryptically.

I wondered why the hell he knew the sleeping habits of this flying mammal so intimately. I was beginning to get an eerie feeling, and decided I didn't want to be in this isolated corner of the library anymore. It was no wonder I hadn't ever come here before, I reflected—this guy probably never left this room, and the strange vibes he gave off must've kept me away.

"Whatever," I said. "Catch you later."

Before I could turn to leave, he gestured, and the door closed behind me, as if by magic.

I spun around in surprise.

But there was nothing magical involved—two men stood behind me, and they had come into the small room before closing the door. This did not make me feel any less nervous, of course.

"We have been studying you," the guy at the desk continued.

Why me? I wondered, turning back toward him. I had a feeling I was about to get an offer I couldn't refuse. I wondered if I could escape, despite there being three of them; they all looked weak, since none of them was especially muscular, and all of them had ridiculously pale complexions, despite their blond hair. That delicate Anglo heritage, inbred a few generations too many.

Nerves made me quip sarcastically, even when I knew I should keep my mouth shut. "I hadn't realized the University had created a new major to study me. I guess you want me to be your advisor, right?"

"You are not so far from the truth in your jest. We need new knowledge, young knowledge, knowledge of this strange world we have woken in. We need experience that one can't get from a book."

Cue *Twilight Zone* theme song, I mentally instructed the soundtrack for my life.

"I don't know if I'm up for whatever kind of experience it is you're looking for," I began. I wondered what drugs they were on, but I'd decided I didn't want to try them—or to take part in whatever they had in mind.

"Look, I'm sorry to break up this little party, but I've got an exam tomorrow and if I don't get back to studying, bye-bye graduating with honors." I moved toward the door.

"You will be one of us," the guy in front of the door said, blocking my exit.

They were, I realized suddenly, beginning to sound exactly like a cult.

"We're already all sons of Yale," I said, still trying to make my way past him to the door. He stood his ground.

"Come," the guy at the desk said.

I turned back toward him. He was holding a knife.

"Is that really necessary?" I said, while my mind raced furiously but didn't get anywhere; it was as trapped in its thinking, running over the same few thoughts—what can I do? how can I get out of here?—as I was trapped in this room.

"We have chosen," he said.

I remembered all those years of grade school gym class, my desperate longing to be picked for the right team. This was one of those few times when I wished I'd been overlooked.

"Can't we discuss this?" I pleaded. "What the hell have I been chosen for?"

"Each century, we choose another to join us. We will drink your blood, and you shall drink ours. Then we will sleep, and we will think your thoughts, share your experiences, as you will share ours."

I visualized all sorts of headlines that would appear about my death in the *Yale Daily News*. No, this was weird enough to make the *New York Times*—at least, I hoped my getting killed for this bizarre vampire cult made the *Times*.

Once again I wondered, why me?

As if he read my thoughts, he answered my rhetorical question. "You have been chosen because, like us, you thirst for knowledge."

"It sounds like you're trying to slake a different thirst. Can't we do this without drinking blood. I'm not crazy about the stuff, and I really don't have enough to spare, so . . ."

I felt I was talking to myself, so I shut up. I stared at them, one after another. The guy at the desk was still holding the knife. It looked silver.

"Is that knife silver?" I asked.

"Yes."

"Doesn't that bother you?" I said, trying to keep him talking. If he was talking, he wasn't sticking that thing into me. "You being a vampire and all."

"Silver does not bother me," he said.

"I guess those stories are all lies, then," I complained. Maybe I could talk them out of thinking they were vampires, and thereby save my skin. I tried to remember all the psychology classes I'd taken, all the tricks of logic. "About silver being harmful to vampires," I continued, "and garlic and crosses. And turning into bats. All lies."

"Ah, you do not believe," he said. He laid the knife down on the desk again, and I let out a breath I hadn't realized I was holding. I was amazed I could have so much breath to expel when I'd been rattling on so much, but fear does amazing things to the body, once the adrenaline kicks in.

My worldview dropped away suddenly, and I was catching my breath in surprise half a moment later when a bat flapped in the space where he'd been sitting a moment before.

Suddenly I realized they were completely serious. About everything. This was not a drug-crazed cult, but the real thing.

Part of my brain was fascinated. My first brush with the supernatural, and while half of me was trying to figure out how to stay alive, the other part was furiously taking notes. Maybe I'd change majors, and do an anthropological study of vampires, I mused—if I ever got out of here alive.

The bat disappeared and the guy was sitting at the desk again. He picked up the silver knife.

"Why don't you have fangs?" I asked.

He smiled. "The fangs are part of the lies." His teeth looked normal.

I didn't exactly have a choice. I could follow along, and maybe they'd make me a vampire and not just kill me outright. Or I could resist, and maybe they'd just kill me. I wondered if that weren't the better choice to make—otherwise I'd have to drink blood. I thought of all the things I'd ever heard about vampires and wondered which of them were true and which weren't. These guys didn't seem like creatures of evil—although I wasn't sure I liked their insistence that I had to become one of them. I wanted free will!

I could scream, but it wouldn't do any good, I was sure. If I'd never been to this part of the library, I was sure no one else frequented it, either.

"Can I sit down?" I asked. "This is all kind of sudden for me. You've been studying me, but I've had maybe fifteen minutes to think this through, and most of those have been with you pointing a knife at me. I don't think well when someone's pointing a knife at me. This is a big decision I'm making, and I want to give it some thought before I make it."

I was impressed with my own bravado, as he stood and offered me his seat at the desk. I sat, and noticed a chalice, like the ones down at Mory's.

"You don't expect me to fill that, do you?"

He nodded.

"No way. It's enormous! I'd die."

"You will be reborn through our blood. That is the gift we give in exchange for your experience and knowledge. You will have centuries in which to think, and each century we will wake and choose one who thirsts for knowledge, like us, to join our ranks."

Despite myself—I wanted to rebel entirely at the very thought of his existence—parts of his spiel sounded appealing. Could the sharing of blood also be a sharing of experience? I'd walk around in their veins, as it were, rather than their shoes. What could be more fascinating than that?

I hated the fact that I had no choice in the matter, but I was damned curious about what they were offering anyway.

What could I lose from trying it, when I didn't have a choice anyway? And there was so much I could gain.

I took a deep breath. I would say yes. I opened my mouth.

No voice came out.

I exhaled again, thinking and rethinking. I opened my mouth again and said, "Yes."

He smiled again, that goofy smile of his, and lifted the silver knife.

My stomach flipped over again in fear. "Must you keep waving that thing around?" I said, but I knew that he did.

He didn't bother to answer.

I held my arm above the chalice, baring my wrist for him. I felt like I was about to have blood drawn at the doctor's. "Don't expect me to watch," I said, as the blade hovered above my flesh. I turned away. Cold metal touched and then bit my skin.

My wrist exploded warmth. I felt my head go light. It was nerves, of course, I'd hardly begun to lose blood to make me dizzy like this.

My arm bled. The chalice filled. I realized the two other men were humming. No, they were singing, though I couldn't quite make out the words. But I recognized the tune—the Whiffenpoofs song. They weren't the words I knew, although I couldn't help singing along in my mind. But only one phrase from the song kept running through my brain, "Damned from here to eternity / God have mercy on such as we."

The words certainly fit this situation.

I glanced over at my arm. That was when I fainted. I've never had a strong stomach for the sight of blood, especially not my own.

When I came to, I was still sitting in the chair. I hoped my memories were all a bad dream, that I'd fallen asleep while study-ing. But I opened my arms and took in the small room around me. Three young men stood, passing a chalice between them.

My life flashed before their eyes, as it drained from my body.

I closed my eyes again. I felt hot, like the room was too stuffy. I felt like I was buried under too many comforters, but I didn't have the energy to push them off of me.

I was roused awake. The chalice was in my hands. I opened my eyes and looked down. It was full of blood.

No way, I thought. I was grateful I didn't have the energy to lift the cup to my lips.

But then I heard the singing, though I still couldn't make out the words. And my arms, of their own accord, lifted the heavy sil-ver cup.

There is something about tradition which almost becomes rit-ual. I tasted of the blood, and shared experience flooded through me. Three centuries of life, of knowledge, hit me all at once. My mind felt like it would short circuit trying to process all this infor-mation. I wanted to choke (especially when I realized I was drink-ing blood) anything to stop this flow of input and experience. I began to lose consciousness again, trying to assimilate every-thing.

I let go.

I stopped fighting it. I stopped trying to understand. I listened to the song and let ritual command me. I drank until the cup was drained and the singing stopped.

I was numinous.

I was multiple.

I was Life itself, pure energy, pure knowledge.

I could spend eternity trying to decipher what I was feeling just then. And that was what I was about to do, I knew, with the col-lective knowledge of my new blood brothers.

I did not know them, I *was* them—their totality of experience and knowledge. We had no separate identities any longer; we were only the one.

We had left the library, though I hadn't been cognizant of mov-ing, caught up in the rush of experience and memory. Snow swirled around us, wind blew through my hair; I was not cold.

We moved through the night—I do not know if we walked or flew, that distinction no longer mattered. My mind was absorbed with the totality of Life.

We arrived at the tomb where we would sleep for a century, lost in our thought, sifting and assimilating and contemplating.

I lay down beside my brothers in knowledge.

My last thought before I settled into the coffin they had prepared for me, was that I would, at last, have years now to think about my thesis—and so much more.

Lawrence Schimel is the editor of The American Vampire Series, in addition to more than a dozen other anthologies, including *Tarot Fantastic* and *The Fortune Teller.* His stories and poems have appeared in over one hundred anthologies, ranging from *The Time of the Vampires* to *The Random House Treasury of Light Verse,* and in numerous periodicals.

There are many types of parasites in this world. . . .

Luella Miller

BY MARY E. WILKINS-FREEMAN

lose to the village street stood the one-story house in which Luella Miller, who had an evil name in the village, had dwelt. She had been dead for years, yet there were those in the village who, in spite of the clearer light which comes on a vantage-point from a long-past danger, half believed in the tale which they had heard from their childhood. In their hearts, although they scarcely would have owned it, was a survival of the wild horror and frenzied fear of their ancestors who had dwelt in the same age with Luella Miller. Young people even would stare with a shudder at the old house as they passed, and children never played around it as was their wont around an untenanted building. Not a window in the old Miller house was broken: the panes reflected the morning sunlight in patches of emerald and blue, and the latch of the sagging front door was never lifted, although no bolt secured it. Since Luella Miller had been carried out, the house had had no tenant except one friendless old soul who had no choice between that and the far-off shelter of the open sky. This old woman, who had survived her kindred and friends, lived in the house one week, then one morning no smoke came out of the chimney, and a body of neighbors, a score strong, entered and found her dead in her bed.

There were dark whispers as to the cause of her death, and there were those who testified to an expression of fear so exalted that it showed forth the state of the departing soul upon the dead face. The old woman had been hale and hearty when she entered the house, and in seven days she was dead; it seemed that she had fallen a victim to some uncanny power. The minister talked in the pulpit with covert severity against the sin of superstition; still the belief prevailed. Not a soul in the village but would have chosen the almshouse rather than that dwelling. No vagrant, if he heard the tale, would seek shelter beneath that old roof, unhallowed by nearly half a century of superstitious fear.

There was only one person in the village who had actually known Luella Miller. That person was a woman well over eighty, but a marvel of vitality and unextinct youth. Straight as an arrow, with the spring of one recently let loose from the bow of life, she moved about the streets, and she always went to church rain or shine. She had never married, and had lived alone for years in a house across the road from Luella Miller's.

This woman had none of the garrulousness of age, but never in all her life had she ever held her tongue for any will save her own, and she never spared the truth when she essayed to present it. She it was who bore testimony to the life, evil, though possibly wittingly or designedly so, of Luella Miller, and to her personal appearance. When this old woman spoke—and she had the gift of description, although her thoughts were clothed in the rude vernacular of her native village—one could seem to see Luella Miller as she had really looked. According to this woman, Lydia Anderson by name, Luella Miller had been a beauty of a type rather unusual in New England. She had been a slight, pliant sort of creature, as ready with a strong yielding to fate and as unbreakable as a willow. She had glimmering lengths of straight, fair hair, which she wore softly looped around a long, lovely face. She had blue eyes full of soft pleading, little slender, clinging hands, and a wonderful grace of motion and attitude.

"Luella Miller used to sit in a way nobody else could if they sat up and studied a week of Sundays," said Lydia Anderson, "and it was a sight to see her walk. If one of them willows over there on the edge of the brook could start up and get its roots free of the

B L O O D   L I N E S

ground, and move off, it would go just the way Luella Miller used to. She had a green shot silk she used to wear, too, and a hat with green ribbon streamers, and a lace veil blowing across her face and out sideways, and a green ribbon flyin' from her waist. That was what she came out bride in when she married Erastus Miller. Her name before she was married was Hill. There was always a sight of 'l's' in her name, married or single. Erastus Miller was good lookin', too, better lookin' than Luella. Sometimes I used to think that Luella wa'n't so handsome after all. Erastus just about worshiped her. I used to know him pretty well. He lived next door to me, and we went to school together. Folks used to say he was waitin' on me, but he wa'n't. I never thought he was except once or twice when he said things that some girls might have suspected meant somethin'. That was before Luella came here to teach the district school. It was funny how she came to get it, for folks said she hadn't any education, and that one of the big girls, Lottie Henderson, used to do all the teachin' for her, while she sat back and did embroidery work on a cambric pocket-handkerchief. Lottie Henderson was a real smart girl, a splendid scholar, and she just set her eyes by Luella, as all the girls did. Lottie would have made a real smart woman, but she died when Luella had been here about a year—just faded away and died: nobody knew what ailed her. She dragged herself to that schoolhouse and helped Luella teach till the very last minute. The committee all knew how Luella didn't do much of the work herself, but they winked at it. It wa'n't long after Lottie died that Erastus married her. I always thought he hurried it up because she wa'n't fit to teach. One of the big boys used to help her after Lottie died, but he hadn't much government, and the school didn't do very well, and Luella might have had to give it up, for the committee couldn't have shut their eyes to things much longer. The boy that helped her was a real honest, innocent sort of fellow, and he was a good scholar, too. Folks said he overstudied, and that was the reason he was took crazy the year after Luella married, but I don't know. And I don't know what made Erastus Miller go into consumption of the blood the year after he was married: consumption wa'n't in his family. He just grew weaker and weaker, and went almost bent double when he tried to wait on Luella, and he spoke feeble, like an old man. He worked terrible hard till the last trying to save up a little to leave Luella. I've seen him out in the worst storms on a wood-sled—he used to cut and sell wood—and he was hunched up on top lookin' more dead than alive. Once I couldn't stand it: I went over and helped him pitch some wood on the cart—I was always strong in my arms. I wouldn't stop for all he told me to, and I guess he was glad enough for the help. That was only a week before he died. He fell on the kitchen floor while he was gettin' breakfast. He always got the breakfast and let Luella lay abed. He did all the sweepin' and the washin' and the ironin' and most of the cookin'. He couldn't bear to have Luella lift her finger, and she let him do for her. She lived like a queen for all the work she did. She didn't even do her sewin'. She said it made her shoulder ache to sew, and poor Erastus' sister Lily used to do all her sewin'. She wa'n't able to, either; she was never strong in her back, but she did it beautifully. She had to, to suit Luella, she was so dreadful particular. I never saw anythin' like the fagottin' and hemstitchin' that Lily Miller did for Luella. She made all Luella's weddin' outfit, and that green silk dress, after Maria Babbit cut it. Maria she cut it for nothin', and she did a lot more cuttin' and fittin' for nothin' for Luella, too. Lily Miller went to live with Luella after Erastus died. She gave up her home, though she was real attached to it and wa'n't a mite afraid to stay alone. She rented it and she went to live with Luella right away after the funeral."

Then this old woman, Lydia Anderson, who remembered Luella Miller, would go on to relate the story of Lily Miller. It seemed that on the removal of Lily Miller to the house of her dead brother, to live with his widow, the village people first began to talk. This Lily Miller had been hardly past her first youth, and a most robust and blooming woman, rosy cheeked, with curls of strong, black hair overshadowing round, candid temples and bright dark eyes. It was not six months after she had taken up her residence with her sister-in-law that her rosy color faded and her pretty curves became wan hollows. White shadows began to show in the black rings of her hair, and the light died out of her eyes, her features sharpened, and there were pathetic lines at her mouth, which yet wore always an expression of utter sweetness and even happiness. She was devoted to her sister; there was no doubt that she loved her with her whole heart, and was perfectly content in her service. It was her sole anxiety lest she should die and leave her alone.

"The way Lily Miller used to talk about Luella was enough to make you mad and enough to make you cry," said Lydia Anderson. "I've been in there sometimes toward the last when she was too feeble to cook and carried her some blanc-mange or custard—somethin' I thought she might relish, and she'd thank me, and when I asked her how she was, say she felt better than she did yesterday, and asked me if I didn't think she looked better, dreadful pitiful, and say poor Luella had an awful time takin' care of her and doin' the work—she wa'n't strong enough to do anythin'—when all the time Luella wa'n't liftin' her finger and poor Lily didn't get any care except what the neighbors gave her, and Luella eat up everythin' that was carried in for Lily. I had it real straight that she did. Luella used to just sit and cry and do nothin'. She did act real fond of Lily, and she pined away considerable, too. There was those that thought she'd go into a decline herself. But after Lily died, her Aunt Abby Mixter came, and then Luella picked up and grew as fat and rosy as ever. But poor Aunt Abby begun to droop just the way Lily had, and I guess somebody wrote to her married daughter, Mrs. Sam Abbot, who lived in Barre, for she wrote her mother that she must leave right away and come and make her a visit, but Aunt Abby wouldn't go. I can see her now. She was a real good lookin' woman, tall and large, with a big, square face and a high forehead that looked of itself kind of benevolent and good. She just tended out on Luella as if she had been a baby, and when her married daughter sent for her she wouldn't stir one inch. She'd always thought a lot of her daughter, too, but she said Luella needed her and her married daughter didn't. Her daughter kept writin' and writin', but it didn't do any good. Finally she came, and when she saw how bad her mother looked, she broke down and cried and all but went on her knees to have her come away. She spoke her mind out to Luella, too. She told her that she'd killed her husband and everybody that had anythin' to do with her, and she'd thank her to leave her mother alone. Luella went into hysterics, and Aunt Abby was so frightened that she called me after her daughter went. Mrs. Sam Abbot she went away fairly cryin' out loud in the buggy, the neighbors heard her, and well she might, for she never saw her mother again alive. I went in that night when Aunt Abby called for me standin' in the door with her little green-checked shawl over her head. I can see her now. 'Do come over here, Miss Anderson,' she sung out, kind of gasping for breath. I didn't stop for anythin'. I put over as fast as I could, and when I got there, there was Luella laughin' and cryin' all together, and Aunt Abby trying to hush her, and all the time she herself was white as a sheet and shakin' so she could hardly stand. "For the land sakes, Mrs. Mixter,' says I, 'you look worse than she does. You ain't fit to be up out of your bed.'

"'Oh, there ain't anythin' the matter with me,' says she. Then she went on talkin' to Luella. 'There, there, don't, don't, poor little lamb,' says she. 'Aunt Abby is here. She ain't goin' away and leave you. Don't, poor little lamb.'

"'Do leave her with me, Mrs. Mixter, and you get back to bed,' says I, for Aunt Abby had been layin' down considerable lately, though somehow she contrived to do the work.

"'I'm well enough,' says she. 'Don't you think she had better have the doctor, Miss Anderson?'

"'The doctor,' says I, 'I think *you* had better have the doctor. I think you need him much worse than some folks I could mention.' And I looked right straight at Luella Miller laughin' and cryin' and goin' on as if she was the center of all creation. All the time she was actin' so—seemed as if she was too sick to sense anythin'—she was keepin' a sharp lookout as to how we took it out of the corner of one eye. I see her. You could never cheat me about Luella Miller. Finally I got real mad and I run home and I got a bottle of valerian I had, and I poured some boilin' hot water on a handful of catnip, and I mixed up that catnip tea with most half a wineglass of valerian, and I went with it over to Luella's. I marched right up to Luella, a-holdin' out that cup, all smokin'. 'Now' says I, 'Luella Miller, *you swaller this!'*

"'What is—what is it, oh, what is it?' she sort of screeches out. Then she goes off a-laughin' enough to kill.

"'Poor lamb, poor little lamb,' says Aunt Abby, standin' over her, all kind of tottery, and tryin' to bathe her head with camphor.

"'*You swaller this right down,*' says I. And I didn't waste any ceremony. I just took hold of Luella Miller's chin and I tipped her

BLOOD LINES

head back, and I caught her mouth open with laughin', and I clapped that cup to her lips, and I fairly hollered at her: 'Swaller, swaller, swaller!' and she gulped it right down. She had to, and I guess it did her good. Anyhow, she stopped cryin' and laughin' and let me put her to bed, and she went to sleep like a baby inside of half an hour. That was more than poor Aunt Abby did. She lay awake all that night and I stayed with her, though she tried not to have me; said she wa'n't sick enough for watchers. But I stayed, and I made some good cornmeal gruel and I fed her a teaspoon every little while all night long. It seemed to me as if she was jest dyin' from bein' all wore out. In the mornin' as soon as it was light I run over to the Bisbees and sent Johnny Bisbee for the doctor. I told him to tell the doctor to hurry, and he come pretty quick. Poor Aunt Abby didn't seem to know much of anythin' when he got there. You couldn't hardly tell she breathed, she was so used up. When the doctor had gone, Luella came into the room lookin' like a baby in her ruffled nightgown. I can see her now. Her eyes were as blue and her face all pink and white like a blossom, and she looked at Aunt Abby in the bed sort of innocent and surprised. 'Why,' says she, 'Aunt Abby ain't got up yet?'

"'No, she ain't,' says I, pretty short.

"'I thought I didn't smell the coffee,' says Luella.

"'Coffee,' says I. 'I guess if you have coffee this mornin' you'll make it yourself.'

"'I never made the coffee in all my life,' says she, dreadful astonished. 'Erastus always made the coffee as long as he lived, and then Lily she made it, and then Aunt Abby made it. I don't believe I *can* make the coffee, Miss Anderson.'

"'You can make it or go without, jest as you please,' says I.

"'Ain't Aunt Abby goin' to get up?' says she.

"'I guess she won't get up,' says I, 'sick as she is.' I was gettin' madder and madder. There was somethin' about that little pink-and-white thing standin' there and talkin' about coffee, when she had killed so many better folks than she was, and had jest killed another, that made me feel 'most as if I wished somebody would up and kill her before she had a chance to do any more harm.

"'Is Aunt Abby sick?' says Luella, as if she was sort of aggrieved and injured.

"'Yes,' says I, 'she's sick, and she's goin' to die, and then you'll be left alone, and you'll have to do for yourself and wait on yourself, or do without things.' I don't know but I was sort of hard, but it was the truth, and if I was any harder than Luella Miller had been I'll give up. I ain't never been sorry that I said it. Well, Luella, she up and had hysterics again at that, and I just let her have 'em. All I did was to bundle her into the room on the other side of the entry where Aunt Abby couldn't hear her, if she wa'n't past it—I don't know but she was—and set her down hard in a chair and told her not to come back into the other room, and she minded. She had her hysterics in there till she got tired.

"When she found out that nobody was comin' to coddle her and do for her she stopped. At least I suppose she did. I had all I could do with poor Aunt Abby tryin' to keep the breath of life in her. The doctor had told me that she was dreadful low, and give me some very strong medicine to give to her in drops real often, and told me real particular about the nourishment. Well, I did as he told me real faithful till she wa'n't able to swaller any longer. Then I had her daughter sent for. I had begun to realize that she wouldn't last any time at all. I hadn't realized it before, though I spoke to Luella the way I did. The doctor he came, and Mrs. Sam Abbot, but when she got there it was too late; her mother was dead. Aunt Abby's daughter just give one look at her mother layin' there, then she turned sort of sharp and sudden and looked at me.

"'Where is she?' says she, and I knew she meant Luella.

"'She's out in the kitchen,' says I. 'She's too nervous to see folks die. She's afraid it will make her sick.'

"The Doctor he speaks up then. He was a young man. Old Doctor Park had died the year before, and this was a young fellow just out of college. 'Mrs. Miller is not strong,' says he, kind of severe, 'and she is quite right in not agitating herself.'

"'You are another, young man; she's got her pretty claw on you,' thinks I, but I didn't say anythin' to him. I just said over to Mrs. Sam Abbot that Luella was in the kitchen, and Mrs. Sam Abbot she went out there, and I went, too, and I never heard anythin' like the way she talked to Luella Miller. I felt pretty hard to Luella myself, but this was more than I ever would have dared to say. Luella she was too scared to go into hysterics. She jest flopped. She seemed to jest shrink away to nothin' in that kitchen chair, with Mrs. Sam Abbot standin' over her and talkin' and tellin' her the truth. I guess the truth was most too much for her and no mistake, because Luella presently actually did faint away, and there wa'n't any sham about it, the way I always suspected there was about them hysterics. She fainted dead away and we had to lay her flat on the floor, and the Doctor he came runnin' out and he said somethin' about a weak heart dreadful fierce to Mrs. Sam Abbot, but she wa'n't a mite scared. She faced him jest as white as even Luella was layin' there lookin' like death and the Doctor feelin' of her pulse.

"'Weak heart,' says she, 'weak heart; weak fiddlesticks! There ain't nothin' weak about that woman. She's got strength enough to hang onto other folks till she kills 'em. Weak? It was my poor mother that was weak: this woman killed her as sure as if she had taken a knife to her.'

"But the Doctor he didn't pay much attention. He was bendin' over Luella layin' there with her yellow hair all streamin' and her pretty pink-and-white face all pale, and her blue eyes like stars gone out, and he was holdin' onto her hand and smoothin' her forehead, and tellin' me to get the brandy in Aunt Abby's room, and I was sure as I wanted to be that Luella had got somebody else to hang onto, now Aunt Abby was gone, and I thought of poor Erastus Miller, and I sort of pitied the poor young Doctor, led away by a pretty face, and I made up my mind I'd see what I could do.

"I waited till Aunt Abby had been dead and buried about a month, and the Doctor was goin' to see Luella steady and folks were beginnin' to talk; then one evenin', when I knew the Doctor had been called out of town and wouldn't be round, I went over to Luella's. I found her all dressed up in a blue muslin with white polka dots on it, and her hair curled jest as pretty, and there wa'n't a young girl in the place could compare with her. There was somethin' about Luella Miller seemed to draw the heart right out of you, but she didn't draw it out of *me*. She was settin' rocking in the chair by her sittin'-room window, and Maria Brown had gone home. Maria Brown had been in to help her, or rather to do the work, for Luella wa'n't helped when she didn't do anythin'. Maria Brown was real capable and she didn't have any ties;

she wa'n't married, and lived alone, so she'd offered. I couldn't see why she should do the work any more than Luella; she wa'n't any too strong; but she seemed to think she could and Luella seemed to think so, too, so she went over and did all the work—washed, and ironed, and baked, while Luella sat and rocked. Maria didn't live long afterward. She began to fade away just the same fashion the others had. Well, she was warned, but she acted real mad when folks said anythin': said Luella was a poor, abused woman, too delicate to help herself, and they'd ought to be ashamed, and if she died helpin' them that couldn't help themselves she would—and she did.

"'I s'pose Maria has gone home,' says I to Luella, when I had gone in and sat down opposite her.

"'Yes, Maria went half an hour ago, after she had got supper and washed the dishes,' says Luella, in her pretty way.

"'I suppose she has got a lot of work to do in her own house tonight,' says I, kind of bitter, but that was all thrown away on Luella Miller. It seemed to her right that other folks that wa'n't any better able than she was herself should wait on her, and she couldn't get it through her head that anybody should think it *wa'n't* right.

"'Yes,' says Luella, real sweet and pretty, 'yes, she said she had to do her washin' tonight. She has let it go for a fortnight along of comin' over here.'

"'Why don't she stay home and do her washin' instead of comin' over here and doin' *your* work, when you are just as well able, and enough sight more so, than she is to do it?' says I.

"Then Luella she looked at me like a baby who has a rattle shook at it. She sort of laughed as innocent as you please. 'Oh, I can't do the work myself, Miss Anderson,' says she. 'I never did. Maria *has* to do it.'

"Then I spoke out: 'Has to do it!' says I. 'Has to do it!' She don't have to do it, either. Maria Brown has her own home and enough to live on. She ain't beholden to you to come over here and slave for you and kill herself!'

"Luella she jest set and stared at me for all the world like a doll-baby that was so abused that it was come to life.

"'Yes,' says I, 'she's killin' herself. She's goin' to die just the way

Erastus did, and Lily, and your Aunt Abby. You're killin' her jest as you did them. I don't know what there is about you, but you seem to bring a curse,' says I. 'You kill everybody that is fool enough to care anythin' about you and do for you.'

"She stared at me and she was pretty pale.

"'And Maria ain't the only one you're goin' to kill,' says I. 'You're goin' to kill Doctor Malcom before you're done with him.'

"Then a red color came flamin' all over her face. 'I ain't goin' to kill him, either,' says she, and she begun to cry.

"'Yes, you be!' says I. Then I spoke as I had never spoke before. You see, I felt it on account of Erastus. I told her that she hadn't any business to think of another man after she'd been married to one that had died for her: that she was a dreadful woman; and she was, that's true enough, but sometimes I have wondered lately if she knew it—if she wa'n't like a baby with scissors in its hand cuttin' everybody without knowin' what it was doin'.

"Luella she kept gettin' paler and paler, and she never took her eyes off my face. There was somethin' awful about the way she looked at me and never spoke one word. After awhile I quit talkin' and I went home. I watched that night, but her lamp went out before nine o'clock, and when Doctor Malcom came drivin' past and sort of slowed up he see there wa'n't any light and he drove along. I saw her sort of shy out of meetin' the next Sunday, too, so he shouldn't go home with her, and I begun to think mebbe she did have some conscience after all. It was only a week after that that Maria Brown died—sort of sudden at the last, though everybody had seen it was comin'. Well, then there was a good deal of feelin' and pretty dark whispers. Folks said the days of witchcraft had come again, and they were pretty shy of Luella. She acted sort of offish to the Doctor and he didn't go there, and there wa'n't anybody to do anythin' for her. I don't know how she *did* get along. I wouldn't go in there and offer to help her—not because I was afraid of dyin' like the rest, but I thought she was just as well able to do her own work as I was to do it for her, and I thought it was about time that she did it and stopped killin' other folks. But it wa'n't very long before folks began to say that Luella herself was goin' into a decline jest the way her husband, and Lily, and Aunt Abby and the others had, and I saw myself that she looked pretty bad. I used to see her goin' past from the store with a bundle as if she could hardly crawl, but I remembered how Erastus used to wait and tend when he couldn't hardly put one foot before the other, and I didn't go out to help her.

"But at last one afternoon I saw the Doctor come drivin' up like mad with his medicine chest, and Mrs. Babbit came in after supper and said that Luella was real sick.

"'I'd offer to go in and nurse her,' says she, 'but I've got my children to consider, and mebbe it ain't true what they say, but it's queer how many folks that have done for her have died.'

"I didn't say anythin', but I considered how she had been Erastus's wife and how he had set his eyes by her, and I made up my mind to go in the next mornin', unless she was better, and see what I could do; but the next mornin' I see her at the window, and pretty soon she came steppin' out as spry as you please, and a little while afterward Mrs. Babbit came in and told me that Doctor had got a girl from out of town, a Sarah Jones, to come there, and she said she was pretty sure that the Doctor was goin' to marry Luella.

"I saw him kiss her in the door that night myself, and I knew it was true. The woman came that afternoon, and the way she flew around was a caution. I don't believe Luella had swept since Maria died. She swept and dusted, and washed and ironed; wet clothes and dusters and carpets were flyin' over there all day, and every time Luella set her foot out when the Doctor wa'n't there there was that Sarah Jones helpin' her up and down the steps, as if she hadn't learned to walk.

"Well, everybody knew that Luella and the Doctor were goin' to be married, but it wa'n't long before they began to talk about his lookin' so poorly, jest as they had about the others; and they talked about Sarah Jones, too.

"Well, the Doctor did die, and he wanted to be married first, so as to leave what little he had to Luella, but he died before the minister could get there, and Sarah Jones died a week afterward.

"Well, that wound up everything for Luella Miller. Not another soul in the whole town would lift a finger for her. There got to be a sort of panic. Then she began to droop in good earnest. She used to have to go to the store herself, for Mrs. Babbit was afraid to let Tommy go for her, and I've seen her goin' past and stoppin' every two or three steps to rest. Well, I stood it as long as I could, but one day I see her comin' with her arms full and stoppin' to lean against the Babbit fence, and I run out and took her bundles and carried them to her house. Then I went home and never spoke one word to her though she called after me dreadful kind of pitiful. Well, that night I was taken sick with a chill, and I was sick as I wanted to be for two weeks. Mrs. Babbit had seen me run out to help Luella and she came in and told me I was goin' to die on account of it. I didn't know whether I was or not, but I considered I had done right by Erastus's wife.

"That last two weeks Luella she had a dreadful hard time, I guess. She was pretty sick, and as near as I could make out nobody dared go near her. I don't know as she was really needin' anythin' very much, for there was enough to eat in her house and it was warm weather, and she made out to cook a little flour gruel every day, I know, but I guess she had a hard time, she that had been so petted and done for all her life.

"When I got so I could go out, I went over there one morning. Mrs. Babbit had just come in to say she hadn't seen any smoke and she didn't know but it was somebody's duty to go in, but she couldn't help thinkin' of her children, and I got right up, though I hadn't been out of the house for two weeks, and I went in there, and Luella she was layin' on the bed, and she was dyin'.

"She lasted all that day and into the night. But I sat there after the new doctor had gone away. Nobody else dared to go there. It was about midnight that I left her for a minute to run home and get some medicine I had been takin', for I begun to feel rather bad.

"It was a full moon that night, and just as I started out of my door to cross the street back to Luella's, I stopped short, for I saw something."

Lydia Anderson at this juncture always said with a certain defiance that she did not expect to be believed, and then proceeded in a hushed voice:

"I saw what I saw, and I know I saw it, and I will swear on my death bed that I saw it. I saw Luella Miller and Erastus Miller, and Lily, and Aunt Abby, and Maria, and the Doctor, and Sarah, all goin' out of her door, and all but Luella shone white in the moonlight, and they were all helpin' her along till she seemed to fairly fly in the midst of them. Then it all disappeared. I stood a minute with my heart poundin', then I went over there. I thought of goin' for Mrs. Babbit, but I thought she'd be afraid. So I went alone, though I knew what had happened. Luella was layin' real peaceful, dead on her bed."

This was the story that the old woman, Lydia Anderson, told, but the sequel was told by the people who survived her, and this is the tale which has become folklore in the village.

Lydia Anderson died when she was eighty-seven. She had continued wonderfully hale and hearty for one of her years until about two weeks before her death.

One bright moonlight evening she was sitting beside a window in her parlor when she made a sudden exclamation, and was out of the house and across the street before the neighbor who was taking care of her could stop her. She followed as fast as possible and found Lydia Anderson stretched on the ground before the door of Luella Miller's deserted house, and she was quite dead.

The next night there was a red gleam of fire athwart the moonlight and the old house of Luella Miller was burned to the ground. Nothing is now left of it except a few old cellar stones and a lilac bush, and in summer a helpless trail of morning glories among the weeds, which might be considered emblematic of Luella herself.

Mary E. Wilkins-Freeman was the author of twelve novels and more than two hundred short stories at the turn of the century; she is best remembered, however, for her handful of supernatural tales. "Luella Miller" is typical of Wilkins-Freeman's intensely "regional" writing, which she maintained could be elevated to universal appeal.

Ah, the classic vampire—arrogant, sensual, powerful.
Ah, the classic young lady—intelligent, lovely, longing for something more. . . .

When the Red Storm Comes

BY SARAH SMITH

o you believe in vampires?" he said.

I snapped *Dracula* closed and pushed it under the tapestry bag containing my neglected cutwork. "Mr. Stoker writes amusingly," I said. "I believe I don't know you, sir."

"What a shame," he said, putting his hand on the café chair across from me. I looked up—and up; he was tall, blond; his uniform blazed crimson, a splash of blood against the green trees and decent New Hampshire brick of Market Square. The uniform was Austro-Hungarian; his rank I did not know, but clearly he was an officer.

"You should be better acquainted with vampires." He clicked heels and bowed. "Count Ferenc Zohary." Without invitation he sat down, smiling at me.

In this August 1905, in Portsmouth where I was spending the summer before my debutante year, negotiations were being held that might finish the long Russo-Japanese War. Aboard his yacht *Mayflower* at the naval yard, President Roosevelt had hosted the first meeting between the Russian and Japanese plenipotentiaries,

Count Serge Witte and the Marquis Komura. Now the opponents met officially at the naval yard and schemed betweentimes at the Wentworth Hotel. My aunt Mildred did not encourage newspaper reading for unmarried women, so I was out-of-date, but knew the negotiations were supposed to be going badly. The town was crowded with foreign men; there was a storminess in the air, a feel of heavy male energy, of history and importance. Danger, blood, and cruelty, like Mr. Stoker's book: it made my heart beat more strongly than any woman's should. *Don't talk to any of them,* Aunt Mildred had said. But for once my aunt was out of sight.

"You are part of the negotiations? Pray tell me how they proceed."

"I am an observer only."

"Will they make peace?"

"I hope not, for my country's sake." He looked amused at my surprise. "If they continue the war, Russia and Japan will bleed, Russia will lose, turn west; they will make a little war and probably lose. But if they sign their treaty, Russia will fight us five years from now, when they are stronger; and then the Germans will come in, and the French to fight the Germans, and the English with the French. Very amusing. My country cannot survive."

"Is it not wearying, to have such things decided and to be able to do nothing?"

"I am never wearied." My companion stretched out his hand, gathered together my half-finished cutwork linen, and waved it in the air for a moment like a handkerchief before dropping it unceremoniously on the ground. "Your mother makes you do this," he said, "but you prefer diplomacy. Or vampires. Which?"

I flushed. "My aunt controls my sewing," I said. Cutwork had been my task for this summer, sitting hour after hour on Aunt Mildred's verandah, sewing hundreds of tiny stitches on the edges of yards of linen, then clipping out patterns with my sharp-pointed scissors. Linen for my trousseau, said Aunt Mildred, who would not say the word "sheets." In the fall I would go to New York, planning my strategies for marriage like a powerless general. The battle was already hopeless; without greater wealth than I commanded, I could not hope to be in the center of events. I would become what I was fit for by looks but not by soul, the showy useless wife of some businessman, whose interest in war extended only to the army's need for boots or toothbrushes.

But now, because Admiral Togo had won at Tsushima, I had my taste of war, however faraway and tantalizing; I was sitting with a soldier, here in the hot thick sunlight and green leaves of Market Square.

"Do you like war," my companion asked, "or simply blood?"

An interesting question. "I think they both concern power."

"Precisely." He leafed through the book while I watched him secretly. In the exquisitely tailored crimson uniform, he had a look of coarseness combined with power. Above the stiff gold-braided collar, his neck was thick with muscle. His hands were short and broad-nailed, his fingertips square against the yellow-and-red binding of *Dracula*. Perhaps feeling my eyes on him, he looked up and smiled at me. He had assurance, a way of looking at me as though I were already attracted to him, though he was not handsome: a thick-lipped mouth, a scar on his jaw, and a nick out of his ear. And he had thrown my cutwork on the ground.

"My name is Susan Wentworth," I said.

"Wentworth, like the hotel. That is easy to remember." No sweet words about my face being too beautiful for my name to be forgotten. "Do you stay at the hotel?" he asked.

A gentleman never asked directly where a lady lived, to save her the embarrassment of appearing to desire his company.

"My aunt has a cottage at Kittery Point."

"That is not far. Do you come to the tea dances at the hotel?"

"Seldom, Count Zohary. My aunt thinks the diplomatic guests are not suitable company."

"Very true. But exciting, no? Do you find soldiers exciting, Miss Wentworth?"

"Soldiering, yes, and diplomacy; I admit that I do."

"A certain amount of blood . . . that is nice with the tea dances." With his thumbnail he marked a passage in the book and showed it to me. *As she arched her neck she actually licked her lips like an animal,* I read. "Do you find that exciting?"

"I am not a vampire, Count Zohary," I said, uneasily amused.

"I know that." My companion smiled at me, showing regular

even teeth. "I, for instance, I am a vampire, and I can assure you that you are not one yet."

"You, Count Zohary?"

"Of course, not as this man Stoker describes. I walk in the sun, I see my face in my shaving mirror; I assure you I sleep in sheets, not dirt." He reached out and touched the thin gold cross I wore around my neck. "A pretty thing. It does not repel me." His fingers hovered very close to my neck and bosom. "The vampire is very sensual, Miss Wentworth, especially when he is also a soldier. Very attractive. You should try."

I had let him go too far. "I think you dare overmuch, Count Zohary."

"Ah, why I dare, that is the vampire in me. But you don't hold up your cross and say, 'Begone, *necuratul!*'" he said. "And that is the vampire in you. Do you like what you read, Miss Susan Wentworth? You look as though you would like it very much. Are you curious? If you will come to the tea dance at the hotel, I will show you the handsome hotel sheets, and teach you that vampires are—almost—as civilized as diplomats."

He looked at me, gauging my response: and for a moment, horrified, I felt I would respond. I wanted the brutal crude power of the man. "Count Zohary, you have mistaken me, I am respectable." I snatched the book away from him and stuffed it deep into my tapestry bag. "I have—*certainly* no desire to see your—" I would not give him the satisfaction of finishing the sentence. "You're making me talk nonsense."

He brushed his mustache with his finger, then lifted one corner of his lip. "What will convince you, dear respectable Miss Wentworth? My fangs? Shall I turn into a wolf for you? Come into your chamber like a red mist, or charge in like cavalry?" Over our head the leaves rattled and wind soughed through the square. Count Zohary looked up. "Shall I tell you the future in your blood? Shall I control the sea for you, or call a storm? That is my best parlor trick. Let us have a thunderstorm, Miss Wentworth, you and I."

The tide controlled the sea, and the Piscatequa River called thunderstorms once or twice a week in August, without help from Hungarian counts. "If you can tell the future, Count Zohary, you know that everything you say is useless."

"It is not my most reliable gift, Miss Wentworth," he said. "Unfortunately, or I would not be here watching Witte and Komura, but back in New York drinking better coffee at the embassy. It works best after I have had a woman, or drunk blood. Shall we find out together what Witte and Komura will do? No? You do not wish to know?" On the café table there was a ring of condensation from my glass of ice water. With mock solemnity he shook salt from the table shaker over it and stared at the water as if into a crystal ball, making passes like a fortune-teller. "Seawater is better to look into; blood best. Ice water—*ach*, Miss Wentworth, you make me work. But I see you will come to the tea dance. Today, Wednesday, or Thursday you will come."

"I will not," I said. "Of course I will not."

"Tomorrow?"

"Certainly not."

"Thursday, then." From the direction of the ocean, thunder muttered above the white tower of First Church. Count Zohary made a gesture upward and smiled at me. I began to gather up my things, and he bent down, stretching out his long arm to pick up my fallen linen. "This is almost done; you must come Thursday."

"Why Thursday?" I asked unwillingly.

"Because I have made a bet with myself. Before you have finished this *Quatsch*," he said, "I will give you what you want. I shall have turned you into a vampire."

A sea-salt wave of breeze rolled over the square, hissing; the leaves were tossed pale side up like dead fish. I stared at him, the smell of the sea in my mouth, an acrid freshness. He smiled at me, slightly pursing his lips. Flushing, I pushed my chair away. Count Zohary rose, clicked his heels, raised my hand to his lips; and through the first drops of rain I saw him stride away, his uniform the color of fresh blood against the brick and white of the Athenaeum, darkening in the rain. A soldier, his aide-de-camp, came forward with a black cape for him. Unwillingly I thought of vampires.

◊◊◊

That night the rain shook the little-paned windows of my white bedroom. *This monster has done much harm already,* I read. Moisture in the air made the book's binding sticky, so that both my palms were printed with fragments of the red name backward. *The howling of wolves.* There were no wolves around Portsmouth, nor vampires either. I could tell my own future without help from him: This fall in New York would decide it, whatever my strategies. Women of my sort all had the same future.

How much less alive could I be if I were a vampire's prey?

I pictured myself approaching young men of my acquaintance and sinking my teeth into their throat. This was fancy; I had no access even to the ordinary powers of men such as the count.

But he had told me one quite specific thing, and it intrigued me: he was with the embassy in New York.

The next day, though I was tired, I assiduously sewed at my cutwork and pricked at it with my scissors, and finishing this respectable task, I felt as though I were again in control of myself, triumphant over Count Zohary, and ready to face him.

At my instigation, Mrs. Lathrop, my aunt's friend, proposed that we visit the Wentworth, and Aunt Mildred was persuaded to agree.

On Thursday, Elizabeth Lathrop and her daughter Lucilla, Aunt Mildred and I, all fit ourselves into the Lathrop barouche, and at a gentle pace we were driven through the curving streets of Kittery and past the Federal mansions of Portsmouth. It was a perfect day, the breeze from the sea just enough to refresh us, late day lilies and heliotrope blooming behind old-fashioned wooden trellis fences; a day for a pleasant, thoughtless excursion; yet as we passed through Market Square, I looked for his glittering red figure, and as we pulled into the handsome gravel driveway of the Wentworth, I found myself excited, as if I were going to a meeting of some consequence.

Aunt Mildred and Mrs. Lathrop found us a table by the dance floor, which was not large but modern and well appointed. An orchestra was playing waltzes; a few couples practiced their steps on the floor, and many soldiers sat at tables under the potted palms, flirting with young women. Mrs. Lathrop and Lucilla intended a sight of Count Witte, whose manners were reported to be so uncouth that he must eat behind a screen. I saw no sign of Count Zohary. At one table, surrounded by a retinue of men, the notorious Mme. N. held court, a laughing, pretty woman who was rumored to have brought down three governments. While the orchestra played, Mrs. Lathrop and my aunt Mildred gossiped about her. Lucilla Lathrop and I discovered nothing in common. From under my eyelashes I watched clever Mme. N.

Three women from the Japanese legation entered the dining room, causing a sensation with their kimonos, wigs, and plastered faces. I wondered if there were Japanese vampires, and if the painted Japanese ladies felt the same male energy from all those soldiers. Were those Japanese women's lives as constrained as mine?

"The heat is making me uneasy, Aunt Mildred; I will go and stroll on the terrace." Under my parasol, I let the sea wind cool my checks; I stared over the sandy lawn, over the sea.

"Miss Wentworth. Have you come to see my sheets?"

"By no means, Count Zohary." He was sitting at one of the little café tables on the terrace. Today he was in undress uniform, a brownish-gray. In the sea light his blond hair had a foxy tint. Standing, he bowed elaborately, drawing out a chair. "I would not give you the satisfaction of refusing." I inclined my head and sat down.

"Then you will satisfy by accepting?"

"Indeed not. What satisfaction is that?" I looked out over the sea, the calm harbor. While yachts swayed at anchor, the Star Island ferry headed out toward the shoals, sun gleaming off its windows and rail. I had seen this view for years from Aunt Mildred's house; there was nothing new in it.

"Come now, turn you head, Miss Wentworth. You don't know what I offer. Look at me." On his table was a plate of peaches, ripe and soft; I smelled them on the warm air, looked at them but not at him. A fly buzzed over them; he waved it away, picked up a fruit, and took a bite out of it. I watched his heavy muscular hand. "You think you are weary of your life, but you have never tasted it. What is not tasted has no flavor. I offer everything you are missing—ah, now you look at me." His eyes were reddish-brown with flecks of light. He sucked at the juice, then offered the peach to me, the same he had tasted; he held it close to my lips. "Eat."

"I will have another, but not this."

"Eat with me; then you will have as many as you want." I took a tiny nip from the fruit's pink flesh. Soft, hairy skin; sweet flesh. He handed the plate of fruit to me; I took one and bit. My mouth was full of pulp and juice.

"I could have your body," he said in a soft voice. "By itself, like that peach; that is no trouble. But you can be one of us, I saw it in the square. I want to help you, to make you what you are."

"One of us? What do you mean?"

"One who wants power," he said with the same astonishing softness. "Who can have it. A vampire. Eat your peach, Miss Wentworth, and I will tell you about your Dracula. Vlad *Drăculeşti*, son of Vlad the Dragon. On Tîmpa Hill by Braşov, above the chapel of St. Jacob, he had his enemies' limbs lopped and their bodies impaled; and as they screamed, he ate his meal beside them, dipping his bread into the blood of the victims, because the taste of human blood is the taste of power. The essence of the vampire is power." He reached out his booted foot and, under the table, touched mine. "Power is not money, or good looks, or rape or seduction. It is simple, life and death; to kill; to drink the blood of the dying; but oneself to survive, to beget, to make one's kind, to flourish. Komura and Witte have such power, they are making a great red storm, with many victims. I too have power, and I will have blood on my bread. Will you eat and drink with me?"

"Blood—?"

He looked at me with his light-flecked eyes. "Does blood frighten you, do you faint at the sight of blood, like a good little girl? I think not." He took a quick bite from his peach. "Have you ever seen someone die? Did they bleed? Did you look away? No, I see you did not; you were fascinated, more than a woman should be. You like the uniforms, the danger, the soldiers, but what you truly like, Miss Wentworth, is red. When you read about this war in the newspapers, will you pretend you are shocked and say Oh, how *dreadful*, while you look twice and then again at the pictures of blood, and hope you do not know why your heart beats so strong? Will you say, I can never be so much alive as to drink blood? Or will you know yourself, and be glad when the red storm comes?" He tapped my plate of peaches with his finger. "To become what you are is simpler than eating one of those, Miss Wentworth, and much more pleasant."

"I wish some degree of power—who does not—but to do this—" He was right; I had been fascinated. The next day I had come back to the scene, had been disappointed that the blood was washed away. "This is ridiculous, you must wish to make me laugh or to disgust me. You are making terrible fun of me."

"Drink my blood," he said. "Let me drink yours. I will not kill you. Have just a little courage, a little curiosity. Sleep with me; that last is not necessary, but is very amusing. Then—a wide field, and great power, Miss Wentworth."

I swallowed. "You simply mean to make me your victim."

"If it seems to you so, then you will be my victim. I want to give you life, because you might take it and amuse me. But you undervalue yourself. Are you my victim?" For a moment, across a wide oval in front of the hotel, wind flattened the water, and through some trick of light and wave, it gleamed red. "See, Miss Wentworth. My parlor trick again."

"No—I often see such light on the water."

"Not everyone does."

"Then I see nothing."

By his plate he had a little sharp fruit knife. He picked it up and drew a cut across his palm; as the blood began to well, he cupped his palm and offered it to me. "The blood is a little sea, a little red sea, the water I like best to control. I stir it up, Miss Wentworth; I drink it; I live." With one finger of his right hand he touched his blood, then the vein on my wrist. "I understand its taste; I can make it flow like tide, Miss Wentworth, I can make your heart beat, Miss Wentworth, until you would scream at me to stop. Do you want to understand blood, do you want to taste blood, do you want your mouth full of it, salty, sweet, foul blood? Do you want the power of the blood? Of course you do not, the respectable American girl. Of course you do; you do."

He took my hand, he pulled me close to him. He looked at me with his insistent animal eyes, waiting, his blood cupped in his hand. I knew that at that moment I could break away from his grip and return to Aunt Mildred and the Lathrops. They would not so much as notice I had gone or know what monstrous things had been said to me. I could sit down beside them, drink tea, and listen to the orchestra for the rest of my life. For me there would be no vampires.

The blood, crusted at the base of his fingers, still welled from the slit he had made in his palm. It was bright, bright red. I bent down and touched my tongue to the wound. The blood was salty, intimate, strong, the taste of my own desire.

◊◊◊

The white yacht was luxuriously appointed, with several staterooms. We sailed far out to sea. Count Zohary had invited the Lathrops and my aunt to chaperone me. On deck, Mr. Lathrop, a freckled man in a white suit, trolled for bluefish and talked with Count Zohary. I heard the words *Witte, Sakhalin, reparations;* this evening there was to be an important meeting between the plenipotentiaries. Aunt Mildred and Mrs. Lathrop talked and played whist, while Lucilla Lathrop's crocheting needle flashed through yards of cream-white tatting. I began still another piece of cutwork, but abandoned it and stood in the bow of the boat, feeling the sea waves in my body, long and slow. In part I was convinced Count Zohary merely would seduce me; I did not care. I had swallowed his blood and now he would drink mine.

Under an awning, sailors served luncheon from the hotel. Oysters Rockefeller, cream of mushroom soup with Parker House rolls, salmon steaks, mousse of hare, pepper dumplings, matchsticked sugared carrots, corn on the cob, a salad of cucumbers and Boston lettuce, summer squash. For dessert, almond biscuits, a praline and mocha-buttercream glazed cake, and ice cream in several flavors. With the food came wine, brandy with dessert, and a black bottle of champagne. I picked at the spinach on my oysters, but drank the wine thirstily. In the post-luncheon quiet, the boat idled on calm water; the sailors went below.

Mr. Lathrop fell asleep first, a handkerchief spread over his red face; then Lucilla Lathrop began snoring gently in a deck chair under the awning, her tatting tangled in her lap. Mr. Lathrop's fishing rod trailed from his nerveless hand; I reeled it in and laid it on the deck, and in the silent noon the thrum of fishing line was as loud as the engine had been. Aunt Mildred's cards sank into her lap. She did not close her eyes, but when I stood in front of her, she seemed not to see me. Alone, Mrs. Lathrop continued to play her cards, slowly, one by one, onto the little baize-colored table between her and my aunt, as if she were telling fortunes.

"Mrs. Lathrop?" She looked up briefly, her eyes dull as raisins in her white face, nodded at me, and went back to her cards.

"They have eaten and drunk," Count Zohary said, "and they are tired." A wave passed under the boat; Aunt Mildred's head jerked sideways and she fell across the arm of her chair, limply, rolling like a dead person. I almost cried out, almost fell; Count Zohary caught me and put his hand across my mouth.

"If you scream you will wake them."

Grasping my hand, he led me down the stairs, below decks, through a narrow corridor. On one side was the galley, and there, his head on his knees, sat the cook, asleep; near him a handsome sailor had fallen on the floor, sleeping too; I saw no others.

The principal stateroom was at the bow of the ship, white in the hot afternoon. The bed was opened, the sheets drawn back; the cabin had an odor of lemon oil, a faint musk of ocean. "Sheets," he said. "You see?" I sank down on the bed, my knees would not hold me. I had not known, at the last, how my body would fight me; I wanted to be not here, to know the future that was about to happen, to have had it happen, to have it happening now. I heard the snick of the bolt, and then he was beside me, unbuttoning the tiny buttons at my neck. So quiet it was, so quiet, I could not breathe. He bent down and touched the base of my neck with his tongue, and then I felt the tiny prick of his teeth, the lapping of his tongue and the sucking as he began to feed.

It was at first a horror to feel the blood drain, to sense my will struggle and fail; and then the pleasure rose, shudders and trembling so exquisite I could not bear them; the hot white cabin turned to shadows and cold and I fell across the bed. I am in my coffin, I thought, in my grave. He laid me back against the pillows, bent over me, pushed up my skirts and loosened the strings of my petticoats; I felt his hand on my skin. This was what I had feared, but now there was no retreat, I welcomed what was to come. I guided him forward; he lay full on me, his body was heavy on me, pressed against me, his uniform braid bruising my breasts. Our clothes were keeping us from each other. I slid the stiff fastenings open, fumbled out of my many-buttoned dress, struggled free of everything that kept me from him. *Now*, I whispered. *You must.*

We were skin to skin, and then, in one long agonizing push, he invaded me, he was *in me*, in my very body. Oh, the death pangs as I became a vampire, the convulsion of all my limbs! I gasped, bit his shoulder, made faces to keep from screaming. Yet still I moved with him, felt him moving inside me, and his power flowed into me. I laughed at the pain and pleasure unimaginable, as the sea waves pulsed through the cabin and pounded in my blood.

"Are you a vampire now, little respectable girl?" he gasped.

"Oh, yes, I have power, yes, I am a vampire."

He laughed.

When I dressed, I found blood on my bruised neck; my privates were bloody and sticky with juice, the signs of my change. I welcomed them. In the mirror, I had a fine color in my cheeks, and my white linen dress was certainly no more creased than might be justified by spending an afternoon on the water. My blood beat heavy and proud, a conquering drum.

I went on deck and ate a peach to still my thirst, but found it watery and insipid. It was late, toward sunset, the light failing, the sea red. In the shadows of the water I saw men silently screaming. I desired to drink the sea.

Mr. Lathrop opened his eyes and asked me, "Did you have a pleasant afternoon, Miss Wentworth?" His eyes were fixed, his color faded next to mine. Lucilla's face, as she blinked and yawned, was like yellow wax under her blond hair. Flies were buzzing around Mrs. Lathrop's cards, and Mrs. Lathrop gave off a scent of spoiled meat, feces, and blood. "Good afternoon, Aunt Mildred, how did you nap?" She did not answer me. Oh, they are weary, I thought, weary and dead.

Count Zohary came up the stairs, buttoning his uniform collar gingerly, as if his neck were bruised too. To amuse him, I pressed my sharp cutwork scissors against the vein of Aunt Mildred's neck, and held a Parker House roll underneath it; but he and I had no taste for such as Aunt Mildred. I threw my scissors into the blood-tinged sea: they fell, swallowed, corroded, gone.

Under a red and swollen sky, our ship sailed silent back to the white hotel. Count Zohary and I were the first to be rowed to shore. Across the red lawn, lights blazed, and outside the hotel a great crowd had assembled. "In a moment we will see the future," he said.

"I saw men dying in the ocean," I answered.

We walked across the lawn together, my arm in his; under my feet, sea sand hissed.

"Count Zohary, perhaps you have friends who share those interests that you have taught me to value? I would delight to be introduced to them. Though I know not what I can do, I wish for wide horizons."

"I have friends who will appreciate you. You will find a place in the world."

As we entered the even more crowded foyer, Count Sergei Witte and the Marquis Komura stood revealed, shaking hands. From a thousand throats a shout went up. "Peace! It is peace!"

"It is the great storm," said Count Zohary. For a moment he looked pensive, as though even vampires could regret.

He and I gained the vantage point of the stairs, and I looked down upon the crowd as if I were their general. Many of the young men were dead, the Americans as well as the foreign observers. I looked at the victims with interest. Some had been shot in the eye, forehead, cheekbone; some were torn apart as if by bombs. Their blood gleamed fresh and red. The flesh of some was gray and dirt-abraded, the features crushed, as if great weights had fallen on them. Next to me stood a woman in a nurse's uniform; as she cheered, she coughed gouts of blood and blinked blind eyes. Outside, Roman candles began to stutter, and yellow-green light fell over the yellow and gray faces of the dead.

But among them, bright as stars above a storm, I saw us, the living. How we had gathered for this! Soldiers and civilians; many on the Russian and Japanese staff, and not a few of the observers; the eminent Mme. N., who bowed to me distantly but cordially across the room; by a window a nameless young man, still as obscure as I; and my bright, my blazing Count Zohary. The hotel staff moved among us, gray-faced, passing us glasses of champagne; but my glass was hot and salty, filled with the sea of blood to come. For the first time, drinking deep, I was a living person with a future.

That autumn I was in New York, but soon traveled to Europe; and wherever I went, I helped to call up the storm.

Sarah Smith is the author of two compelling historical novels, *The Vanished Child* and *The Knowledge of Water.*

Where there is love, life and unlife have no meaning.

The Beautiful, the Damned

BY KRISTINE KATHRYN RUSCH

1

come from the Middle West, an unforgiving land with little or no tolerance for imagination. The wind blows harsh across the prairies, and the snows fall thick. Even with the conveniences of the modern age, life is dangerous there. To lose sight of reality, even for one short romantic moment, is to risk death.

I didn't belong in that country, and my grandfather knew it. I was his namesake, and somehow, being the second Nick Carraway in a family where the name had a certain mystique had forced that mystique upon me. He had lived in the East during the twenties, and had had grand adventures, most of which he would not talk about. When he returned to St. Paul in 1928, he met a woman—my grandmother Nell—and with her solid, common sense had shed himself of the romance and imagination that had led to his adventures in the first place.

Although not entirely. For when I announced, fifty years later, that I intended to pursue my education in the East, he paid four years of Ivy League tuition. And, when I told him, in the early eighties, that, despite my literary background and romantic nature, I planned a career in the securities business, he regaled me with stories of being a bond man in New York City in the years before the crash.

He died while I was still learning the art of the cold call, stuck on the sixteenth floor of a windowless high-rise, in a tiny cubicle that matched a hundred other tiny cubicles, distinguished only by my handprint on the phone set and the snapshots of my family thumbtacked to the indoor-outdoor carpeting covering the small barrier that separated my cubicle from all the others. He never saw the house in Connecticut which, although it was not grand, was respectable, and he never saw my rise from a cubicle employee to a man with an office. He never saw the heady Reagan years, although he would have warned me about the awful Black Monday well before it appeared. For despite the computers, jets, and televised communications, the years of my youth were not all that different from the years of his.

He never saw Fitz either, although I knew, years later, when my mother mailed me my grandfather's diaries, that my grandfather would have understood my mysterious neighbor, too.

◊◊◊

My house sat at the bottom of a hill, surrounded by trees whose russet leaves are—in my mind—in a state of perpetual autumn. I think the autumn melancholy comes from the overlay of hindsight upon what was, I think, the strangest summer of my life, a summer which, like my grandfather's summer of 1925, I do not discuss, even when asked. In that tiny valley, the air always had a damp chill and rich smell of loam. The scent grew stronger upon that winding dirt path that led to Fitz's house on the hill's crest—not a house really, but more of a mansion in the conservative New England style, white walls hidden by trees, with only the wide walk and the entry visible from the gate. Once behind, the walls and windows seemed to go on forever, and the manicured lawn with its neatly mowed grass and carefully arranged marble fountains seemed like a throwback from a simpler time.

The house had little life in the daytime, but at night the windows were thrown open and cars filled the driveway. The cars were all sleek and dark—blue Saabs and midnight BMWs, black Jaguars, and ebony Carreras. Occasionally a white stretch limo or a silver DeLorean would mar the darkness, but those guests rarely returned for a second visit, as if someone had asked them to take their ostentation elsewhere. Music trickled down the hill with the light, usually music of a vanished era, waltzes and marches and Dixieland jazz, music both romantic and danceable, played to such perfection that I envied Fitz his sound system until I saw several of the better known New York Philharmonic members round the corner near my house early on a particular Saturday evening.

Laughter, conversation and the tinkle of ice against fine crystal filled the gaps during the musicians' break, and in those early days, as I sat on my porch swing and stared up at the light, I imagined parties like those I had only seen on film—slender, beautiful women in glittery gowns, and athletic men who wore tuxedos like a second skin, exchanging witty and wry conversation under a dying moon.

I never trudged up the hill, although later I learned I could have, and dropped into a perpetual party that never seemed to have a guest list; but I still had enough of my Midwestern politeness to wait for an invitation and enough of my practical Midwestern heritage to know that such an invitation would never come.

Air conditioners have done little to change Manhattan in the summer. If anything, the heat from their exhausts adds to the oppression in the air, the stench of garbage rotting on the sidewalks and the smell of sweaty human bodies pressed too close. Had my cousin Arielle not discovered me, I might have spent the summer in the cool loam of my Connecticut home, monitoring the markets through my personal computer, and watching Fitz's parties with a phone wedged between my shoulder and ear.

Arielle always had an ethereal, otherworldly quality. My sensible aunt, with her thick ankles and dishwater-blonde hair, must have recognized that quality in the newborn she had given birth to in New Orleans, and committed the only romantic act of her life by deciding that Arielle was not a Mary or a Louise, family names that had suited Carraways until then.

I had never known Arielle well. At family reunions held on the shores of Lake Superior, she was always a beautiful, unattainable ghost, dressed in white gauze with silver blonde hair that fell to her waist, wide blue eyes, and skin so pale it seemed as fragile as my mother's bone china. We had exchanged perhaps five words over all those reunions, held each July, and always I had bowed my head and stammered in the presence of such royalty. Her voice was sultry and musical, lacking the long "a"s and soft "d"s that made my other relations sound like all their years of education had made no impression at all.

Why she called me when she and her husband Tom discovered that I had bought a house in a village only a mile from theirs I will never know. Perhaps she was lonely for a bit of family, or perhaps the otherworldliness had absorbed her, even then.

2

I drove to Arielle's and Tom's house in my own car, a BMW, navy blue and spit-polished, bought used because all of my savings had gone into the house. They lived on a knoll in a mock-Tudor style house with young saplings that had obviously been transplanted. The lack of tall trees gave the house a vulnerable air, as if the neighbors who lived on higher hills could look down upon it and find it flawed. The house itself was twice the size of mine, with a central living area flanked by a master bedroom wing and a guest wing, the wings more of an architect's affectation than anything else.

Tom met me at the door. He was a beefy man in his late twenties whose athletic build was beginning to show signs of softening into fat. He still had the thick neck, square jaw, and massive shoulders of an offensive lineman, which, of course, he had been. After one season with the Green Bay Packers—in a year unremarkable for its lackluster performance—he was permanently sidelined by a knee injury. Not wanting to open a car dealership that would forever capitalize on his one season of glory, he took his wife and his inheritance and moved east. When he saw me, he clapped his hand on my back as if we were old friends when, in fact, we had only met once, at the last and least of the family reunions.

"Ari's been waiting to see you," he said, and the broad, flat, uneducated vowels of the Midwest brought with them the sense of the stifling summer afternoons of the reunions, children's laughter echoing over the waves of the lake as if their joy would last forever.

He led me through a dark foyer and into a room filled with light. Nothing in the front of the house had prepared me for this room, with its floor to ceiling windows and their view of an English garden beyond the patio. Arielle sat on a loveseat beneath the large windows, the sunlight reflecting off her hair and white dress, giving her a radiance that was almost angelic. She held out her hand, and as I took it, she pulled me close and kissed me on the cheek.

"Nicky," she murmured. "I missed you."

The softness with which she spoke, the utter sincerity in her gaze made me believe her and, as on those summer days of old, I blushed.

"Not much to do in Connecticut." Tom's booming voice made me draw back. "We've been counting the nails on the walls."

"Now, Tom," Ari said without taking her hand from mine, "we belong here."

I placed my other hand over hers, capturing the fragile fingers for a moment before releasing her. "I rather like the quiet," I said.

"You would," Tom said. He spun on the toe of a well-polished shoe and strode across the hardwood floor, always in shadow despite the light pouring in from the windows.

His abruptness took me aback, and I glanced at Ari. She shrugged. "I think we'll eat on the terrace. The garden is cool this time of day."

"Will Tom join us?"

She frowned in a girlish way, furrowing her brow, and making her appear, for a moment, as if she were about to cry. "He will when he gets off the phone."

I hadn't heard a phone ring, but I had no chance to ask her any more because she placed her slippered feet on the floor and stood. I had forgotten how tiny she was, nearly half my height, but each feature perfectly proportioned. She took my arm and I caught the fresh scent of lemons rising from her warm skin.

The Beautiful, the Damned

"You must tell me everything that's happened to you," she said, and I did. Under her intense gaze my life felt important, my smallest accomplishments a pinnacle of achievement. When I had finished, we had reached the terrace. A glass table, already set for three, stood in the shade of a maple tree. The garden spread before us, lush and green. Each plant had felt the touch of a pruning shears and all were trimmed back so severely that nothing was left to chance.

I pulled out a chair for Ari and she sat daintily, her movements precise. I took the chair across from her, feeling cloddish, afraid that my very size would cause me to break something. I wondered how Tom, with his linebacker's build, felt as he moved through his wife's delicate house.

She shook out a linen napkin and placed it on her lap. A man appeared beside her dressed as a waiter—he had moved so silently that I hadn't noticed him—and poured water into our crystal glasses. He filled Tom's as well, and Ari stared at the empty place. "I wish he wouldn't call her before lunch," she said. "It disturbs my digestion."

I didn't want to ask what Ari was referring to. I didn't want to get trapped in their private lives.

She sighed and brushed a strand of hair out of her face. "But I don't want to talk about Tom's awful woman. I understand you live next door to the man they call Fitz."

I nodded as the waiter appeared again, bringing fresh bread in a ceramic basket.

"I would love," she said, leaning forward just enough to let me know this was the real reason behind my invitation, "to see the inside of his home."

◊◊◊

Tom never joined us. We finished our lunch, walked through the garden, and had mint juleps in the late afternoon, after which everything seemed a bit funnier than it had before. As I left in the approaching twilight, it felt as if Ari and I had been friends instead of acquaintances linked by a happenstance of birth.

By the time I got home, it was dark. The house retained the

heat of the day, and so I went into the backyard and stared at the path that led up to Fitz's mansion. The lights blazed on the hillside, and the sound of laughter washed down to me like the blessing of a god. Perhaps Ari's casual suggestion put something in my mind, or perhaps I was still feeling the effects of the mint juleps, but whatever the cause, I walked up the path feeling drawn to the house like a moth to light.

My shoes crunched against the hardpacked earth, and my legs, unused to such strenuous exercise, began to ache.

Midway up, the coolness of the valley had disappeared, and perspiration made my shirt cling to my chest. The laughter grew closer, and with it, snatches of conversation—women's voices rising with passion, men speaking in low tones, pretending that they couldn't be overheard.

I stopped at a small rock formation just before the final rise to Fitz's house. The rocks extended over the valley below like a platform, and from them, I could see the winding road I had driven that afternoon to Ari's house. A car passed below, and I followed the trail of its headlights until they disappeared into the trees.

As I turned to leave the platform, my desire to reach the party gone, I caught a glimpse of a figure moving against the edge of the path. A man stood on the top of the rise, staring down at the road, as I had. He wore dark evening dress with a white shirt and a matching white scarf draped casually around his neck. The light against his back caused his features to be in shadow—only when he cupped his hands around a burning match to light a cigarette already in his mouth did I get a sense of his face.

He had an older beauty—clean-shaven, almost womanish, with a long nose, high cheekbones, and wide, dark eyes. A kind of beauty that had been fashionable in men when my grandfather was young—the Rudolph Valentino, Leslie Howard look that seemed almost effete by the standards of today.

As he tossed the match away, a waltz started playing behind him, and it gave him context. He stared down at the only other visible point of light—Ari's knoll—and his posture suggested such longing that I half expected the music to swell, to add too much violin in the suggestion of a world half-forgotten.

I knew, without being told, that this was my neighbor. I almost called to him, but felt that to do so would ruin the perfection of the moment. He stared until he finished his cigarette, then dropped it, ground it with his shoe, and slipping his hands in his pockets, wandered back to the party—alone.

3

The next afternoon I was lounging on my sofa with the air conditioning off, lingering over the book review section of the Sunday *Times* when the crunch of gravel through the open window alerted me to a car in my driveway. I stood up in time to see a black Rolls Royce stop outside my garage. The driver's door opened, and a chauffeur got out, wearing, unbelievably, a uniform complete with driving cap. He walked up to the door, and I watched him as though he were a ghost. He clasped one hand behind his back and, with the other, rang the bell.

The chimes pulled me from my stupor. I opened the door, feeling ridiculously informal in my polo shirt and my stocking feet. The chauffeur didn't seem to notice. He handed me a white invitation embossed in gold and said, "Mr. Fitzgerald would like the pleasure of your company at his festivities this evening."

I stammered something to the effect that I would be honored. The chauffeur nodded and returned to the Rolls, backing it out of the driveway with an ease that suggested years of familiarity. I watched until he disappeared up the hill. Then I took the invitation inside and stared at it, thinking that for once, my Midwestern instincts had proven incorrect.

◊◊◊

The parties began at sundown. In the late afternoon, I would watch automobiles with words painted on their sides climb the winding road to Fitz's mansion. *Apple Valley Caterers. Signal Wood Decorators.* Musicians of all stripes, and extra service personnel, preparing for an evening of work that would last long past dawn. By the time I walked up the hill, the sun had set and the lights strung on the trees and around the frame of the house sent a glow bright as daylight down the walk to greet me.

Cars still drove past—the sleek models this time—drivers often visible, but the passengers hidden by shaded windows. As I trudged, my face heated. I looked like a schoolboy, prowling the edges of an adult gathering at which he did not belong.

By the time I arrived, people flowed in and out of the house like moths chasing the biggest light. The women wore their hair short or up, showing off cleavage and dresses so thin that they appeared to be gauze. Most of the men wore evening clothes, some of other eras, long-waisted jackets complete with tails and spats. One man stood under the fake gaslight beside the door, his skin so pale it looked bloodless, his hair slicked back like a thirties gangster, his eyes hollow dark points in his empty face. He supervised the attendants parking the cars, giving directions with the flick of a bejeweled right hand. When he saw me, he nodded, as if I were expected, and inclined his head toward the door.

I became a moth and flitted through. A blonde woman, her hair in a marcel, gripped my arm as if we had come together, her bow-shaped lips painted a dark wine red. The crowd parted for us, and she said nothing, just squeezed my arm, and then disappeared up a flight of stairs to the right.

It was impossible to judge the house's size or decor. People littered its hallways, sprawled along its stairs. Waiters, carrying trays of champagne aloft, slipped through the crowd. Tables heaped in ice and covered in food lined the walls. The orchestra played on the patio, and couples waltzed around the pool. I recognized a few faces from the jumble of Wall Street, others from the occasional evening at the Met, but saw no one I knew well enough to speak to, no one with whom to have even a casual conversation.

When I arrived, I made an attempt to find my host, but the two or three people of whom I asked his whereabouts stared at me in such an amazed way, and denied so vehemently any knowledge of his movements that I slunk off in the direction of the open bar—the only place on the patio where a single man could linger without looking purposeless and alone.

I ordered a vodka martini although I rarely drank hard liquor—it seemed appropriate to the mood—and watched the crowd's mood switch as the orchestra slid from the waltz to a jitterbug. Women dressed like flappers, wearing no-waisted fringed dresses and pearls down to their thighs danced with an abandon I had only seen in movies. Men matched their movements, sweat marring the perfection of their tailored suits.

A hand gripped my shoulder, the feeling tight but friendly, unlike Tom's clap of the week before. As l looked up, I realized that the crowd of single men around the bar had eased, and I was standing alone, except for the bartender and the man behind me.

Up close, he was taller and more slender than he had looked in the moonlight. His cheekbones were high, his lips thin, his eyes hooded. "Your face looks familiar," he said. "Perhaps you're related to the Carraways of St. Paul, Minnesota."

"Yes," I said. The drink had left an unpleasant tang on my tongue. "I grew up there."

"And Nick Carraway, the bondsman, would be your—grandfather? great-grandfather?"

That he knew my grandfather startled me. Fitz looked younger than that, more of an age with me. Perhaps there were family ties I did not know about. "Grandfather," I said.

"Odd," he murmured. "How odd, the way things grow beyond you."

He had kept his hand on my shoulder, making it impossible to see more than half of his face. "I wanted to thank you for inviting me," I said.

"It would be churlish not to," he said. "Perhaps, in the future, we'll actually be able to talk."

He let go of my shoulder. I could still feel the imprint of his hand as he walked away. He had an air of invisibleness to him, a way of moving unnoticed through a crowd. When he reached the edge of the dancers, he stopped and looked at me with a gaze piercing in its intensity.

"Next time, old sport," he said, the old-fashioned endearment tripping off his tongue like a new and original phrase, "bring your cousin. I think she might like the light."

At least, that was what I thought he said. Later, when I had time to reflect, I wondered if he hadn't said, "I think she might like the night."

4

Men with little imagination often have a clarity of vision that startles the mind. For all their inability to imagine beauty, they seem able to see the ugliness that lies below any surface. They have a willingness to believe in the baser, cruder side of life.

On the following Wednesday afternoon, I found myself in a bar at the edge of the financial district, a place where men in suits rarely showed their faces, where the average clientele had muscles thick as cue balls and just as hard. Tom had corralled me as I left the office, claiming he wanted to play pool and that he knew a place, but as we walked in, it became clear that we were not there for a game, but for an alibi.

The woman he met was the antithesis of Ari. She was tall, big-chested with thick ankles, more a child of my aunt than Ari ever could be. The woman—Rita—wore her clothes like an ill-fitting bathrobe, slipping to one side to reveal a mound of flesh and a bit of nipple. Lipstick stained the side of her mouth and the edges of her teeth. She laughed loud and hard, like a man, and her eyes were bright with too much drink.

I stuck my tie in my pocket, pulled off my suit jacket and draped it over a chair, rolling up my sleeves before I challenged one of the large men in a ripped T-shirt to a game of eight-ball. I lost fifty dollars to him before he decided there was no challenge in it; by then Tom and Rita had reappeared, her clothing straight and her lipstick neatly applied.

Tom clapped my back before I could step away, and the odors of sweat, musk, and newly applied cologne swept over me. "Thanks, man," he said, as if my accompanying him on this trip had deepened our friendship.

I could not let the moment slide without exacting my price. "My neighbor asked that Ari come to one of his parties this week."

Rita slunk back as if Ari's name lessened Rita's power. Tom stepped away from me.

"Fitzgerald's a ghoul," he said. "They say people go to his house and never come back."

"I was there on Sunday."

"You're lucky to get out with your life."

"Hundreds of people go each night." I unrolled my sleeves, buttoned them, and then slipped into my suit coat. "I plan to take Ari."

Tom stared at me for a moment, the male camaraderie gone. Finally he nodded, the acknowledgment of a price paid.

"Next time you go," Rita said, the only words she would ever say to me, "take a good look at his guests."

◊◊◊

I drove Ari up in my car. Even though I had spent the afternoon washing and polishing it, the car's age showed against the sleek new models, something in the lack of shine of the bumpers, the crude design of a model year now done. The attendant was polite as he took my place, but lacked the enthusiasm he had shown over a Rolls just moments before.

Ari stared at the house, her tiny mouth agape, her eyes wide. The lights reflected in her pupils like a hundred dancing stars. She left my side immediately and ran up the stairs as if I were not even there.

I tipped the attendant and strode in, remembering Rita's admonishment. The faces that looked familiar had a photographic edge to them—the patina of images I had seen a thousand times in books, in magazines, on film. But as I scanned, I could not see Ari. It was as if she had come into the mammoth house and vanished.

I grabbed a flute of champagne from a passing waiter and wandered onto the patio. The orchestra was playing "Alexander's Ragtime Band" and the woman with the marcel danced in the center, alone, as if she were the only one who understood the music.

Beside me, a burly man with dark hair and a mustache that absorbed his upper lip spoke of marlin fishing as if it were a combat sport. A lanky and lean man who spoke with a Mississippi accent told a familiar story about a barn-burning to a crowd of women who gazed adoringly at his face. Behind him, a tiny woman with an acid tongue talked in disparaging terms of the

Algonquin, and another man with white hair, a face crinkled from too much drink, and a body so thin it appeared dapper, studied the edges of the conversation as if the words were written in front of him.

They all had skin as pale as Fitz's, and a life force that seemed to have more energy than substance.

There were others scattered among the crowd: a man with an unruly shock of white hair who spoke of his boyhood in Illinois, his cats, and the workings of riverboats powered by steam; the demure brown-haired woman wearing a long white dress, standing in a corner, refusing to meet anyone's gaze. "She's a poet," a young girl beside me whispered, and I nodded, recognizing the heart-shaped face, the quiet, steady eyes.

In that house, on that night, I never questioned their presence, as if being in the company of people long-dead were as natural as speaking to myself. I avoided them: They had nothing to do with me. I was drawn to none of them, except, perhaps, Fitz himself.

He was as invisible as Ari. I wandered through the manse three times, pushing past bodies flushed from dancing, bright with too much drink, letting the conversation flow over me like water over a stone. Most of my colleagues spoke of Fitz himself, how he had favored them in one way or another, with a commission or, in the case of the women, with time alone. They spoke with a sigh, their eyes a bit glazed, as if the memory were more of a dream, and as they spoke, they touched their throats, or played with pearl chokers around their necks. A shudder ran through me and wondered what I had brought Arielle into.

I found her at three a.m., waltzing in the empty grand ballroom with Fitz. He wore an ice cream suit, perfectly tailored, his hair combed back, and she wore a white gown that rippled around her like her hair. She gazed at him like a lover, her lips parted and moist, her body pressed against his, and as they whirled to the imaginary music, I caught glimpses of his face, his brows brought together in concentration, his eyes sparkling and moist. He looked like a man caught in a dream from which he could not wake, a dream which had gone bad, a dream which, when he remembered it, he would term a nightmare.

Then she saw me, and her expression changed. "Nick," she

said. "Nick Carraway." And she laughed. The voice was not hers. It had more music than before, but beneath it, a rasp older women gained from too many cigarettes, too much drink. "He will never leave us alone, Scott."

Fitz looked at me. If anything, he appeared paler than he had before. The sparkle in his eyes was not tears, but the hard glare of a man who could not cry. "Thanks for all your help, old man," he said, and with that I knew I had been dismissed.

5

About a week before, an ambitious young reporter appeared on Fitz's doorstep as one of the parties began. He managed to find Fitz at the edge of the pool and asked him if he had anything to say.

"About what?" Fitz asked.

"About anything."

It transpired after a few minutes that the young man had heard Fitz's name around the office in a connection he wouldn't or couldn't reveal and, it being his day off, had hurried out to Connecticut "to see."

It was a random shot and yet the reporter's instinct had been right. Fitz's reputation, as spread by the people who saw him, the people who came to his gatherings, had that summer fallen just short of news. Stories of his mysterious past persisted, and yet none came close to the truth.

You see, he did not die of a heart attack in 1940. Instead he fell in, as he later said, with the ghouls of the Hollywood crowd. Obsessed with immortality, glamour, and youth, they convinced him to meet a friend, a person whose name remains forever elusive. He succumbed to the temptation, as he had so often before, and discovered only after he had changed that in giving up life he had given up living and that the needs which drove his fiction disappeared with his need for food and strong drink.

He watched his daughter from afar and occasionally brought others into the fold, as the loneliness ate at him. He began throwing large parties and in them found sustenance, and others like him who had managed to move from human fame into a sort of shadowed, mythical existence. But the loneliness did not abate, and over time he learned that he had only one more chance, another opportunity to make things right. And so he monitored the baby wards in the South, allowing his own brush with the supernatural to let him see when her soul returned. For his love affair with her was more haunting and tragic than those he wrote about, and he hoped, with his new understanding, that he could make amends.

Some of this I learned, and some of this he told me. I put it down here as a way of noting that the rumors about him weren't even close to the truth, that the truth was, in fact, as strange as fiction, and I would not believe it if I had not seen it with my own eyes. What he did tell me, he said at a time of great confusion, and I might not have believed him, even then, if later that year, I hadn't found the books, the novels, the biographies, that somehow even with my literary education, I had managed to overlook.

◊◊◊

That night, I did not sleep. The phone rang three times, and all three times, the machine picked up. Tom's coarse accent echoed in the darkness of my bedroom, demanding to know why Ari had not returned home. Finally I slipped on a faded pair of jeans and loafers, and padded up the hill to see if I could convince her to leave before Tom created trouble.

Only the light in the ballroom remained on, casting a thin glow across the yard. The cars were gone as were their occupants. Discarded cigarette butts, broken champagne glasses, and one woman's shoe with the heel missing were the only evidence of the gaiety that had marked the evening. Inside, I heard Ari sobbing hysterically, and as I walked up the steps, a hand pushed against my chest.

I hadn't seen him in the dark. He had been sitting on the steps, staring at the detritus in the driveway, an unlit cigarette in his hands. "You can't help her," he said, and in his voice, I heard the weariness of a man whose dreams were lost.

Still, I pushed past him and went inside. Ari sat on the floor, her bare feet splayed in front of her, her dress still the white of pure snow. When she saw me, the crying stopped. "Nicky," she said in that raspy, not-her voice, and then the laughter started, as uncontrolled as the crying. I went to her, put my arm around her shoulder, and tried to lift her up. She shook her head and pulled out of my grasp. For a moment, the horrible laughter stopped and she gazed up at me, her eyes as clear as the sky on a summer morning. "You don't understand, do you?" she asked. "When I'm here, this is where I belong."

Then the laughter began again, a harsh, almost childish sound too close to tears. Fitz glided past me, still wearing the white suit he had worn earlier. He picked her up and shushed her, and she buried her face against his shoulder as if he gave her strength.

Her thin, fragile neck was clear and unmarked. God help me, I checked. But he had not touched her, at least in that way.

He carried her to the plush sofa pushed back to the wall beneath the windows. Then he pushed the hair off her face, wiped the tears from her cheeks, and whispered to her, hauntingly: *"Sleep."* Her eyes closed and her breathing evened, and once again she was the Arielle I had always known, pink-cheeked and delicate.

He looked at me, and said, "This is why Daisy had to leave Gatsby, because he was wrong for her. The better part of me knew that being with me shattered her spirit. But I could not let her go. You knew that, didn't you, old man? That I could not let her go?"

But I didn't know, and I didn't understand until much later. So I remained quiet. Wisely, as it turned out.

"Ah, Nick," he said, his fingers brushing her brow. "Your arrival surprised me. I never thought—I never realized—how the characters live on, even when the story's over. I could believe in my own transformation but not your existence. And I never understood the past, so here I am repeating it."

He smiled then, a self-deprecating smile that made all his words seem like the foolish ravings of a man who had had little sleep.

"Go home, old sport," he said. "Everything will look different in the light of day."

I must have glanced at Arielle with concern, for he cupped her cheek possessively. "Don't worry," he said. "I'll take good care of her."

Something in the throb of his voice made me trust him, made me turn on my heel even though I knew it was wrong, and leave him there with her. Some warble, some imperative, as if he were the creator and I the created. I wandered down the hill in the dark, and didn't return until the light of day.

6

I had slept maybe twenty minutes when I woke to the sound of tires peeling on the road outside my house. An engine raced, powering a fast-moving car up the hill. As I sat up, brakes squealed and a voice raised in a shout that echoed down the valley. The shouts continued until they ended abruptly—mid sentence—followed by a moment of silence and a woman's high-pitched scream.

It was still dark, although the darkness had that gray edge that meant dawn wasn't far away. I picked up the phone and called the police which, in my compulsion-fogged mind, felt like an act of defiance. Then I rose from my bed a second time, dressed, and ran out of the house.

I didn't think to take the car until I was halfway up the path. By then to run back and get it would have taken twice as long as continuing. The sun rose, casting orange and gold tendrils across the sky. The silence in Fitz's house unnerved me and I was shaking by the time I reached the driveway.

I had never seen the car before—a light gray sedan that lacked pretension—but the Wisconsin vanity plate made its ownership clear. It had parked on the shattered glass. A woman's black glove lay beneath one of the tires. In the early morning glow, Fitz's manse seemed ancient and old: the lawn filled with bottles and cans from the night before; the shutters closed and unpainted; the steps cracked and littered with ashes and gum. The door stood open and I slipped inside, careful to touch nothing.

A great gout of blood rose in an arch along one wall and dripped to the tile below. Drops led me to the open French doors. Through them, I saw the pool.

Tiny waves still rippled the water. The laden air mattress moved irregularly along the surface, the man's dark suit already telling me this was not whom I had expected. His eyes were open and appeared to frown in confusion, his skin chalk-white, and his neck a gaping hole that had been licked clean of blood.

◊◊◊

Of Ari and Fitz we never found a trace. A man who had lived on the fringes as long as he had knew how to disappear. I had half hoped for an acknowledgment—a postcard, a fax, a phone message—something that recognized the dilemma he had put me in. But, as he said, an author never realizes that the characters live beyond the story, and I suspect he never gave me a second thought.

Although I thought of *him* as I read the articles, the biographies, the essays and dissertations based on his life—his true life. I saved his novels for last and his most famous for last of all. And in it, I heard my grandfather's voice, and understood why he never spoke of his life before he returned from the East all those years ago. For that life had not been his but a fiction created by a man my grandfather had never met. My grandfather's life began in 1925 and he lived it fully until the day he died.

I sold the house at the bottom of the hill, and moved back to the Middle West. I found that I prefer the land harsh and the winds of reality cold against my face. It reminds me that I am alive. And, although I bear my grandfather's name in a family where that name has a certain mystique, that mystique does not belong to me. Nor must I hold it hallowed against my breast. The current my grandfather saw drawing him into the past pushes me toward the future, and I shall follow it with an understanding of what has come before.

For, although we are all created by someone, that someone does not own us. We pick our own paths. To do anything else condemns us to a glittering world of all-night parties hosted by Fitz and his friends, the beautiful and the damned.

Kristine Kathryn Rusch is the author of more than twenty books in various genres, including horror, mystery, fantasy, and science fiction.

There are some things best left alone in the dark—
things so terrifying they move beyond our ability to comprehend.

The Shunned House

BY H. P. LOVECRAFT

1

rom even the greatest of horrors irony is seldom absent. Sometimes it enters directly into the composition of the events, while sometimes it relates only to their fortuitous position among persons and places. The latter sort is splendidly exemplified by a case in the ancient city of Providence, where in the late forties Edgar Allan Poe used to sojourn often during his unsuccessful wooing of the gifted poetess, Mrs. Whitman. Poe generally stopped at the Mansion House in Benefit Street—the renamed Golden Ball Inn whose roof has sheltered Washington, Jefferson, and Lafayette—and his favourite walk led northward along the same street to Mrs. Whitman's home and the neighbouring hillside churchyard of St. John's, whose hidden expanse of eighteenth-century gravestones had for him a peculiar fascination.

Now the irony is this. In this walk, so many times repeated, the world's greatest master of the terrible and the bizarre was obliged to pass a particular house on the eastern side of the street; a dingy, antiquated structure perched on the abruptly rising side-hill, with a great unkempt yard dating from a time when the region was partly open country. It does not appear that he ever wrote or spoke of it, nor is there any evidence that he even noticed it. And yet that house, to the two persons in possession of certain information, equals or outranks in horror the wildest phantasy of the genius who so often passed it unknowingly, and stands starkly leering as a symbol of all that is unutterably hideous.

The house was—and for that matter still is—of a kind to attract the attention of the curious. Originally a farm or semi-farm building, it followed the average New England colonial lines of the middle eighteenth century—the prosperous peaked-roof sort, with two stories and dormerless attic, and with the Georgian doorway and interior panelling dictated by the progress of taste at that time. It faced south, with one gable end buried to the lower windows in the eastward rising hill, and the other exposed to the foundations toward the street. Its construction, over a century and a half ago, had followed the grading and straightening of the road in that especial vicinity; for Benefit Street—at first called Back Street—was laid out as a lane winding amongst the graveyards of the first settlers, and straightened only when the removal of the bodies to the North Burial Ground made it decently possible to cut through the old family plots.

At the start, the western wall had lain some twenty feet up a precipitous lawn from the roadway; but a widening of the street at about the time of the Revolution sheared off most of the intervening space, exposing the foundations so that a brick basement wall had to be made, giving the deep cellar a street frontage with door and two windows above ground, close to the new line of public travel. When the sidewalk was laid out a century ago the last of the intervening space was removed; and Poe in his walks must have seen only a sheer ascent of dull grey brick flush with the sidewalk and surmounted at a height of ten feet by the antique shingled bulk of the house proper.

The farm-like grounds extended back very deeply up the hill, almost to Wheaton Street. The space south of the house, abutting on Benefit Street, was of course greatly above the existing sidewalk level, forming a terrace bounded by a high bank wall of damp, mossy stone pierced by a steep flight of narrow steps which led inward between canyon-like surfaces to the upper region of mangy lawn, rheumy brick walls, and neglected gardens whose dismantled cement urns, rusted kettles fallen from tripods of knotty sticks, and similar paraphernalia set off the weather-beaten front door with its broken fanlight, rotting Ionic pilasters, and wormy triangular pediment.

What I heard in my youth about the shunned house was merely that people died there in alarmingly great numbers. That, I was told, was why the original owners had moved out some twenty years after building the place. It was plainly unhealthy, perhaps because of the dampness and fungous growth in the cellar, the general sickish smell, the draughts of the hallways, or the quality of the well and pump water. These things were bad enough, and these were all that gained belief among the persons whom I knew. Only the notebooks of my antiquarian uncle, Dr. Elihu Whipple, revealed to me at length the darker, vaguer surmises which formed an undercurrent of folklore among old-time servants and humble folk; surmises which never travelled far, and which were largely forgotten when Providence grew to be a metropolis with a shifting modern population.

The general fact is, that the house was never regarded by the solid part of the community as in any real sense "haunted". There were no widespread tales of rattling chains, cold currents of air, extinguished lights, or faces at the window. Extremists sometimes said the house was "unlucky", but that is as far as even they went. What was really beyond dispute is that a frightful proportion of persons died there; or more accurately, *had* died there, since after some peculiar happenings over sixty years ago the building had become deserted through the sheer impossibility of renting it. These persons were not all cut off suddenly by any one cause; rather did it seem that their vitality was insidiously sapped, so that each one died the sooner from whatever tendency to weakness he may have naturally had. And those who did not die displayed in varying degree a type of anaemia or consumption, and sometimes a decline of the mental faculties, which spoke ill for the salubriousness of the building. Neighbouring houses, it must be added, seemed entirely free from the noxious quality.

This much I knew before my insistent questioning led my uncle to shew me the notes which finally embarked us both on our hideous investigation. In my childhood the shunned house was vacant, with barren, gnarled, and terrible old trees, long, queerly pale grass, and nightmarishly misshapen weeds in the high terraced yard where birds never lingered. We boys used to overrun the place, and I can still recall my youthful terror not only at the morbid strangeness of this sinister vegetation, but at the eldritch atmosphere and odour of the dilapidated house, whose unlocked front door was often entered in quest of shudders. The small-paned windows were largely broken, and a nameless air of desolation hung round the precarious panelling, shaky interior shutters, peeling wall-paper, falling plaster, rickety staircases, and such fragments of battered furniture as still remained. The dust and cobwebs added their touch of the fearful; and brave indeed was the boy who would voluntarily ascend the ladder to the attic, a vast raftered length lighted only by small blinking windows in the gable ends, and filled with a massed wreckage of chests, chairs, and spinning-wheels which infinite years of deposit had shrouded and festooned into monstrous and hellish shapes.

But after all, the attic was not the most terrible part of the house. It was the dank, humid cellar which somehow exerted the strongest repulsion on us, even though it was wholly above ground on the street side, with only a thin door and window-pierced brick wall to separate it from the busy sidewalk. We scarcely knew whether to haunt it in spectral fascination, or to shun it for the sake of our souls and our sanity. For one thing, the bad odour of the house was strongest there; and for another thing, we did not like the white fungous growths which occasionally sprang up in rainy summer weather from the hard earth floor. Those fungi, grotesquely like the vegetation in the yard outside, were truly horrible in their outlines; detestable parodies of toadstools and Indian pipes, whose like we had never seen in any other situation. They rotted quickly, and at one stage became slightly phosphorescent; so that nocturnal passers-by sometimes spoke of witch-fires glowing behind the broken panes of the foetor-spreading windows.

We never—even in our wildest Hallowe'en moods—visited this cellar by night, but in some of our daytime visits could detect the phosphorescence, especially when the day was dark and wet.

There was also a subtler thing we often thought we detected—a very strange thing which was, however, merely suggestive at most. I refer to a sort of cloudy whitish pattern on the dirt floor—a vague, shifting deposit of mould or nitre which we sometimes thought we could trace amidst the sparse fungous growths near the huge fireplace of the basement kitchen. Once in a while it struck us that this patch bore an uncanny resemblance to a doubled-up human figure, though generally no such kinship existed, and often there was no whitish deposit whatever. On a certain rainy afternoon when this illusion seemed phenomenally strong, and when, in addition, I had fancied I glimpsed a kind of thin, yellowish, shimmering exhalation rising from the nitrous pattern toward the yawning fireplace, I spoke to my uncle about the matter. He smiled at this odd conceit, but it seemed that his smile was tinged with reminiscence. Later I heard that a similar notion entered into some of the wild ancient tales of the common folk—a notion likewise alluding to ghoulish, wolfish shapes taken by smoke from the great chimney, and queer contours assumed by certain of the sinuous tree-roots that thrust their way into the cellar through the loose foundation-stones.

2

Not till my adult years did my uncle set before me the notes and data which he had collected concerning the shunned house. Dr. Whipple was a sane, conservative physician of the old school, and for all his interest in the place was not eager to encourage young thoughts toward the abnormal. His own view, postulating simply a building and location of markedly unsanitary qualities, had nothing to do with abnormality; but he realised that the very picturesqueness which aroused his own interest would in a boy's fanciful mind take on all manner of gruesome imaginative associations.

The doctor was a bachelor; a white-haired, clean-shaven, old-fashioned gentleman, and a local historian of note, who had often broken a lance with such controversial guardians of tradition as Sidney S. Rider and Thomas W. Bicknell. He lived with one man-servant in a Georgian homestead with knocker and iron-railed steps, balanced eerily on a steep ascent of North Court Street beside the ancient brick court and colony house where his grand-father—a cousin of that celebrated privateersman, Capt. Whipple, who burnt His Majesty's armed schooner *Gaspee* in 1772—had voted in the legislature on May 4, 1776, for the independence of the Rhode Island Colony. Around him in the damp, low-ceiled library with the musty white panelling, heavy carved overmantel, and small-paned, vine-shaded windows, were the relics and records of his ancient family, among which were many dubious allusions to the shunned house in Benefit Street. That pest spot lies not far distant—for Benefit runs ledgewise just above the court-house along the precipitous hill up which the first settlement climbed.

When, in the end, my insistent pestering and maturing years evoked from my uncle the hoarded lore I sought, there lay before me a strange enough chronicle. Long-winded, statistical, and drearily genealogical as some of the matter was, there ran through it a continuous thread of brooding, tenacious horror and preternatural malevolence which impressed me even more than it had impressed the good doctor. Separate events fitted together uncannily, and seemingly irrelevant details held mines of hideous possibilities. A new and burning curiosity grew in me, compared to which my boyish curiosity was feeble and inchoate. The first revelation led to an exhaustive research, and finally to that shuddering quest which proved so disastrous to myself and mine. For at last my uncle insisted on joining the search I had commenced, and after a certain night in that house he did not come away with me. I am lonely without that gentle soul whose long years were filled only with honour, virtue, good taste, benevolence, and learning. I have reared a marble urn to his memory in St. John's churchyard—the place that Poe loved—the hidden grove of giant willows on the hill, where tombs and headstones huddle quietly between the hoary bulk of the church and the houses and bank walls of Benefit Street.

The history of the house, opening amidst a maze of dates, revealed no trace of the sinister either about its construction or about the prosperous and honourable family who built it. Yet from the first a taint of calamity, soon increased to boding significance, was apparent. My uncle's carefully compiled record began

BLOOD LINES

with the building of the structure in 1763, and followed the theme with an unusual amount of detail. The shunned house, it seems, was first inhabited by William Harris and his wife Rhoby Dexter, with their children, Elkanah, born in 1755, Abigail, born in 1757, William, Jr., born in 1759, and Ruth, born in 1761. Harris was a substantial merchant and seaman in the West India trade, connected with the firm of Obadiah Brown and his nephews. After Brown's death in 1761, the new firm of Nicholas Brown & Co. made him master of the brig *Prudence*, Providence-built, of 120 tons, thus enabling him to erect the new homestead he had desired ever since his marriage.

The site he had chosen—a recently straightened part of the new and fashionable Back Street, which ran along the side of the hill above crowded Cheapside—was all that could be wished, and the building did justice to the location. It was the best that moderate means could afford, and Harris hastened to move in before the birth of a fifth child which the family expected. That child, a boy, came in December; but was still-born. Nor was any child to be born alive in that house for a century and a half.

The next April sickness occurred among the children, and Abigail and Ruth died before the month was over. Dr. Job Ives diagnosed the trouble as some infantile fever, though others declared it was more of a mere wasting-away or decline. It seemed, in any event, to be contagious; for Hannah Bowen, one of the two servants, died of it in the following June. Eli Liddeason, the other servant, constantly complained of weakness; and would have returned to his father's farm in Rehoboth but for a sudden attachment for Mehitabel Pierce, who was hired to succeed Hannah. He died the next year—a sad year indeed, since it marked the death of William Harris himself, enfeebled as he was by the climate of Martinique, where his occupation had kept him for considerable periods during the preceding decade.

The widowed Rhoby Harris never recovered from the shock of her husband's death, and the passing of her first-born Elkanah two years later was the final blow to her reason. In 1768 she fell victim to a mild form of insanity, and was thereafter confined to the upper part of the house; her elder maiden sister, Mercy Dexter, having moved in to take charge of the family. Mercy was a plain, raw-boned woman of great strength; but her health visibly declined from the time of her advent. She was greatly devoted to her unfortunate sister, and had an especial affection for her only surviving nephew William, who from a sturdy infant had become a sickly, spindling lad. In this year the servant Mehitabel died, and the other servant, Preserved Smith, left without coherent explanation—or at least, with only some wild tales and a complaint that he disliked the smell of the place. For a time Mercy could secure no more help, since the seven deaths and case of madness, all occurring within five years' space, had begun to set in motion the body of fireside rumour which later became so bizarre. Ultimately, however, she obtained new servants from out of town; Ann White, a morose woman from that part of North Kingstown now set off as the township of Exeter, and a capable Boston man named Zenas Low.

It was Ann White who first gave definite shape to the sinister idle talk. Mercy should have known better than to hire anyone from the Nooseneck Hill country, for that remote bit of backwoods was then, as now, a seat of the most uncomfortable superstitions. As lately as 1892 an Exeter community exhumed a dead body and ceremoniously burnt its heart in order to prevent certain alleged visitations injurious to the public health and peace, and one may imagine the point of view of the same section in 1768. Ann's tongue was perniciously active, and within a few months Mercy discharged her, filling her place with a faithful and amiable Amazon from Newport, Maria Robbins.

Meanwhile poor Rhoby Harris, in her madness, gave voice to dreams and imaginings of the most hideous sort. At times her screams became insupportable, and for long periods she would utter shrieking horrors which necessitated her son's temporary residence with his cousin, Peleg Harris, in Presbyterian-Lane near the new college building. The boy would seem to improve after these visits, and had Mercy been as wise as she was well-meaning, she would have let him live permanently with Peleg. Just what Mrs. Harris cried out in her fits of violence, tradition hesitates to say; or rather, presents such extravagant accounts that they nullify themselves through sheer absurdity. Certainly it sounds absurd to hear that a woman educated only in the rudiments of French

BLOOD LINES

often shouted for hours in a coarse and idiomatic form of that language, or that the same person, alone and guarded, complained wildly of a staring thing which bit and chewed at her. In 1772 the servant Zenas died, and when Mrs. Harris heard of it she laughed with a shocking delight utterly foreign to her. The next year she herself died, and was laid to rest in the North Burial Ground beside her husband.

Upon the outbreak of trouble with Great Britain in 1775, William Harris, despite his scant sixteen years and feeble constitution, managed to enlist in the Army of Observation under General Greene; and from that time on enjoyed a steady rise in health and prestige. In 1780, as a Captain in Rhode Island forces in New Jersey under Colonel Angell, he met and married Phebe Hetfield of Elizabethtown, whom he brought to Providence upon his honourable discharge in the following year.

The young soldier's return was not a thing of unmitigated happiness. The house, it is true, was still in good condition; and the street had been widened and changed in name from Back Street to Benefit Street. But Mercy Dexter's once robust frame had undergone a sad and curious decay, so that she was now a stooped and pathetic figure with hollow voice and disconcerting pallor—qualities shared to a singular degree by the one remaining servant Maria. In the autumn of 1782 Phebe Harris gave birth to a stillborn daughter, and on the fifteenth of the next May Mercy Dexter took leave of a useful, austere, and virtuous life.

William Harris, at last thoroughly convinced of the radically unhealthful nature of his abode, now took steps toward quitting it and closing it forever. Securing temporary quarters for himself and his wife at the newly opened Golden Ball Inn, he arranged for the building of a new and finer house in Westminster Street, in the growing part of the town across the Great Bridge. There, in 1785, his son Dutee was born; and there the family dwelt till the encroachments of commerce drove them back across the river and over the hill to Angell Street, in the newer East Side residence district, where the late Archer Harris built his sumptuous but hideous French-roofed mansion in 1876. William and Phebe both succumbed to the yellow fever epidemic of 1797, but Dutee was brought up by his cousin Rathbone Harris, Peleg's son.

Rathbone was a practical man, and rented the Benefit Street house despite William's wish to keep it vacant. He considered it an obligation to his ward to make the most of all the boy's property, nor did he concern himself with the deaths and illnesses which caused so many changes of tenants, or the steadily growing aversion with which the house was generally regarded. It is likely that he felt only vexation when, in 1804, the town council ordered him to fumigate the place with sulphur, tar, and gum camphor on account of the much-discussed deaths of four persons, presumably caused by the then diminishing fever epidemic. They said the place had a febrile smell.

Dutee himself thought little of the house, for he grew up to be a privateersman, and served with distinction on the *Vigilant* under Capt. Cahoone in the War of 1812. He returned unharmed, married in 1814, and became a father on that memorable night of September 23, 1815, when a great gale drove the waters of the bay over half the town, and floated a tall sloop well up Westminster Street so that its masts almost tapped the Harris windows in symbolic affirmation that the new boy, Welcome, was a seaman's son.

Welcome did not survive his father, but lived to perish gloriously at Fredericksburg in 1862. Neither he nor his son Archer knew of the shunned house as other than a nuisance almost impossible to rent—perhaps on account of the mustiness and sickly odour of unkempt old age. Indeed, it never was rented after a series of deaths culminating in 1861, which the excitement of the war tended to throw into obscurity. Carrington Harris, last of the male line, knew it only as a deserted and somewhat picturesque centre of legend until I told him my experience. He had meant to tear it down and build an apartment house on the site, but after my account decided to let it stand, install plumbing, and rent it. Nor has he yet had any difficulty in obtaining tenants. The horror has gone.

3

It may well be imagined how powerfully I was affected by the annals of the Harrises. In this continuous record there seemed to me to brood a persistent evil beyond anything in Nature as I had known it; an evil clearly connected with the house and not with the family. This impression was confirmed by my uncle's less systematic array of miscellaneous data—legends transcribed from servant gossip, cuttings from the papers, copies of death-certificates by fellow-physicians, and the like. All of this material I cannot hope to give, for my uncle was a tireless antiquarian and very deeply interested in the shunned house; but I may refer to several dominant points which earn notice by their recurrence through many reports from diverse sources. For example, the servant gossip was practically unanimous in attributing to the fungous and malodorous *cellar* of the house a vast supremacy in evil influence. There had been servants—Ann White especially—who would not use the cellar kitchen, and at least three well-defined legends bore upon the queer quasi-human or diabolic outlines assumed by tree-roots and patches of mould in that region. These latter narratives interested me profoundly, on account of what I had seen in my boyhood, but I felt that most of the significance had in each case been largely obscured by additions from the common stock of local ghost lore.

Ann White, with her Exeter superstition, had promulgated the most extravagant and at the same time most consistent tale; alleging that there must lie buried beneath the house one of those vampires—the dead who retain their bodily form and live on the blood or breath of the living—whose hideous legions send their preying shapes or spirits abroad by night. To destroy a vampire one must, the grandmothers say, exhume it and burn its heart, or at least drive a stake through that organ; and Ann's dogged insistence on a search under the cellar had been prominent in bringing about her discharge.

Her tales, however, commanded a wide audience, and were the more readily accepted because the house indeed stood on land once used for burial purposes. To me their interest depended less on this circumstance than on the peculiarly appropriate way in which they dovetailed with certain other things—the complaint of the departing servant Preserved Smith, who had preceded Ann and never heard of her, that something "sucked his breath" at night; the death-certificates of fever victims of 1804, issued by

Dr. Chad Hopkins, and shewing the four deceased persons all unaccountably lacking in blood; and the obscure passages of poor Rhoby Harris's ravings, where she complained of the sharp teeth of a glassy-eyed, half-visible presence.

Free from unwarranted superstition though I am, these things produced in me an odd sensation, which was intensified by a pair of widely separated newspaper cuttings relating to deaths in the shunned house—one from the Providence *Gazette and Country-Journal* of April 12,1815, and the other from the *Daily Transcript and Chronicle* of October 27, 1845—each of which detailed an appallingly grisly circumstance whose duplication was remarkable. It seems that in both instances the dying person, in 1815 a gentle old lady named Stafford and in 1845 a schoolteacher of middle age named Eleazar Durfee, became transfigured in a horrible way; glaring glassily and attempting to bite the throat of the attending physician. Even more puzzling, though, was the final case which put an end to the renting of the house—a series of anaemia deaths preceded by progressive madnesses wherein the patient would craftily attempt the lives of his relatives by incisions in the neck or wrist.

This was in 1860 and 1861, when my uncle had just begun his medical practice; and before leaving for the front he heard much of it from his elder professional colleagues. The really inexplicable thing was the way in which the victims—ignorant people, for the ill-smelling and widely shunned house could now be rented to no others—would babble maledictions in French, a language they could not possibly have studied to any extent. It made one think of poor Rhoby Harris nearly a century before, and so moved my uncle that he commenced collecting historical data on the house after listening, some time subsequent to his return from the war, to the first-hand account of Drs. Chase and Whitmarsh. Indeed, I could see that my uncle had thought deeply on the subject, and that he was glad of my own interest—an open-minded and sympathetic interest which enabled him to discuss with me matters at which others would merely have laughed. His fancy had not gone so far as mine, but he felt that the place was rare in its imaginative potentialities, and worthy of note as an inspiration in the field of the grotesque and macabre.

For my part, I was disposed to take the whole subject with profound seriousness, and began at once not only to review the evidence, but to accumulate as much more as I could. I talked with the elderly Archer Harris, then owner of the house, many times before his death in 1916; and obtained from him and his still surviving maiden sister Alice an authentic corroboration of all the family data my uncle had collected. When, however, I asked them what connexion with France or its language the house could have, they confessed themselves as frankly baffled and ignorant as I. Archer knew nothing, and all that Miss Harris could say was that an old allusion her grandfather, Dutee Harris, had heard of might have shed a little light. The old seaman, who had survived his son Welcome's death in battle by two years, had not himself known the legend; but recalled that his earliest nurse, the ancient Maria Robbins, seemed darkly aware of something that might have lent a weird significance to the French ravings of Rhoby Harris, which she had so often heard during the last days of that hapless woman. Maria had been at the shunned house from 1769 till the removal of the family in 1783, and had seen Mercy Dexter die. Once she hinted to the child Dutee of a somewhat peculiar circumstance in Mercy's last moments, but he had soon forgotten all about it save that it was something peculiar. The granddaughter, moreover, recalled even this much with difficulty. She and her brother were not so much interested in the house as was Archer's son Carrington, the present owner, with whom I talked after my experience.

Having exhausted the Harris family of all the information it could furnish, I turned my attention to early town records and deeds with a zeal more penetrating than that which my uncle had occasionally shewn in the same work. What I wished was a comprehensive history of the site from its very settlement in 1636— or even before, if any Narragansett Indian legend could be unearthed to supply the data. I found, at the start, that the land had been part of the long strip of home lot granted originally to John Throckmorton; one of many similar strips beginning at the Town Street beside the river and extending up over the hill to a line roughly corresponding with the modern Hope Street. The Throckmorton lot had later, of course, been much subdivided;

and I became very assiduous in tracing that section through which Back or Benefit Street was later run. It had, a rumour indeed said, been the Throckmorton graveyard; but as I examined the records more carefully, I found that the graves had all been transferred at an early date to the North Burial Ground on the Pawtucket West Road.

Then suddenly I came—by a rare piece of chance, since it was not in the main body of records and might easily have been missed— upon something which aroused my keenest eagerness, fitting in as it did with several of the queerest phases of the affair. It was the record of a lease, in 1697, of a small tract of ground to an Etienne Roulet and wife. At last the French element had appeared—that, and another deeper element of horror which the name conjured up from the darkest recesses of my weird and heterogeneous reading—and I feverishly studied the platting of the locality as it had been before the cutting through and partial straightening of Back Street between 1747 and 1758. I found what I had half expected, that where the shunned house now stood the Roulets had laid out their graveyard behind a one-story and attic cottage, and that no record of any transfer of graves existed. The document, indeed, ended in much confusion; and I was forced to ransack both the Rhode Island Historical Society and Shepley Library before I could find a local door which the name Etienne Roulet would unlock. In the end I did find something; something of such vague but monstrous import that I set about at once to examine the cellar of the shunned house itself with a new and excited minuteness.

The Roulets, it seemed, had come in 1696 from East Greenwich, down the west shore of Narragansett Bay. They were Huguenots from Caude, and had encountered much opposition before the Providence selectmen allowed them to settle in the town. Unpopularity had dogged them in East Greenwich, whither they had come in 1686, after the revocation of the Edict of Nantes, and rumour said that the cause of dislike extended beyond mere racial and national prejudice, or the land disputes which involved other French settlers with the English in rivalries which not even Governor Andros could quell. But their ardent Protestantism—too ardent, some whispered—and their evident

BLOOD LINES

distress when virtually driven from the village down the bay, had moved the sympathy of the town fathers. Here the strangers had been granted a haven; and the swarthy Etienne Roulet, less apt at agriculture than at reading queer books and drawing queer diagrams, was given a clerical post in the warehouse at Pardon Tillinghast's wharf, far south in Town Street. There had, however, been a riot of some sort later on— perhaps forty years later, after old Roulet's death—and no one seemed to hear of the family after that.

For a century and more, it appeared, the Roulets had been well remembered and frequently discussed as vivid incidents in the quiet life of a New England seaport. Etienne's son Paul, a surly fellow whose erratic conduct had probably provoked the riot which wiped out the family, was particularly a source of speculation; and though Providence never shared the witchcraft panics of her Puritan neighbours, it was freely intimated by old wives that his prayers were neither uttered at the proper time nor directed toward the proper object. All this had undoubtedly formed the basis of the legend known by old Maria Robbins. What relation it had to the French ravings of Rhoby Harris and other inhabitants of the shunned house, imagination or future discovery alone could determine. I wondered how many of those who had known the legends realised that additional link with the terrible which my wider reading had given me; that ominous item in the annals of morbid horror which tells of the creature *Jacques Roulet, of Caude* who in 1598 was condemned to death as a daemoniac but afterward saved from the stake by the Paris parliament and shut in a madhouse. He had been found covered with blood and shreds of flesh in a wood, shortly after the killing and rending of a boy by a pair of wolves. One wolf was seen to lope away unhurt. Surely a pretty hearthside tale, with a queer significance as to name and place; but I decided that the Providence gossips could not have generally known of it. Had they known, the coincidence of names would have brought some drastic and frightened action—indeed, might not its limited whispering have precipitated the final riot which erased the Roulets from the town?

I now visited the accursed place with increased frequency; studying the unwholesome vegetation of the garden, examining all the walls of the building, and poring over every inch of the earthen cellar floor. Finally, with Carrington Harris's permission, I fitted a key to the disused door opening from the cellar directly upon Benefit Street, preferring to have a more immediate access to the outside world than the dark stairs, ground floor hall, and front door could give. There, where morbidity lurked most thickly, I searched and poked during long afternoons when the sunlight filtered in through the cobwebbed above-ground windows, and a sense of security glowed from the unlocked door which placed me only a few feet from the placid sidewalk outside. Nothing new rewarded my efforts—only the same depressing mustiness and faint suggestions of noxious odours and nitrous outlines on the floor—and I fancy that many pedestrians must have watched me curiously through the broken panes.

At length, upon a suggestion of my uncle's, I decided to try the spot nocturnally; and one stormy midnight ran the beams of an electric torch over the mouldy floor with its uncanny shapes and distorted, half-phosphorescent fungi. The place had dispirited me curiously that evening, and I was almost prepared when I saw—or thought I saw—amidst the whitish deposits a particularly sharp definition of the "huddled form" I had suspected from boyhood. Its clearness was astonishing and unprecedented—and as I watched I seemed to see again the thin, yellowish, shimmering exhalation which had startled me on that rainy afternoon so many years before.

Above the anthropomorphic patch of mould by the fireplace it rose; a subtle, sickish, almost luminous vapour which as it hung trembling in the dampness seemed to develop vague and shocking suggestions of form, gradually trailing off into nebulous decay and passing up into the blackness of the great chimney with a foetor in its wake. It was truly horrible, and the more so to me because of what I knew of the spot. Refusing to flee, I watched it fade—and as I watched I felt that it was in turn watching me greedily with eyes more imaginable than visible. When I told my uncle about it he was greatly aroused; and after a tense hour of reflection, arrived at a definite and drastic decision. Weighing in his mind the importance of the matter, and the significance of our relation to it, he insisted that we both test—and if possible destroy—the horror of the house by a joint night or nights of aggressive vigil in that musty and fungus-cursed cellar.

4

On Wednesday, June 25, 1919, after a proper notification of Carrington Harris which did not include surmises as to what we expected to find, my uncle and I conveyed to the shunned house two camp chairs and a folding camp cot, together with some scientific mechanism of greater weight and intricacy. These we placed in the cellar during the day, screening the windows with paper and planning to return in the evening for our first vigil. We had locked the door from the cellar to the ground floor; and having a key to the outside cellar door, we were prepared to leave our expensive and delicate apparatus—which we had obtained secretly and at great cost—as many days as our vigils might need to be protracted. It was our design to sit up together till very late, and then watch singly till dawn in two-hour stretches, myself first and then my companion; the inactive member resting on the cot.

The natural leadership with which my uncle procured the instruments from the laboratories of Brown University and the Cranston Street Armoury, and instinctively assumed direction of our venture, was a marvellous commentary on the potential vitality and resilience of a man of eighty-one. Elihu Whipple had lived according to the hygienic laws he had preached as a physician, and but for what happened later would be here in full vigour today. Only two persons suspect what did happen—Carrington Harris and myself. I had to tell Harris because he owned the house and deserved to know what had gone out of it. Then too, we had spoken to him in advance of our quest; and I felt after my uncle's going that he would understand and assist me in some vitally necessary public explanations. He turned very pale, but agreed to help me, and decided that it would now be safe to rent the house.

To declare that we were not nervous on that rainy night of watching would be an exaggeration both gross and ridiculous. We were not, as I have said, in any sense childishly superstitious, but scientific study and reflection had taught us that the known universe of three dimensions embraces the merest fraction of the whole cosmos of substance and energy. In this case an overwhelming preponderance of evidence from numerous authentic sources pointed to the tenacious existence of certain forces of great power and, so far as the human point of view is concerned, exceptional malignancy. To say that we actually believed in vampires or werewolves would be a carelessly inclusive statement. Rather must it be said that we were not prepared to deny the possibility of certain unfamiliar and unclassified modifications of vital force and attenuated matter; existing very infrequently in three-dimensional space because of its more intimate connexion with other spatial units, yet close enough to the boundary of our own to furnish us occasional manifestations which we, for lack of a proper vantage-point, may never hope to understand.

In short, it seemed to my uncle and me that an incontrovertible array of facts pointed to some lingering influence in the shunned house; traceable to one or another of the ill-favoured French settlers of two centuries before, and still operative through rare and unknown laws of atomic and electronic motion. That the family of Roulet had possessed an abnormal affinity for outer circles of entity—dark spheres which for normal folk hold only repulsion and terror—their recorded history seemed to prove. Had not, then, the riots of those bygone seventeen-thirties set moving certain kinetic patterns in the morbid brain of one or more of them—notably the sinister Paul Roulet—which obscurely survived the bodies murdered and buried by the mob, and continued to function in some multiple-dimensioned space along the original lines of force determined by a frantic hatred of the encroaching community?

Such a thing was surely not a physical or biochemical impossibility in the light of a newer science which includes the theories of relativity and intra-atomic action. One might easily imagine an alien nucleus of substance or energy, formless or otherwise, kept alive by imperceptible or immaterial subtractions from the life-force or bodily tissues and fluids of other and more palpably living things into which it penetrates and with whose fabric it sometimes completely merges itself. It might be actively hostile, or it might be dictated merely by blind motives of self-preservation. In any case such a monster must of necessity be in our scheme of things an anomaly and an intruder, whose extirpation forms a primary duty with every man not an enemy to the world's life, health, and sanity.

What baffled us was our utter ignorance of the aspect in which we might encounter the thing. No sane person had even seen it, and few had ever felt it definitely. It might be pure energy—a form ethereal and outside the realm of substance—or it might be partly material; some unknown and equivocal mass of plasticity, capable of changing at will to nebulous approximations of the solid, liquid, gaseous, or tenuously unparticled states. The anthropomorphic patch of mould on the floor, the form of the yellowish vapour, and the curvature of the tree-roots in some of the old tales, all argued at least a remote and reminiscent connexion with the human shape; but how representative or permanent that similarity might be, none could say with any kind of certainty.

We had devised two weapons to fight it; a large and specially fitted Crookes tube operated by powerful storage batteries and provided with peculiar screens and reflectors, in case it proved intangible and opposable only by vigorously destructive ether radiations, and a pair of military flame-throwers of the sort used in the world-war, in case it proved partly material and susceptible of mechanical destruction—for like the superstitious Exeter rustics, we were prepared to burn the thing's heart out if heart existed to burn. All this aggressive mechanism we set in the cellar in positions carefully arranged with reference to the cot and chairs, and to the spot before the fireplace where the mould had taken strange shapes. That suggestive patch, by the way, was only faintly visible when we placed our furniture and instruments, and when we returned that evening for the actual vigil. For a moment I half doubted that I had ever seen it in the more definitely limned form—but then I thought of the legends.

Our cellar vigil began at 10 p.m., daylight saving time, and as it continued we found no promise of pertinent developments. A weak, filtered glow from the rain-harassed street-lamps outside, and a feeble phosphorescence from the detestable fungi within, shewed the dripping stone of the walls, from which all traces of whitewash had vanished; the dank, foetid, and mildew-tainted hard earth floor with its obscene fungi; the rotting remains of what had been stools, chairs, and tables, and other more shapeless furniture; the heavy planks and massive beams of the ground floor overhead; the decrepit plank door leading to bins and chambers beneath other parts of the house; the crumbling stone staircase with ruined wooden hand-rail; and the crude and cavernous fireplace of blackened brick where rusted iron fragments revealed the past presence of hooks, andirons, spit, crane, and a door to the Dutch oven—these things, and our austere cot and camp chairs, and the heavy and intricate destructive machinery we had brought.

We had, as in my own former explorations, left the door to the street unlocked; so that a direct and practical path of escape might lie open in case of manifestations beyond our power to deal with. It was our idea that our continued nocturnal presence would call forth whatever malign entity lurked there; and that being prepared, we could dispose of the thing with one or the other of our provided means as soon as we had recognised and observed it sufficiently. How long it might require to evoke and extinguish the thing, we had no notion. It occurred to us, too, that our venture was far from safe; for in what strength the thing might appear no one could tell. But we deemed the game worth the hazard, and embarked on it alone and unhesitatingly; conscious that the seeking of outside aid would only expose us to ridicule and perhaps defeat our entire purpose. Such was our frame of mind as we talked—far into the night, till my uncle's growing drowsiness made me remind him to lie down for his two-hour sleep.

Something like fear chilled me as I sat there in the small hours alone—I say alone, for one who sits by a sleeper is indeed alone; perhaps more alone than he can realise. My uncle breathed heavily, his deep inhalations and exhalations accompanied by the rain outside, and punctuated by another nerve-racking sound of distant dripping water within—for the house was repulsively damp even in dry weather, and in this storm positively swamp-like. I studied the loose, antique masonry of the walls in the fungus-light and the feeble rays which stole in from the street through the screened windows; and once, when the noisome atmosphere of the place seemed about to sicken me, I opened the door and looked up and down the street, feasting my eyes on familiar sights and my nostrils on the wholesome air. Still nothing occurred to reward my watching; and I yawned repeatedly, fatigue getting the better of apprehension.

Then the stirring of my uncle in his sleep attracted my notice. He had turned restlessly on the cot several times during the latter half of the first hour, but now he was breathing with unusual irregularity, occasionally heaving a sigh which held more than a few of the qualities of a choking moan. I turned my electric flashlight on him and found his face averted, so rising and crossing to the other side of the cot, I again flashed the light to see if he seemed in any pain. What I saw unnerved me most surprisingly, considering its relative triviality. It must have been merely the association of any odd circumstance with the sinister nature of our location and mission, for surely the circumstance was not in itself frightful or unnatural. It was merely that my uncle's facial expression, disturbed no doubt by the strange dreams which our situation prompted, betrayed considerable agitation, and seemed not at all characteristic of him. His habitual expression was one of kindly and well-bred calm, whereas now a variety of emotions seemed struggling within him. I think, on the whole, that it was this *variety* which chiefly disturbed me. My uncle, as he gasped and tossed in increasing perturbation and with eyes that had now started open, seemed not one but many men, and suggested a curious quality of alienage from himself.

All at once he commenced to mutter, and I did not like the look of his mouth and teeth as he spoke. The words were at first indistinguishable, and then—with a tremendous start—I recognised something about them which filled me with icy fear till I recalled the breadth of my uncle's education and the interminable translations he had made from anthropological and antiquarian articles in the *Revue des Deux Mondes*. For the venerable Elihu Whipple was muttering *in French*, and the few phrases I could distinguish seemed connected with the darkest myths he had ever adapted from the famous Paris magazine.

Suddenly a perspiration broke out on the sleeper's forehead, and he leaped abruptly up, half awake. The jumble of French changed to a cry in English, and the hoarse voice shouted excitedly, "My breath, my breath!" Then the awakening became complete, and with a subsidence of facial expression to the normal state my uncle seized my hand and began to relate a dream whose nucleus of significance I could only surmise with a kind of awe.

He had, he said, floated off from a very ordinary series of dream-pictures into a scene whose strangeness was related to nothing he had ever read. It was of this world, and yet not of it— a shadowy geometrical confusion in which could be seen elements of familiar things in most unfamiliar and perturbing combinations. There was a suggestion of queerly disordered pictures superimposed one upon another; an arrangement in which the essentials of time as well as of space seemed dissolved and mixed in the most illogical fashion. In this kaleidoscopic vortex of phantasmal images were occasional snapshots, if one might use the term, of singular clearness but unaccountable heterogeneity.

Once my uncle thought he lay in a carelessly dug open pit, with a crowd of angry faces framed by straggling locks and three-cornered hats frowning down on him. Again he seemed to be in the interior of a house—an old house, apparently—but the details and inhabitants were constantly changing, and he could never be certain of the faces or the furniture, or even of the room itself, since doors and windows seemed in just as great a state of flux as the more presumably mobile objects. It was queer—damnably queer—and my uncle spoke almost sheepishly, as if half expecting not to be believed, when he declared that of the strange faces many had unmistakably borne the features of the Harris family. And all the while there was a personal sensation of choking, as if some pervasive presence had spread itself through his body and sought to possess itself of his vital processes. I shuddered at the thought of those vital processes, worn as they were by eighty-one years of continuous functioning, in conflict with unknown forces of which the youngest and strongest system might well be afraid; but in another moment reflected that dreams are only dreams, and that these uncomfortable visions could be, at most, no more than my uncle's reaction to the investigations and expectations which had lately filled our minds to the exclusion of all else.

Conversation, also, soon tended to dispel my sense of strangeness; and in time I yielded to my yawns and took my turn at slumber. My uncle seemed now very wakeful, and welcomed his period of watching even though the nightmare had aroused him far ahead of his allotted two hours. Sleep seized me quickly, and I was at once haunted with dreams of the most disturbing kind. I felt, in my visions, a cosmic and abysmal loneness; with hostility surging from all sides upon some prison where I lay confined. I seemed bound and gagged, and taunted by the echoing yells of distant multitudes who thirsted for my blood. My uncle's face came to me with less pleasant associations than in waking hours, and I recall many futile struggles and attempts to scream. It was not a pleasant sleep, and for a second I was not sorry for the echoing shriek which clove through the barriers of dream and flung me to a sharp and startled awakeness in which every actual object before my eyes stood out with more than natural clearness and reality.

5

I had been lying with my face away from my uncle's chair, so that in this sudden flash of awakening I saw only the door to the street, the more northerly window, and the wall and floor and ceiling toward the north of the room, all photographed with morbid vividness on my brain in a light brighter than the glow of the fungi or the rays from the street outside. It was not a strong or even a fairly strong light; certainly not nearly strong enough to read an average book by. But it cast a shadow of myself and the cot on the floor, and had a yellowish, penetrating force that hinted at things more potent than luminosity. This I perceived with unhealthy sharpness despite the fact that two of my other senses were violently assailed. For on my ears rang the reverberations of that shocking scream, while my nostrils revolted at the stench which filled the place. My mind, as alert as my senses, recognised the gravely unusual; and almost automatically I leaped up and turned about to grasp the destructive instruments which we had left trained on the mouldy spot before the fireplace. As I turned, I dreaded what I was to see; for the scream had been in my uncle's voice, and I knew not against what menace I should have to defend him and myself.

Yet after all, the sight was worse than I had dreaded. There are horrors beyond horrors, and this was one of those nuclei of all dreamable hideousness which the cosmos saves to blast an accursed and unhappy few. Out of the fungus-ridden earth steamed up a vaporous corpse-light, yellow and diseased, which bubbled and lapped to a gigantic height in vague outlines half-human and half-monstrous, through which I could see the chimney and fireplace beyond. It was all eyes—wolfish and mocking—and the rugose insect-like head dissolved at the top to a thin stream of mist which curled putridly about and finally vanished up the chimney. I say that I saw this thing, but it is only in conscious retrospection that I ever definitely traced its damnable approach to form. At the time it was to me only a seething, dimly phosphorescent cloud of fungous loathsomeness, enveloping and dissolving to an abhorrent plasticity the one object to which all my attention was focussed. That object was my uncle—the venerable Elihu Whipple—who with blackening and decaying features leered and gibbered at me, and reached out dripping claws to rend me in the fury which this horror had brought.

It was a sense of routine which kept me from going mad. I had drilled myself in preparation for the crucial moment, and blind training saved me. Recognising the bubbling evil as no substance reachable by matter or material chemistry, and therefore ignoring the flame-thrower which loomed on my left, I threw on the current of the Crookes tube apparatus, and focussed toward that scene of immortal blasphemousness the strongest ether radiations which man's art can arouse from the spaces and fluids of Nature. There was a bluish haze and a frenzied sputtering, and the yellowish phosphorescence grew dimmer to my eyes. But I saw the dimness was only that of contrast, and that the waves from the machine had no effect whatever.

Then, in the midst of that daemoniac spectacle, I saw a fresh horror which brought cries to my lips and sent me fumbling and staggering toward that unlocked door to the quiet street, careless of what abnormal terrors I loosed upon the world, or what thoughts or judgments of men I brought down upon my head.

BLOOD LINES

In that dim blend of blue and yellow the form of my uncle had commenced a nauseous liquefaction whose essence eludes all description, and in which there played across his vanishing face such changes of identity as only madness can conceive. He was at once a devil and a multitude, a charnel-house and a pageant. Lit by the mixed and uncertain beams, that gelatinous face assumed a dozen—a score—a hundred—aspects; grinning, as it sank to the ground on a body that melted like tallow, in the caricatured likeness of legions strange and yet not strange.

I saw the features of the Harris line, masculine and feminine, adult and infantile, and other features old and young, coarse and refined, familiar and unfamiliar. For a second there flashed a degraded counterfeit of a miniature of poor mad Rhoby Harris that I had seen in the School of Design Museum, and another time I thought I caught the raw-boned image of Mercy Dexter as I recalled her from a painting in Carrington Harris's house. It was frightful beyond conception; toward the last, when a curious blend of servant and baby visages flickered close to the fungous floor where a pool of greenish grease was spreading, it seemed as though the shifting features fought against themselves, and strove to form contours like those of my uncle's kindly face. I like to think that he existed at that moment, and that he tried to bid me farewell. It seems to me I hiccoughed a farewell from my own parched throat as I lurched out into the street; a thin stream of grease following me through the door to the rain-drenched sidewalk.

The rest is shadowy and monstrous. There was no one in the soaking street, and in all the world there was no one I dared tell. I walked aimlessly south past College Hill and the Athenaeum, down Hopkins Street, and over the bridge to the business section where tall buildings seemed to guard me as modern material things guard the world from ancient and unwholesome wonder. Then grey dawn unfolded wetly from the east, silhouetting the archaic hill and its venerable steeples, and beckoning me to the place where my terrible work was still unfinished. And in the end I went, wet, hatless, and dazed in the morning light, and entered that awful door in Benefit Street which I had left ajar, and which still swung cryptically in full sight of the early householders to whom I dared not speak.

The grease was gone, for the mouldy floor was porous. And in front of the fireplace was no vestige of the giant doubled-up form in nitre. I looked at the cot, the chairs, the instruments, my neglected hat, and the yellowed straw hat of my uncle. Dazedness was uppermost, and I could scarcely recall what was dream and what was reality. The thought trickled back, and I knew that I had witnessed things more horrible than I had dreamed. Sitting down, I tried to conjecture as nearly as sanity would let me just what had happened, and how I might end the horror, if indeed it had been real. Matter it seemed not to be, nor ether, nor any-thing else conceivable by mortal mind. What, then, but some exotic *emanation;* some vampirish vapour such as Exeter rustics tell of as lurking over certain churchyards? This I felt was the clue, and again I looked at the floor before the fireplace where the mould and nitre had taken strange forms. In ten minutes my mind was made up, and taking my hat I set out for home, where I bathed, ate, and gave by telephone an order for a pickaxe, a spade, a military gas-mask, and six carboys of sulphuric acid, all to be delivered the next morning at the cellar door of the shunned house in Benefit Street. After that I tried to sleep; and failing, passed the hours in reading and in the composition of inane verses to counteract my mood.

At 11 a.m. the next day I commenced digging. It was sunny weather, and I was glad of that. I was still alone, for as much as I feared the unknown horror I sought, there was more fear in the thought of telling anybody. Later I told Harris only through sheer necessity, and because he had heard odd tales from old peo-ple which disposed him ever so little toward belief. As I turned up the stinking black earth in front of the fireplace, my spade caus-ing a viscous yellow ichor to ooze from the white fungi which it severed, I trembled at the dubious thoughts of what I might uncover. Some secrets of inner earth are not good for mankind, and this seemed to me one of them.

My hand shook perceptibly, but still I delved; after a while stand-ing in the large hole I had made. With the deepening of the hole, which was about six feet square, the evil smell increased; and I lost all doubt of my imminent contact with the hellish thing whose emanations had cursed the house for over a century and a half. I

222   B L O O D   L I N E S

wondered what it would look like—what its form and substance would be, and how big it might have waxed through long ages of life-sucking. At length I climbed out of the hole and dispersed the heaped-up dirt, then arranging the great carboys of acid around and near two sides, so that when necessary I might empty them all down the aperture in quick succession. After that I dumped earth only along the other two sides; working more slowly and donning my gas-mask as the smell grew. I was nearly unnerved at my proximity to a nameless thing at the bottom of a pit.

Suddenly my spade struck something softer than earth. I shuddered, and made a motion as if to climb out of the hole, which was now as deep as my neck. Then courage returned, and I scraped away more dirt in the light of the electric torch I had provided. The surface I uncovered was fishy and glassy—a kind of semi-putrid congealed jelly with suggestions of translucency. I scraped further, and saw that it had form. There was a rift where a part of the substance was folded over. The exposed area was huge and roughly cylindrical; like a mammoth soft blue-white stovepipe doubled in two, its largest part some two feet in diameter. Still more I scraped, and then abruptly I leaped out of the hole and away from the filthy thing; frantically unstopping and tilting the heavy carboys, and precipitating their corrosive contents one after another down that charnel gulf and upon the unthinkable abnormality whose titan *elbow* I had seen.

The blinding maelstrom of greenish-yellow vapour which surged tempestuously up from that hole as the floods of acid descended, will never leave my memory. All along the hill people tell of the yellow day, when virulent and horrible fumes arose from the factory waste dumped in the Providence River, but I know how mistaken they are as to the source. They tell, too, of the hideous roar which at the same time came from some disordered water-pipe or gas main underground—but again I could correct them if I dared. It was unspeakably shocking, and I do not see how I lived through it. I did faint after emptying the fourth carboy, which I had to handle after the fumes had begun to penetrate my mask; but when I recovered I saw that the hole was emitting no fresh vapours.

The two remaining carboys I emptied down without particular

result, and after a time I felt it safe to shovel the earth back into the pit. It was twilight before I was done, but fear had gone out of the place. The dampness was less foetid, and all the strange fungi had withered to a kind of harmless greyish powder which blew ash-like along the floor. One of earth's nethermost terrors had perished forever; and if there be a hell, it had received at last the daemon soul of an unhallowed thing. And as I patted down the last spadeful of mould, I shed the first of the many tears with which I have paid unaffected tribute to my beloved uncle's memory.

The next spring no more pale grass and strange weeds came up in the shunned house's terraced garden, and shortly afterward Carrington Harris rented the place. It is still spectral, but its strangeness fascinates me, and I shall find mixed with my relief a queer regret when it is torn down to make way for a tawdry shop or vulgar apartment building. The barren old trees in the yard have begun to bear small, sweet apples, and last year the birds nested in their gnarled boughs.

H. P. Lovecraft is one of the masters of horror and supernatural tales, having haunted (and inspired) generations of readers (and writers). "The Shunned House" is a tale of a vampiric creature older than the version popularized by Stoker in *Dracula*, and makes reference to many of the historical accounts of vampires that appeared in newspapers throughout New England in the 1880s.

Look for other books in
THE AMERICAN VAMPIRE SERIES!

Southern Blood

EDITED BY
LAWRENCE SCHIMEL
AND MARTIN H. GREENBERG

Perhaps more than any region, the American South is haunted by the past. Ghosts of history, of the dead, of wars and lineages, of slights to honor—all linger vividly in the minds and lives of southerners. The South is a region rich in superstitions, both petty and grand, that arise from the many different sources and traditions that make up southern cultures. One of the strongest is the myth of the vampire, returned from the dead to drain life from the living.

All the stories in *Southern Blood* are set in the South, from Florida to Texas, North Carolina to Arkansas.

FROM CUMBERLAND HOUSE
PUBLISHERS